A.T. Thomson

I0651012

The Life and Times of George Villiers, Duke of Buckingham
Volume III

Outlook

A.T. Thomson

The Life and Times of George Villiers, Duke of Buckingham
Volume III

1. Auflage | ISBN: 978-3-73262-988-6

Erscheinungsort: Frankfurt am Main, Deutschland

Erscheinungsjahr: 2018

Outlook Verlag GmbH, Frankfurt.

THE LIFE AND TIMES
OF
GEORGE VILLIERS,
DUKE OF BUCKINGHAM.

FROM ORIGINAL AND AUTHENTIC SOURCES.

BY MRS. THOMSON,

AUTHOR OF

"MEMOIRS OF THE COURT OF HENRY THE EIGHTH,"

"LIFE OF SIR WALTER RALEGH,"

"MEMOIRS OF SARAH, DUCHESS OF MARLBOROUGH,"

&c., &c.

IN THREE VOLUMES.

VOL. III.

LONDON:

HURST AND BLACKETT, PUBLISHERS,

SUCCESSORS TO HENRY COLBURN,

13, GREAT MARLBOROUGH STREET.

1860.

LONDON:

PRINTED BY R. BORN, GLOUCESTER STREET,

REGENT'S PARK.

LIFE AND TIMES OF

GEORGE VILLIERS.

CHAPTER I.

Whilst these matters were in agitation, the death of the Earl of Suffolk, Chancellor of the University of Cambridge, afforded the King an opportunity of evincing his unbounded favour to the Duke of Buckingham, even whilst he lay under the very shadow of a parliamentary impeachment.

A few years previously, the unpopularity of the Duke at Cambridge had been manifested by a play, in which his measures were satirized, and which had been acted by the scholars of Ben'et College.

The ancient discipline of the University appears, indeed, to have so greatly relaxed, that in 1625-6—in compliance with a letter from the King—Lord Suffolk had found it expedient to address the Heads of Houses, whom he styled "Gentlemen, and my loving friends," exhorting them to restore order and "consequent prosperity to their University."

The last sentence had an ominous sound, for there were few cases in which the King thought it necessary to interfere, in which Buckingham did not prompt the royal mind to active measures.

Notwithstanding the unpopularity of his minister, disregarding the public notion that, as the patron and personal friend of Laud, Buckingham was the patron of Roman Catholics, and in direct defiance of the impeachment, all the influence of the Crown was employed to procure the Duke's election to the office of Chancellor.

That dignity was considered then, as it now is, one of the highest tributes to personal character, as well as to political eminence, that the nation could offer. It happened that Doctor Mew, the Master of Trinity College, was the King's Chaplain. No fewer than forty-three votes were obtained by his means; nevertheless, there was a powerful opponent in Lord Thomas Howard, son of the late Chancellor; a hundred and three votes against the Duke were secured by him, and with more exertion, it is supposed, that he might have defeated the Duke's partisans.[1]

Buckingham therefore was elected: thus did Charles, to use the words of Sir Henry Wotton, "add to the facings or fringings of the Duke's greatness the embroiderings or listing of one favour upon another." But the King, in point of fact, was doing his favourite the greatest injury, by thus marking him out as an object for the justly-aroused indignation of the public.

His doom was, however, at hand. Whatsoever he may have intended to do for Cambridge was cut short by the hands of destiny. There remains, however, a very characteristic memorial of Buckingham in that University. The silver maces still in use, carried by the Esquire Bedells, were a present from the ill-fated Duke,[2] whose presiding office was of so short continuance.

It was to be expected that the House of Commons would receive with great anger this fresh proof of the King's contempt for their body. Regarding this election as a reflection upon them, a resolution was passed to send to the University a remonstrance against their choice. Charles, however, considering —and with some justice—that this remonstrance would be an invasion of the privileges of the University, despatched a message to the House, by Sir Richard Weston, desiring them not to interfere; inditing, at the same time, a letter to the University, expressing his approbation of their election of the Duke.[3]

The Duke's answer to the impeachment was put in on the tenth of June: on the fourteenth the Commons presented a petition, praying for liberty to proceed in the discharge of their duty—and entreating that Buckingham might, during the impeachment, be removed from the royal presence.

Had the King yielded to a prayer so reasonable and equitable, the fury of the public might have been appeased. But he viewed the most important question of this early period of his reign, as between man and man, not as between a monarch and his subject. Buckingham's great fault, he considered, was being his favourite. No criminality could be proved in any department of his conduct as minister.[4] Nor could Charles, who had hung over the death-bed of his father, treat with anything but contempt the accusation of poison. The King believed that all the other articles of the impeachment were prompted by a resolution, after attacking his minister, to assail his own prerogative. He had been reared in the greatest jealousy on that one point, and with the strongest and most conservative value for the sovereign authority. Charles, accomplished as a man, was profoundly ignorant and prejudiced as a king: his views were narrow, and his knowledge of the constitution of his country limited. His notions had been warped by a residence at the courts of France and Spain. The immediate effects of a despotic rule are to a superficial observer imposing. It is only to those who look into the interior circumstances of a people, and who well consider the tendencies of an arbitrary government to blight honest ambition, to cramp and weaken the national character, that its real misery and degradation are apparent.

In Spain, with Buckingham ever at his side; in a court full of picturesque splendour; in youth, with hope and love before him, Charles had probably forgotten the aching hearts in the prisons of the Inquisition. In France, the irresistible fascinations of Richelieu had not, it is reasonable to suppose, been wanting to bias the mind of one likely to be so nearly allied to the royal family of France. Most of all those influences that betrayed Charles to his ruin must, however, be ascribed to the dogmatic fallacies of his father. James had educated according to his own contracted opinions not only his son, but the favourite who was hereafter, as it is expressed by Sir Henry Wotton, to be "the chief concomitant" of the future sovereign of England.[5]

Of late years, before the quarrel with the Commons, the popularity of Buckingham had increased. The whole scene of affairs had been changed from Spain to France; the alteration was satisfactory to many, and was ascribed to the Duke—and he had not only become suddenly a favourite with the public, but had been extolled in Parliament.[6] This was, indeed, says Wotton, "but a mere bubble or blast, and like an ephemeral fit of applause, as eftsoon will appear in the sequel and train of his life." The contrast, therefore, between a success so recent and the present odium into which he had fallen, was no doubt the cause of much chagrin to the harassed favourite, who seems, like most men of sensitive natures, to have valued popularity, and to have been fully aware that his political life depended upon it. He knew that no man could long resist the force of public opinion in this country. Even in those days, suppressed as it was by a fettered press, and by the gaunt spectre of injustice in Star-chambers, it had exploded into one burst of forcible indignation in the House of Commons. Somewhere the dauntless spirit of an Englishman must speak out, and it then began to make itself heard in that great assembly which had hitherto been almost as subservient to Court influence as the French Chamber of the present day.

The answer of the Duke to the Impeachment was drawn out with much skill by Sir Nicholas Hyde,[7] the uncle of Edward Hyde, afterwards Lord Clarendon. Sir Nicholas was considered to be a sound lawyer, and a man of honourable character. He was a "staunch stickler," says Lord Campbell, "for prerogative; but this was supposed to arise rather from the sincere opinion he formed of what the English constitution was or ought to be, than from a desire to recommend himself for promotion."[8] He succeeded Sir Randolf Crewe, who was suddenly removed from his seat to make room for one who had no objection to the arbitrary acts by which Charles endeavoured to support Buckingham, and who was ready to conduct the war with France without the aid of parliament.

The debates which were now carried on with vehemence seemed to produce little impression on the counsels which incited Charles and Buckingham to acts of insanity. The chief orators on the side of the parliament were Selden, Noy, and Thomas Wentworth, member for Oxford, and, before their commitment, Sir Dudley Digges, and Sir John Eliot. To this list several others must be added; amongst the most notable were those of Burton and Prynne. Burton had been one of the clerks of the closet to King Charles when Prince of Wales, and had been offended by not accompanying his royal master to Spain, but grew still more indignant at the preferment of Laud; and by being himself regarded as an "underling." He was afterwards dismissed the court for various acts of insolence, and became, as a matter of course, the bitterest enemy of his late patron.[9]

There were now, to use the language of Sir Edward Coke, "two leaks in the ship," or State. "Two leaks," he declared, "would drown any ship;"[10] yet Lord Campbell, as well as other historians, is of opinion that had it not been for the attempt to force episcopacy on Scotland, Charles, and even his descendants, might have continued to rule by absolute power, until, in the course of centuries, the public voice might have forced a revolution upon the country.

Whilst the levying of a loan, by which Charles hoped to supply the place of a grant from Parliament, was going on, Buckingham was using every effort to return to that country where, either as a lover or as a conqueror, he hoped to see Anne of Austria once more. According to Clarendon, he had sworn that he would see the Queen in spite of all the power of France, and that determination had originated the war which was now on the eve of commencing.

In order to challenge reprisals, since there was no pretence to warrant a proclamation of war with France, Buckingham encouraged the capture of French vessels by English ships and privateers, taking the vanquished vessels as prizes. He began, also, to make his great influence available by his efforts to lower the French nation in the eyes of the King, fearing lest the young and beautiful queen should oppose the war. He endeavoured, it is alleged, to alienate the affections of the King from the bride of his choice, and to shew her personally every species of insolence and rudeness. Once, when she did not call upon his mother, as she had promised to do by appointment, Buckingham entered her Majesty's room in a rage; the Queen answered him harshly: upon which he told her that there had been Queens in England who had lost their heads.[11]

Buckingham appears to have been in a fever of jealousy; hitherto he had exercised a sole influence over his royal master. Henceforth, the less public but more sure sway of an idolized wife would for ever interfere with his counsels. Infuriated against the French, yet madly in love with their Queen, Buckingham had only been deterred from returning to France as a private individual by a dread of assassination on the part of Richelieu, who had, it appears, entertained that design. Having persuaded Charles to send back, contrary to treaties, the Queen's French attendants, he now drove the inexperienced and irritated Henrietta Maria to despair; and finding herself in a foreign country, where all around her were inimical to her religion, and to herself, she passionately entreated to be allowed to return to France. Buckingham, rejoicing at the success of his schemes, besought Charles to allow him to conduct the Queen home. But that proposal, when transmitted to Paris, was indignantly rejected by the French Court, and the Duke was confirmed in his resolution to commence a war with a nation which had the courage to decline his friendship.

His scheme for sending back the Queen's French servants had been, however, agreeable in the extreme to Charles—and it may even have been suggested by the King, who, in answer to a letter from the Duke, writes to him thus:—"Steenie, I have received your letters by Dic Graeme. This is my answer: I command you to send all the French away to-morrow out of town; if you can, by fair means, but stick not long in dispatching, otherwise force them away like so many wyld beasts, until ye have shipped them, and so the devil go with them. Let me hear no more answer, but of the performance of my command; so trust your faithful and constant friend, CHARLES R. Dated Oaking, 7 Aug. 1626."[12]

His former loan of ships to the French implies a more friendly footing with that nation than these later passages of the Duke's life may seem to indicate. [13] It was in fact his dread of any influence stronger than his own that caused Buckingham to induce Charles to break off the treaty with Spain; and had instigated his animosity to France. Haunted by the dread of being superseded in Charles's favour, there were moments when his overburdened mind was opened to some humble friends, and the apprehensions of the King's regard being alienated were imparted in agony to a confidant.

Buckingham was also aware of that intriguing and uncertain disposition in Henrietta Maria, which, in spite of a certain heroism of character which she possessed, shewed itself in mournful colours in later periods of her chequered life. The patronage which she wished to divide among her French followers was also a source of jealousy to the Duke, who had hitherto disposed of all Court offices to people who would support him in his state of power, or aid him if he fell. Henrietta was attended on her arrival in this country by many younger sons of good families in France, who looked to England as the field where golden honours were plentifully to be reaped. "They devoured so much," we are told, "that all the thrift of Bishop Juxom, who had amassed much, was gulped down by these insatiable sharks."[14] Patronage and influence being withdrawn, the Duke's ruin must, he knew, be complete. He had nothing to expect from his country, for he had never considered the interests of his native land as identified with his own. There were in his mind some motives of a higher class and a more general nature, although we must not look for lofty principles of action in those days.

The intrigues of Richelieu, who was now Buckingham's rival and foe, worked in England through the Queen. The Duke had been overreached by the Cardinal, and thirsted for open revenge. By denying the troops of Count Mansfeldt a passage through France, the army of that celebrated general had perished. There was no doubt of Richelieu's determination to extirpate the Protestants, and all promises of befriending them had long since proved faithless; the Duke, therefore, saw that he had been compromised, and he resented that superiority in trickery, which it is difficult for a mind like his to bear. Whilst he had thus been deceived by France, Buckingham was suffering by the popular cry against recusants; and the Romish priests, adding to that cry, were enjoining on Henrietta Maria, as a penance, that she should walk bare-footed to Tyburn, as a tribute to the memory of the Jesuits, who had been executed at that spot of sad remembrances. Thus, the cause of the suffering Protestants in France had become the cause of the people, and Buckingham hoped to regain his popularity by espousing it—whilst, at the same time, by sending away the French attendants of the Queen, he should banish the emissaries of Richelieu. Much of his conduct has been attributed to the influence of a French Abbot, who was related to the Duke of Orleans, who was also a violent enemy to the Cardinal.[15]

Fortunately for Buckingham's endeavours to regain popularity, the Duc de Soubise, who, together with the Duc de Rohan, his brother, were the great leaders of the Protestant party in France, arrived during the summer, after the dissolution of Parliament in England. The Abbot, it seems, who had incited Buckingham against Richelieu, had at the same time acquainted the Duc de Soubise with the state of affairs in England. The alliance of these two great noblemen was eagerly accepted by Buckingham. The Duc de Rohan engaged to supply 4000 foot and 200 horse, to assist the English on landing in France; which was an enterprize eagerly coveted by Buckingham.[16]

M. de Soubise had at his command a fleet of twenty-three sail, which was to proceed at once to La Rochelle, then closely besieged by Richelieu, and to throw provisions into the town. The English Government engaged to fit these ships up, to victual them, and to store them with provisions for La Rochelle. Private information disclosed, however, that these "ships were miserable rotten things, of little or no force." Their crews amounted to 1,261 wretched French sailors, who had neither bread nor drink till the Duke's vice-admiral went down to Plymouth.[17] Soubise had, afterwards, a supply of beef and pork allowed for two days a week; of fish, for the other four; some small store of butter and cheese, and some eighteen or twenty tons of cider. This seems to have been all the provisions for all the ships; and Admiral Pennington, writing to the Duke, said:—"I wish the Frenchmen had all the rest, for our people will never eat it, only the best of it." So like the English now were the English then. A hundred tons of beer were to be supplied out of the town.[18]

But other unforeseen difficulties occurred, and the greatest was the want of men. The miserable provisions, or, perhaps, the lingering presence of the plague, now produced sickness and death among the seamen; "so that few of the captains," writes Pennington, "have sufficient men to bring their ships about." He begs to have a *strict* command for the "press" sent him;[19] but even that was of no avail, as the strongest men fled up the country and hid themselves in the woods.

Then certain merchants, to whom the Lord-Admiral looked for a supply of ships in war, were unwilling to lend their vessels. They even disabled their vessels to prevent their being used; and it became necessary for Pennington, as he stated, to send his carpenters to repair them—and after all he was obliged to wait for a reinforcement from Ireland.[20] The poor Vice-Admiral wrote anxious letters, praying that the useless merchant-ships might be sent away; whilst the others, French and all, might be well provisioned at once. He entreated that a ship-load of cordage, cables, anchors, and sails for the furnishing of other ships, might come forthwith. This was a miserable beginning of an aggressive war, and Charles must now have seen his folly in having quarrelled with Parliament. Eventually, Pennington informed the Duke that he was obliged to discharge all the merchant ships, except a few from Ireland, which were in good condition.[21]

The situation of the Duke seems, at this moment, to have been truly pitiable. It has been already stated that he received and answered all letters himself; and the applications made to him, in his capacity of High Admiral, seem to have been of the most minute character. Sometimes among his correspondence we find a letter from Admiral Burgh, wanting to know what he was to do with some Newfoundland fish which had come into his possession as Vice-Admiral.[22] Then follow numerous complaints of the dilapidated state of the forts and castles which ought to have guarded the coasts. In 1625, however, they were reported to be in a perfect state for defence.

Often was the Duke addressed as "the most noble Prince George;" whilst in numerous epistles a tribute is paid to his justice and circumspection, which would surprise those who take the ordinary view of his character. His powers and his province were alike important. A Lord High Admiral was, to use the words of an eminent writer, "one to whom is committed the government of all things done upon or beyond the sea in any part of the world—all things done upon the sea-coast in all ports and harbours, and upon all rivers below the first bridge next towards the sea." So far for his powers; the following were among the list of his privileges:—

"To the Lord High Admiral belong all penalties of all transgressions at sea or on the shore, the goods of pirates and felons, all stray goods, wrecks at sea and headlands, a share of all lawful prizes not granted to lords of manors adjoining the sea; all great fishes, as sea-dogs, and other great fishes, called royal fishes, except whales and sturgeon."[23]

Questions arising out of these privileges, and disputes between Lord Zouch and the captains of vessels, on the subject of wrecks, occur incessantly among the documents in the State-paper Office, which almost supply a history of the period.

In the beginning of the year 1626, Buckingham had commenced his naval operations by sending to impress twenty of the best merchant-ships in the Thames or elsewhere; "such," were his instructions, "as shall be most ready to go to sea, and most able to do his Majesty's service in his present employments."[24]

The impressment of these vessels does not seem to have been successful in this instance; and although the captains to command them were appointed by

9

Government, they found great difficulty, as has been before stated, in manning their ships.

Great, meantime, were Buckingham's endeavours to clear the seas of pirates, as well as to recover that dominion over the narrow seas upon which encroachments had been made. The Duke now began to be assisted by Sir Edward Nicholas, whose name appears at this period as the writer of the Duke's answers to suitors, and who was evidently regarded with much confidence by Buckingham.[25]

Although a fleet of twenty sail, of the king's ships, and others had been prepared so early as the 6th of January, 1625-6, for a service of six months,[26] yet it was not until June that the Duke suddenly left the court, and, with all the haste of his impetuous nature, went on board the fleet at Dover so unexpectedly that his secretary Nicholas could not join him before he set out, but was a few hours too late. Neither had due preparations been made; shoes, shirts, and stockings were wanting for three thousand men; the surgeons' chests were not supplied with medicines; many of the soldiers' arms were wanting; the colonels and captains begged to have new colours; the soldiers to have hammocks; and it was represented to the Duke that their food ought not to be so inferior as it then was to that of the sailors.[27]

The Duke, according to Sir Henry Wotton's statement, was personally employed on either element; both "Admiral and General," there seems to have been a deficiency of discipline; several murders were committed by the soldiery, and an enforcement of martial law was recommended.

His haste and secrecy had, perhaps, another object. It precluded those farewells which are the most touching to those who encounter the chances of war. In Buckingham's case, the parting with his wife, whom he might never see again, must have been mingled with self-reproach as well as sorrow. He evaded it therefore by flight, notwithstanding a promise that he should see her again, nay even by an assurance that he should not go with the expedition to Rhé.[28] This conduct wounded the poor Duchess to the heart, and it was perhaps these traits of conduct that alienated her affections, and made her less reluctant to a second marriage than might have been expected from one of her gentle nature. Buckingham's apparent neglect would have been inexplicable were it not remembered how completely an unhallowed passion for another severs and rends all domestic ties; and that, long before the links are broken, they are loosened by the first deviation from duty, even in thought. The following letters were probably found among the Duke's papers at the time of his death, and so conveyed to the State-Paper Office, where they have remained buried—the words of reproach and sorrow, unheeded and unknown. They are evidently strictly confidential; but they explain and excuse, if anything can excuse, the after-conduct of the Duchess. Much that followed the Duke's decease is accounted for in this epistle:—

"MY LORD,—Now as I do to plainly se you have deceved me, and if I judge you according to y^r one[29] words I must condemn you not only in this hut in your accation[30] you so much forswore. I confese I deed ever fere you wood be catched, for there was no other likelyhoode after all that showe but you must needs go—for my part, but I have bine a very miserable woman hitherto that never could have you keepe at home, but now I will ever looke to be so till some blessed ocasion comes to draw you quite from the Cort, for ther is non more miserable than I am, and till you leve this life of a cortyer wch you have bine ever since I knewe you, I shall ever thynke myself unhappye. I am the unfortunate of all outher, that ever when I am wth child I must have so much cause of sorrow as to have you go from me, but I never had so great a cause of greeve as now. I hope God of his mercie give me patience, and if I were sure my soule wood be well I could wish myself to be out of this miserable world, for till then I shall not be happye: now I will no more right to hope you do not goe, but must betake myself to my prayers for your safe and prosperous jorney wch I will not fayle to do, and for your quicke returne: but never, whilst I live, will I trust you agane, nor never will put you to your oathe for any thinge agane. I wonder why you sent me word by *crowe*[31] that you wood se me shortly, to put me in hopes: I pray God never woman may love a man as I have done you that non may fele that wch I have done for you: sence ther is no remedy but that you must go, I pray God to send you gon quickly, that you may be quickly at home again, and whosoever that wisht you to this jorney by side yourselfe, that they may be punished for it, because of a greete dele of greeve to me; but that is no mater now ther is no remedy but patience wch God send me. I pray God to send me wise, and not to hurt myself wth greeving now. I am very well, I thanke God, and so is Mall and so I bid farewell.—Your poor greeved and obedient wife,

"K. BUCKINGHAM.

"I pray give order before you goe for the jewells wch I owe for … burn this: for God's sake, go not to lande: and pity me, for I feel (most miserable) at this time: be not angry with me for righting, for my hart is so full I cannot chuse, because I deed not looke for it.

"I would to Jesus that there were in any way in the world to fetch you out of the jorney with y^r honor, if any prayers or any suffering of mine could do it I were a most happy woman, but you have send y^{r}self and made me miserable: God for give you for it.

"You have forgoten poore Dicke Turpin for all y^r promis to me.[32]

11

"26th June, 1627. To the Duke of Buckingham."[33]

And again, on the sixteenth of June, was sent another epistle, full of affection:—

"My dere Lord,—I was very much joy'd at the receiving y^r leter last night, and I will assure you I do not only right cheerfully, but am so in my hart, and outwardly every on may see it, and so they do, for they tell me they ar glad to see me so cheerfull, and I hop sences. I will assure you I will not fayle to keep my promis wth you; I hope you will not deseve me in breaking yours, for I protest if you should, it woold half kill me: and I give you humble thanks for saying you will likewise keepe your word with me in the outher mane bisnes, [34] as you call it. I am very glad you cam so well to y^r jorneys end, but sorey it was so latt, for Mr. Murey told me it was nine a clocke before you gott thether. I pray lett me here as often from you as you can, and send me word when I shall be so hapye as to se you, for I shall think it very longe, my lord: I thanke God I am very well, so farwelle, my dere Lord, your true loving, and obedient wife,

"K. Buckingham.[35]

"My Lord, for God sake lett some of that money wch you in tended to have at Portsmouth to be left wth Dick Oliver, if it be but five hundred pound to pay Mr. Ward for a ringe and for a cross w^h you gave to my Lady Exeter: for Jesus sake do this, for I am so hanted with them for it, that I do not know what to do; if you will but send me 400*l.* I will dispatch them myself, for I cannot ster for them.[36]

"I beseech you remember my cusin Turpine.

"To the Duke of Buckingham, my dere husband."[37]

This epistle was soon followed by another letter, expressive of great affection—the poor Duchess begging of the Duke not to deceive her, and to love no one but herself. "It was impossible," she writes, "for woman to love a man more than she did him." Again she writes:—"beginning to fear" that some hints in which he had encouraged a hope of their meeting again before he sailed were but deceptions, and that she should not see him again, "she was grieved," she added, "that he had not told her the truth."[38]

The Duke's example and presence, however, after all these delays, had so great an effect both on officers and men, that, on the second of June, Sir Fulke Greville had to write word from Cowes Castle, that he could, with a "perspective," see a part of the fleet in Stokes Bay.[39] The Duke, meantime, was harassed with difficulties; affairs were far from being in a satisfactory condition; there was continual difficulty in getting seamen, and supplies of money were wanting to leave the coast guarded, to repair the navy, to furnish stores, and to pay the sailors on their return from Rhé.[40]

Meantime the town of Portsmouth was gladdened by the presence of the King, who walked round the fortifications; and, judging for himself of the ruinous state of the bulwarks, promised that they should be repaired. It was Buckingham's intention at this time to build a new dock at Portsmouth, in order to supersede that at Chatham, and thus to benefit the naval service incredibly.[41] Charles entered into this admirable plan. Accompanied by Monsieur de Soubise, the Earls of Rutland and Denbigh, Lord Carlisle and the Lord Chamberlain, he went aboard several of the ships, and dined at last in the "Triumph." At table his conversation ran all day on the armament, and he asked Sir John Watts, in his own language, whether "she" (the "Triumph") "could yar or not?" The repast went off with great hilarity: the Duke's musicians playing merrily, and Archie the fool, and Sir Robert Deale, adding to the general jollity. Well might the Duchess, nevertheless, mourn at the departure of her husband. The plague was raging in the fort of La Rochelle with as much fury as in England.

At length, on the 27th of June, the Duke sailed from Portsmouth. If we could accept as sincere the good wishes which attended his departure, no man ever left England with greater assurances of devotion. "Secretary Conway was ready," he declared, "to carry his hand all the world cries for the Duke's service." "The Duke's good works," he said, "came forth with a better grace than he ever observed in the acts of any other man. Besides his own duty, affection, and humble endeavour and thorough hope," he "joyed" to consign to the Duke the duty, thankfulness, faith, and affection of his posterity.[42]

Secretary Cope sent a message of good wishes in these terms: "God direct his ways and his ends, and make them acceptable to himself and all good men."[43] Even the Queen, between whom and the Duke there had been so great a coolness, sent him a letter, with best wishes. Sir George Goring, writing to his "ever and above all most honoured Lord," the Duke of Buckingham, engaged to "keep the Duke safe with the Queen." The Duchess could not, however, he said, reconcile herself to his departure, without one word of farewell; and the Duke's mother thought a "word or two in" excuse would revive her much.[44]

It was not therefore, it seems, the departure alone of her husband, but his neglect, that pained her. Fond, indeed, and true were the hearts that mourned for his absence in peril. His sister, the Countess of Denbigh, shed many a tear when she missed the Duke at chapel on the morning of his departure with the King.

His mother's blessing was given in these few, but very expressive words:—

"My deare and most beloved Sonne,—Your departure lies grevous at my hart, being oprest with many motherly feres, and were it not for the great joy I beheld in your face that presages some good fortunes, I had bene much worse, but since it must be as it is, I will omit all (with you) to God's pleasure, assuring my selfe he that hath done so much for you, will make you a happy instrument of his further glory, and your eternall comfort; to which end I will addres all my prayers to our sweet Saviour Jesus,—being your ever most assured loving Mother,

M. Buckingham.[45]

"To the Duke of Buckingham."

The first letter, written according to the Duke's orders, by Sir James Bagg, who accompanied him, to Secretary Nicholas, shewed how unabated was the impetuous and arbitrary spirit of the favourite. "The Duke," Bagg wrote, "is very desirous to have the refusers of the loan sent for to the council, which will make the western people sensible that Eliot and Coryten do not only lie by the heels for my Lord's sake."[46]

He set out, however, in high spirits, excited by the change of scene, and full of confidence in his projected movements. It is agreeable to find a concern for the comfort and health of the troops, which amounted in all to between six and seven thousand, under his command. On the twelfth of July, the "Triumph," with nineteen great ships of the fleet, was seen near St. Martin's, at Rochelle; King Charles's colours, the white flag, and the St. Andrew's cross, in the main tops, being visible to the dismayed French over in the port; and firing from our ships was instantly commenced. Whilst these operations were going on, we find Buckingham writing to Secretary Nicholas, desiring that victuals may be sent after them with all possible speed; and, above all, to take care that the fleet be furnished out of hand with London beer; "the beer from Portsmouth," adds the Lord-Admiral, "proves naught, and the soldier is better satisfied with his beer, if it is good, than with his victuals."[47] At first the Duke's expedition was attended with success; a landing at St. Martin's point, opposite to Rochelle roads, was effected, and the French, who attacked the invaders, were driven back with considerable slaughter. On the 14th of July the troops advanced inland, and took the small fort of St. Marie, and the town of La Flotte; on the eighteenth they gained possession of the town of St. Martin's. Great praises of the Duke's valour were transmitted to England, by a writer who penned his epistle on a drum's head, near St. Martin's. The forces then beleaguered the fort, erecting a battery of twenty-one pieces of "ordnance." "The Lord-General," wrote Sir Allen Apsley, "is the most industrious, and in all business one of the first in person in dangers. Last night the enemy's ordnance played upon his lodging, and one shot lighted upon his

14

bed, but did him no harm."[48] "Unluckily," adds the same writer, "there was no bread and beer thought of for the soldiers—wheat instead of bread, and wine instead of beer."

There appeared every prospect of a long siege, unless reinforcements from England should arrive to strengthen the Duke's efficiency. Whilst the fort held out, the citizens of La Rochelle knew not which side to take. The Duke, every writer from St. Martin's agreed, behaved in the most admirable manner, shewing qualities which no one suspected him of possessing. "His care is infinite, his courage undauntable, his patience and continual labours beyond what could have been expected." Such was the language of one of Secretary Conway's correspondents. "Himself," continues this writer, "views the grounds, goes to the trenches, visits the batteries, observes where the shell doth light, and what effects it works."[49] The greatest vigilance was indeed necessary, owing to the carelessness of some of the officers; there was no one of any great capacity except the Duke and Sir John Burgh—a brave but rough soldier, whose plain speaking was often offensive to Buckingham. His chief adviser in military affairs was Monsieur Dulbier, a man of great experience, but devoid of any striking talents.[50]

Meantime the poverty of the Treasury at home impeded the speedy supplies for which Buckingham incessantly wrote. It was his urgent necessity that stimulated the unjust and extortionate collection of the loan—in default of contributions to which imprisonment was the instant punishment. Several Frenchmen, also, were about this time committed for trying to allure Sir Sackville Crowe's workmen into France to cast ordnance.[51]

Disheartened by the delay of the supplies, Buckingham wrote word that he was making trenches, but, owing to the stony nature of the ground, they went on slowly, whilst the Fleet was dispersed round the Island of Rhé; so that unless some speedy succour came, the expedition could scarcely be benefited by anything that might be sent. The citadel, he considered, would be impregnable, if once the fortifications were perfected; in its present unfurnished state, the only way would be to take it by famine. Already thirty musketeers who had been sent out to get water had been captured. Toiras, the Governor, was likely "to make the place his death-bed." The enemy were strong, and the siege would doubtless be a long one, but he was confident that the King would not let him want aid. By the advice of the Duc de Soubise, he had issued a proclamation, setting forth that the King's intention was only to assist the Protestants.[52]

But the Protestants in La Rochelle unhappily refused the aid[53] of the ever-hated English. Louis XII. was ill; the court was divided into factions: and favourable terms were even offered the Huguenots, provided that they did not admit the English into the city.[54]

The Duke, during all this time of deep anxiety, attended religious service daily, and was, it is possible, the more inclined to have recourse to the One Source of help and safety, an attempt to assassinate him having been made whilst he was beleaguering Fort St. Martin. No impression was made upon the enemy, who were three thousand strong in garrison. Mines were resorted to; two water-pipes were cut off, and the besieged were driven out of their outworks; but Buckingham wrote word from the camp that his army, without a supply, would soon not only be disabled from continuing the siege, but would lose what they had gained.[55] His anxiety on this point was expressed in every letter, and in the most earnest terms, and it was fully responded to by Charles I., but still a reinforcement of two thousand men which had been promised did not arrive. Money could not be raised, and the King was obliged to wait the issue of "three bargains" offered to him before he could send out either provisions or men.

Nothing could be more vexatious than the position of the Duke. He was within a distance of what was then three or four days' sail from England—his credit, his honour, perhaps his life, were staked on the relief of the Huguenot citizens of La Rochelle. Forty days, nevertheless, elapsed without even a message by fisher-boat reaching the famishing troops, "who were well supplied with wheat, but had neither means to grind, or ovens to bake it."[56]

It was not until the twenty-seventh of August, two calendar months since the expedition had sailed from Portsmouth,that arms, ammunition, and victuals were sent off by Nicholas—"honest Nicholas," as the Duke used to call him; but no money came. Of that which was intended for the Duke, some was raised by his own stewards, but was detained on account of pressing claims in his own affairs. The want of money was almost distracting. Nothing could be extracted from the Lord Treasurer Middlesex; even at home the young Queen Henrietta Maria declared herself to be terribly incommoded for want of it.

"Send us men," was the burden of every letter from the camp; and a small contribution from a quarter little suspected of patriotism was the answer to this appeal—Lady Hatton furnishing six stalwart volunteers from Purbeck, clothed and armed from head to foot.[57]

The Duke's mother, too, after the manner of mothers, remitted him some money, and, at the same time sent him, as mothers do on such occasions, a reproving letter. But, unhappily, she who had implanted the lessons of worldly wisdom, and those alone, and whose whole life had been a commentary on those precepts, could not hope to influence her son for good. She indeed reaped as she had sown. One cannot, however, avoid pitying the alarm which was soon to be so fearfully realized by the events which succeeded the fatal enterprize.

"My deerly beloved sonne—I am very sorrie you have entered into so great busines, and so little care to supply your wants as you see by the little hast that is mad to you. I hop your eys wil be oppened to se what a greate goulfe of businesses you have put your selfe into, and so little regarded at home, wher all is mery and well plesed, though the shepes be not vitiled as yet, nor mariners to go with them: as for monyis the kingdom will not supply your expences, and every man grones under the burden of the tymes. At your departuer from me, you tould me you went to make pece, but it was not from your hart: this is not the way for you to imbroule the hole christian world in warrs, and then to declare it for religion, and make God a partie to this wofull affare so far from God as light and darknes; and the high way to make all christian Princes to bend ther forces against us, that other ways in policie would have taken our parts. You knew the worthy King your master[58] never liked that way, and as far as I can perseve ther is non that crise not out of it. You that acknowleg the infinite mercy and providence of all mightie god in preserving your life amongest so many that false doune ded on every side you, and spares you for more honor to himself, if you would not be wilfully blind and overthro your selfe, body and soule, for he hath not I hope made yᵘ so great and gevin you so many exsellent parts as to suffer you to die in a dich,—let me that is your mother intreat you to spend some of your ouers in prayers, and meditating what is fitting and plesing in His sight that has done so much for you, and that honor you so much strive for: bend it for his honor and glorie, and you will sone find a chang so great that you would not for all the kinddomes in world for goe, if you might have them at your disposing: and do not think it out of fere and timberousnes of a woman I perswad you to this;—no, no, it is that I scorne. I would have you leve this bluddy way in which you are exept into, I am sure contray to your natuer and disposition. God hath blessed you with a vartuis wife and swet daughter, with an other sonne, I hope, if you do not distroy it by this way you take: she can not beleve a word you speke, you have so much deseved herselfe: she works carefully for you in sending monies with the supply that is now in coming, though slowly: it would have bene worse but for her. But now let me come to my selfe. If I had a world you should command it, and whatsoever I have ore shall have it: it is all yours by right, but, alas, I have layd out that mony I had, and mor by a thousand ponds, by your consent in bying of Gouldsmise Grang which I am very sory for now. I never dremed you should have neded any of my helpe, for if I had ther should have wanted all and my selfe before you. I hop this servant will bring us better newes of your resolutions then yett we here of; which I pray hartily for and give almass for you that it will pleas Allmighty God to deret your hart the best way to his honor and glorie. I am ever "your most loving affectionat sad Mother,

"M. Buckingham.

"To the Duke of Buckingham."[59]

Very different was the style in which the affectionate-hearted Duchess thus addressed him. The characters of these two women are singularly contrasted in these letters:—

"My dere Lord—Already do I begine to thinke what a longe time I shall live without seeing you: truly there can be no greater affliction to me in the world than your absences, and I confese you have layd a very harde comand upon me in biding me be merey now in y absences, but I will assure yo nothing can be harde to me when I know I pleas you in the doing of it, thoughe outherways it would be:—remember your promis to me, but do not deseve me, for now I believe any thinge you saye, and love me only still, for it is impossible for woman to love mane more than I do you, and you have left me very well satisfied wth you. *My* Lord, I have sent you a letter which I beseech you give to the Commissioner about my sister Wasington's deat, because without that my Lord Savage can do nothing, and the touther is a warrant to Oliver for the allowances you give her, wch he refuses to paye wth out one:—good my Lord, dispatch Dicke Turpin, and I shall thinke myself infinitely obliged to you for it. I am very well, I thanke God: you shall be sure to heare often, and do not forget to right often to me and remember your promis, thus wishing you all happynes, I rest, your trewe loving and obedent wife,

"K. Buckingham.

"Pray remember my duty to my Father.

"To the Duke of Buckingham."[60]

CHAPTER II.

THE DELAY IN SENDING PROVISIONS—THE IMPOSSIBILITY OF REDUCING THE CITADEL BY FAMINE—THE DUKE'S OWN MEANS WERE EMBARKED IN THE CAUSE—SIR JOHN BURGH—HIS DEATH—LETTER OF SIR EDWARD CONWAY TO HIS FATHER —BUCKINGHAM'S SANGUINE NATURE—EFFORTS OF SIR EDWARD NICHOLAS.

CHAPTER II.

In spite of incessant appeals to the authorities at home, the end of August arrived, and no provisions were received at the camp. The Duke then addressed Sir William Becher, enclosing a letter to be shewn to the King, stating that, if provisions did not arrive within twenty days, it would be impossible to detain the mariners at Rhé. Provisions, the Duke said, were getting low; and the cannon did little harm to the citadel, which would only be subdued by famine.[61] All seemed of no avail. "Everything," as Sir William Becher complained to Nicholas, "seemed to go backwards." Even the Duke's own money, which he had wished to advance to the victuallers, was still kept back by his stewards; and six hundred quarters of wheat belonging to him, which he had left at Portsmouth as a supply, were still in that seaport. One cannot help echoing the exclamation of Sir Edward Conway, in writing to his father, General Conway—"If we lose this island it shall be your faults in England!" Every letter, meantime, spoke of the carelessness of life shown by the Duke, of the sanguine nature that encouraged others, and of his great affection to the King, and to the cause he had undertaken.[62] The difficulties which were encountered in getting provisions together are almost inconceivable at the present day: the merchants refused to supply anything that would not yield them fifteen per cent; but at last, Sir Edward Nicholas prevailed with some Bristol speculators, his friends, to send provisions, on condition that their men should not be pressed into the service, and that the vessels should be laden with salt.[63] This aid was, indeed, timely, for the troops were beginning to consider themselves neglected and forgotten by their country.[64] And a great loss contributed to the general dejection. Sir John Burgh, the brave though uncourtly officer who had quarrelled with the Duke, was shot through the body in the trenches, and killed. Sir Edward Conway, writing to his father, thus simply, and as a true soldier, remarks, that "the sorrow of the Duke, and the honours he doth in his burial, are sufficient encouragements to dying." "There was some difference" he adds, "between Burgh and the Duke, through some inconsiderate words, on the part of former, which were by the Duke so freely forgiven," and through these Conway thought "an honest man and the Duke could not be enemies." By Buckingham's orders the old general's remains were sent home, to be interred in Westminster Abbey. "The army," the same writer relates, "grows daily weaker—purses are empty, ammunition consumes, winter grows, their enemies increase in number and power, and they hear nothing from England."[65] At length, on the twenty-first of September a letter[66] came from one of Buckingham's friends, Sir Robert Pye, who, whilst declaring that the reinforcements were in great forwardness, begged of the Duke to "consider the end," and to reflect on the exhausted state of the revenue, which was forestalled, he states, for three years; much land had been sold, all credit lost, and Government was at the utmost shift with the commonwealth. "Would that I did not know so much as I do," added the courtier. Deputy-Lieutenants were supine, and Justices of the Peace of the better sort willing to be put out of the commission:—every man "doubting and providing for the worst," so that all were in a sort of panic. All these discomforts were ascribed to the loan, and the loan was the consequence of the projected war with France and Spain. Too late did Charles, who had hitherto left everything to the Duke, "knit his soul unto business," and endeavour to provide for the fruitless contest.

The month of October proved even more disastrous to the English than September. Hopes were entertained of a surrender. Two gentlemen from the citadel came to treat of surrendering; and, after trying to make conditions, asked leave till the next day to consider them. The night was dark and stormy; notice was given of the approach of an enemy; the Duke put out to sea himself, but the barques took a wrong direction, and the enemy's fleet of thirty-five barques broke through that of the English, and the Admiral of the Fleet was taken prisoner. Fourteen or fifteen of the enemy's barques, however, furnished with a month's provisions, got through to the citadel, which was thus relieved. On account of the sickness produced by the immoderate eating of grapes, and also considering the uncertainty of supplies from England, there were many of the Colonels who now recommended retiring from before Rhé; and so discouraged was the Duke at this failure, that he was on the point of going back to England, when an offer from the citizens of La Rochelle to take a thousand sick into their town, and to send to the camp five hundred men with provisions, encouraged him to wait for reinforcements.

On this incident the fortune of the whole siege seemed to hinge, and it must have been extremely tantalizing, when the citadel was on the very eve of surrendering, to find that relief had been poured into it by the enemy. No one could imagine how it had been managed. There was a nightly watch of six hundred boats; the Duke was generally among the men in these boats, or in the trenches, till near midnight; even the common sailors pitied his exertions, and felt for his anxieties. Then there was a battery of seven cannon, that fired upon the very landing-place, beneath the Fort, besides sunken collies that played on the same spot. The wind was then fair for Rhé, and the merchant ships that had been hired were making for the Island; but the others were detained, since no supplies from England had arrived to enable them to act. In the midst of all his uncertainties the following letter from the Duchess was despatched to the Duke:—

"My Lord—I ded the last night here very good nwse that you had taken the ships wch cam to releve the fort, which I hope will so much discurage them as now they will be out of all hope, and quickly yeelde it upe, and then I hope you will remember your promise in making hast home, for I will assure you both for the publicke, and our private good here in cort, ther is great neede of you, for your great Lady,[67] that you believe is so much your frend, uses your frends something worse then when you were here, and your favour has made her so great as now shee cares for nobody: and poore Gordon is the basist used that ever any creature was, for now you ar not here to take his part they do flie most fercly uppon him, but when you com I hope all things will be mended. I pray say nothing of this, and be sure to burne this leter when you have rede it. I thanke God I am very well. Mall is very well, I thanke God. I thanke you for the orange water you sent me, but yett I dare not us it coming from the Governor,[68] thus praying for your health, in hast, I rest

"your trewe loving and obedent wife,

"K. Buckingham.

"10th Octr."

1627(?)—(on the back of the original letter in pencil.)

Whilst money was thus called for in vain, to carry on the war, the defences at home were daily becoming more and more ruinous. The castles in the Downs were in danger of being swallowed by the sea: and water got into the moat of Deal Castle; the Lanthorn of that fort was wholly destroyed, the loss of which, being a sea-mark, was a source of bitter complaint; Walmer Castle was in ruins.[69] Friends there were who wrote to Buckingham to urge strongly on his attention all that was threatening the country, and to suggest his return; amongst these the Viscount Wilmot[70] was one whose expressions were modified by great kindness, and evident partiality for the Duke; whilst advice came less graciously from Viscount Wimbledon, whose recent failure must have rendered his comments on the affair far from palatable.

Before his letter of suggestion and advice could have arrived, Buckingham had, however, consented to a retreat. The state of despair into which his troops had been thrown by the reinforcement of the citadel, and their discovery of the false representations of the amount of provisions on which the besieged could count, induced him to take this fatal step. Presently, however, better information was obtained; and though the sick had been sent into La Rochelle, and the ordnance embarked, the vacillating Duke again determined to "stay and bide it out."

In the midst of this perplexity, on the fifteenth of October, a valuable auxiliary was sent in the person of Charles, Viscount Wilmot.[71] Lord Holland also set sail, but the Duke now found it difficult to persuade the men to await the long promised assistance. "Pity our misery!" was their cry. The people were "looking themselves and their perspectives" (as telescopes were then styled) "blind in watching for Lord Holland from the tops of houses;" yet that nobleman lingered at Portsmouth, pretending to believe that Buckingham, who, he said, he knew "would stay till the last *bite*," might be supplied with victuals from the west. Then he feared also, as he stated, that the Duke might have sailed towards home; that he was ill supplied with provisions; and that he might be obliged to put back into France or Spain. The King, meantime, was wondering and asking why Holland lingered first at Portsmouth and then in the Downs? Charles's impatience was expressed with a force unusual to his gentle character. Until the eighteenth of October, no one in England, it appears, knew of the great distress into which Buckingham and the forces were plunged by the failure of the supplies.[72]

Whilst the wind was against the Duke's return, no one could suppose that he would throw up the whole end of the expedition, and sail homewards; yet reports of his preparing to do so continually got abroad, as may be seen from the following letters from the Countess of Denbigh, Buckingham's only sister, by whom he was much beloved:—

"Moust deere brother—I hope these nue supplys will give you such advantage to you, that your busines will be ended to your honer and contentment. I pray be not be to hasty to ingage your selfe in any other afares till you see howe you shall be supplyed. I would you could but see our afares here: wee ar sometymes for Ware, some tymes a showe of Peace: poor I must be patiend: I have much to speeke to lett you knowe of all particulars, but I am a bad relater of thinges. I will promis you to play my part in patience, and when you com you well not be lede away with them that doth not love you, and be false to you and all yours. I pray God to bles you: forgit not to rede of the booke I gave you, and if you will take phisick this fall of the leafe you shall do very well, so I take my leave.

"20th Octr. 1627.

"your loving sister,
SU. DENBIGH." [73]

"To the Duke of Buckingham."

"MOUST DEERE BROTHER—I hope you will be sure of supplyes before you undertake to go to Rocchell, for ether ther hath beene some grate mistake or neglicte: that you [should have beene] in any distrecs, it doth grefe my very hart and sole. I heare you have beene in great wantes, but I hope before this you are released. I pray be not to venterus, and I hope you well not forgit the booke I gave you, to looke over it often, at the leaste morning and evening, so with my best love, I take my leave.

"26th Octr. 1627.

"your loveing sister,
SU. DENBIGH."

"To the Duke of Buckingham, my deere Brother."[74]

It must have been peculiarly aggravating, amidst the anxieties of the Duchess and Lady Denbigh, to find that all the Duke's perplexities, privations, and sufferings had not in the slightest degree mitigated his unpopularity at home. It must have been still more irritating to know that, whilst the troops before St. Martin's Fort were in a state of starvation, there was the greatest disorder and carelessness in sending the supplies. "There is," Lord Wilmot wrote to Conway, "neither commissary of victuals, nor any one to give account of arms. They find one thousand muskets, but no pikes nor armour." Meantime the Duke's army were in want of clothes, and mostly went barefoot.[75] Then Lord Holland, when at last on board the fleet, complained that there was no one officer or creature who could tell what there was aboard the provision ships, five of which were Dutch, and might steal away at any moment. There seems to have been neither patriotism at home, in regard to this expedition, nor honour in allies, nor even common honesty in the commanders of hired vessels.

For several days the wind continued contrary to Lord Holland's departure from Plymouth. The twenty-sixth of October had arrived, and the Duke, as it appeared from private letters, had "stayed it out till the last bit of bread:"— such is the expression of John Ashburnham, a devoted partisan of Buckingham's: fears were even entertained that the fleet and army were lost; then "such a rotten, miserable fleet set out to sea as no man ever saw;" "our

24

enemies," Ashburnham adds, "seeing it, may scoff at our nation." Lord Holland, who had been expected by the Duke on the fifteenth, was still waiting for a fair wind at Plymouth on the twenty-seventh,[76] employing himself there in trying to expedite recruits, and to send out a Scottish regiment. "In his responsibility" (as he wrote to the King) "he had provided two or three hundred live sheep, to go out for the sick men, who die for want of fresh meat;"—"three thousand pairs of stockings for the men in the trenches; physic also, and an apothecary." Despair, however, possessed all minds; and a report now began to disquiet even the sanguine, stating that the French were landing an army on the Island of Rhé. The report was true; one fatal mistake had been made by Buckingham—he had left the fort of St. Pré unmolested.

This castle, seated, as its name bespeaks, in a meadow, had appeared too paltry a conquest to the sanguine and impetuous Buckingham, when he had first landed at Rhé. He had passed it untouched, but it was now well garrisoned with French troops from the mainland; still its importance was not fully comprehended until the fatal moment came for a retreat from before Fort St. Martin. It is evident that the Duke had overlooked that which should have been a preliminary step in his march; and that his attention had been distracted by an undertaking too arduous for a man whose life had been passed in a very different battle-field from that on which he now ventured his fortunes. Hitherto, he had been a mere civilian, knowing nothing of war, but in the Tourney—nothing of nautical matters, but in gala-vessels, or some favourite ship; and little of the sea, but on maps. Well might his mother caution him not to engage in too "great business;" it was not, in his case, an idle warning, but desperation had impelled him to make the fatal experiment of being at once General and Admiral in a contest with warriors so perfect as the French. Had he been reinforced in good time,—had the measures at home been directed by energy, or even by good faith merely–the events which so overclouded his later actions with a shade of shame might not have happened. From the moment when the French occupied the Fort St. Pré, the game was, however, virtually lost.

Meantime, Charles I., it is manifest from his letters to Lord Holland, was beginning to be seriously displeased with the negligence of the Commissariat Department. He was also desirous of impressing Lord Holland, not only with the great importance of the result of the expedition, but likewise of his anxiety for the safety of the Duke, "to whom," the King writes, "whosoever does the best service is the most happy, be it for life or death."[77]

So late as the latter end of October, Buckingham was resolved either to stay in the island if supplies came,—or, if they did not arrive, to put himself and the army into La Rochelle, and "run their fortune."[78] This was his last resolution. At one time he had fully determined on leaving, for some of his soldiers were barefooted: others were sick of the siege, and had neither bread, meat, nor beer; but the Duc de Soubise had re-assured him, and, promising eight hundred men from La Rochelle, had encouraged Buckingham to decide on scaling the Fort St. Martin.[79] Meantime, Lord Holland did not appear: he was still at Plymouth. Contrary to the advice of the mariners, he had forced the whole fleet out of the Catwaters into Plymouth Sound; but it was driven back by the "cruellest storms" of twenty hours' duration that had ever been known. Great damage was done: it was now necessary to stay to repair the crazy ships—the wind, as Lord Wilmot expressed it, "did so overblow." The violence of the elements, and the knavery or indifference of man, seemed combined to keep back aid from the hungry soldiers in the Island of Rhé, and to ruin their general.

Perhaps the best, or, as many persons think, the only excuse for Buckingham in the step he eventually took, is contained in a touching letter from Sir Allen Apsley to "Honest Nicholas." Apsley, described in one of the letters from the camp as "very sick and melancholy," dates his letter "from his sick and lately senseless bed on board the Nonsuch."[80] "No man," he begins by saying, "has he more cause more faithfully and more affectionately to love than Nicholas." "His soul melts with tears to think that a State should send so many men, and no provision at all for them. But for Nicholas's provision, through merchants, they had been miserably starved long since." He then goes on to relate that "there were about five thousand seamen and four thousand landsmen in great distress for meat and drink. The army had already lost four thousand men, and all their commanders."

A sort of responsive testimony to the Duke's sufferings, and to the cruel neglect of the authorities at home, is conveyed in a letter from William, Earl of Exeter, to Buckingham. "What cannot be obtained by your courage," writes the descendant of the great Burleigh, "must in the end be submitted to your patience." If the Duke "sowed onions, he would be sure of onions; if he sowed men, they are in danger, for the most part, to come up ingrates." "The indolence," he adds, "which his highness has cause to resent, is as great infidelity as is that of commission." Then he cites examples of great generals, who, without loss of honour, abandoned enterprizes which could not be accomplished; what the Duke had already done was, he said, "miraculous."[81]

Neither did the Duke receive any encouragement to remain, even from one of his best friends, Sir George Goring, the faithful adherent in the great rebellion of Charles I.[82] Goring had, in a former letter, represented to the Duke how futile would be any dependence on supplies; for the "City," he wrote, "whence all present money must now be raised, is so infected by the malignant part of this kingdom, that no man will lend any money upon any security, if they think it will go the way of the Court, which is now made diverse from the State—such is the present distemper." The King, it was said, might choose to break all his bonds, "and then, when should they be paid?" Under these circumstances, Goring strongly advised the Duke to return home, and "to curb the insolence of the French some other way."[83]

On the very day on which this letter was written, a newsletter, dated on board the Triumph, in the Road of Rhé, announced that the embarkation of the troops had already taken place. La Rochelle had by that time been completely blockaded by the French—too late it had declared for the English. For the safety of that city it was essential that Buckingham should remain; but, although he has been almost universally condemned for retiring, it is evident that the want of provisions, and the delay of reinforcements from England, extenuate, if they do not wholly justify, that step. He had now been expecting Lord Holland's arrival for nearly a fortnight, and Lord Holland was still at Teignmouth—having been again driven back by contrary winds.[84]

During all this time, no words could describe all the distress of mind suffered by Buckingham better than those of his biographer and attached adherent, Sir Henry Wotton. "In his countenance, which is the part that all eyes interpret, no open alteration," even after his reverses, could be detected, but the suppressed feelings were the more poignant for that disguise.

"For certain it is," adds Sir Henry, "that to his often-mentioned secretary, Dr. Mason, whom he had in pallet near him, for natural ventilation of all his thoughts, he broke out into passionate expressions of anguish, declaring, in the absence of all other ears and eyes, 'that never his dispatches to divers princes, nor the great business of a fleet, of an army, of a siege, of a treaty, of war, of peace, both on foot together, and all of them in his head at a time, did not so much trouble his repose as a conceit that some at home, under His Majesty, of whom he had well deserved, were now content to forget him.'"[85]

Wotton partly ascribes the Duke's failure to one cause—an improvident confidence, brought with him from a Court where fortune had never deceived him. Besides, he adds, "We must consider him yet but rude in the profession of arms, though greatly of honour, and zealous in the cause."

By others he is considered to have committed an error in not having first attacked the Isle of Oléron, which was not only weakly garrisoned, but well supplied with wine and oil, and other provisions. But his great mistakes arose from his impulsive nature—a disposition often the concomitant of energy. Without waiting for the advice of Soubise, he had invested St. Martin's; in marching to St. Martin's, he had overlooked the Meadow Castle, as St. Pré was called by his soldiers; and that fort was now the chief impediment to his retreat.

Having been urged in vain by Soubise to remain, Buckingham aimed one last blow. He attempted to storm Fort St. Martin. He was perhaps incited to this rash and fruitless act by the taunting conduct of the besieged, who, knowing that he intended to starve them into submission, hung provisions on the walls. No breach was made, and the assault had no other result than the loss of soldiers. A retreat was then decided on. The forces could not now return by St. Pré, and a new route was to be taken. A causeway amid deep salt-marches was their only choice; and this causeway, or mound, was terminated by a bridge that joined to Rhé the second island of Vié. Here no fort to protect the bridge had been erected, and there was therefore no passage over to Vié. The French had all this time been close in pursuit. Buckingham was in the rear, and, as a contemporary observed, "had like to have been snapped,"[86] if he had not ridden through the troops on the narrow causeway, where more than eight or ten could not ride abreast. It was not until the English had reached the Island of Vié that the French chose to attack them; then the delay of forming a bridge gave the pursuers time to make their onset with an advantage they could not have had on the causeway, where a handful of men might have set at defiance a host. The French drove the English horse on Sir Charles Birch's regiment of foot, and both he and Sir John Radcliffe were killed. A hot skirmish ensued. "Our men," says a newsletter, "spoiled one another, and more were drowned than slain. The Duke was the last man in the rear, and carried himself beyond expression bravely."[87] Ultimately the bridge was made good, and on the following day the embarkation of the crest- fallen English was safely effected. Buckingham was of course blamed by one faction, and excused by the other, for this failure. Denzil, afterwards Lord Holles, the great leader of the Presbyterian party, a man who, during his whole life, never changed sides, censured him in forcible terms, quoting the words of one whom he styles "a prophet of their own sides," in saying that the enterprize was "ill begun, badly carried on, and the result accordingly most lamentable." "It was a thousand to one," Holles adds, "that all our ships had not been lost." Ten days' provision alone remained; when that was exhausted the Duke must have submitted to the enemy.[88] No one disputed Buckingham's courage; he brought back, as Hume expresses it, "the vulgar praise of courage and personal bravery." He was justly, nevertheless, condemned for the risk he ran in the retreat; for, it was said, had the General been lost, what would have become of the troops, who had retreated in disorder?

The letters in the State-Paper Office, to which reference has been made, though they do not refute the charge that the enterprize was "ill begun," exonerate Buckingham, nevertheless, from much blame: he had every reason to expect reinforcements, for which he was continually begging; no Commander-in-Chief was ever left in a predicament more cruel; and he was justified in retiring by the certainty that provisions must soon fail, and the uncertainty of any fresh supply from the tardy and corrupt authorities at home.

The confusion in the retreat was stated to be such that "no man," Denzil Holles wrote, "can tell what was done, nor no account can be given how any man was lost—not the lieutenant-colonel how his colonel, nor lieutenant how his captain, which was a sign that things were ill carried." "This every man alone knows—that since England was England, it received not so dishonourable a blow."

The loss was indeed severe; thirty standards had been taken, but more lost; four colonels killed, and about two thousand of our men perished during the retreat.

On the tenth of November the fleet left Rhé, and on the twelfth it was seen in Portsmouth Roads, Buckingham's ship, the Triumph, being distinguished. The Duke, however, who was returning home under such painful circumstances, was not in that vessel. As the fleet neared Plymouth, he quitted his ship, and, getting into a ketch, went into the port, in order to gather some account why the succours so long expected at St. Martin's had never arrived. He had also another step to take—that of sending off an immediate despatch to the King, in order that His Majesty might be apprized by himself alone of the great loss and failure incurred in the attempt on Rhé. The messenger was sworn, on forfeiture of his head, to secrecy.[89]

"Charles received the news," Conway wrote, in reply, "with the wisdom, courage, and constancy of a great king, and has declared so much kingly justice and goodness, with affection, to the Duke, as renders his grace, in the king's judgment, and in the opinion of all those who heard him, clear from all imputation, and honoured by his actions: all guiltiness remaining upon this State for whatsoever fault or misconduct is come to that army." Considering the delay in sending succour, the event was thought to have been better than could have been expected.[90]

A letter soon followed from Sir Edward Nicholas, informing the Duke that, six weeks ago, the state of provisions at Rhé was mentioned to the King and the Lords, "but was not credited." He recommended his patron to do nothing until after his arrival in London: all things were at a stand, he says, until the Duke should give them "life and direction." Secretary Conway, in a letter to his son, even "joyed" to find so few had been killed, and so little, "in point of honour," lost, taking the greatest loss to be in the quality of some half dozen persons.[91]

Three days after the Duke had landed at Plymouth, the Duchess wrote to him:—

"My Lord—Sence I hurd the newse of thy landing I have bine still every hower looking for you, that I cannot now till I see you sleepe in the nights, for every minite, if I do here any noyes, I think it is on from you, to tell me the happy newes what day I shall see you, for I confese I longe for it wth much imptience. I was in great hope that the bisnes you had to do at Portsmouth wood a bine don in a day, and then I should a seene you here to-morrow, but now I cannot tell when to expect you. My Lord, there has bine such ill reports made of the great lose you have had by the man that came furst, as your frends desiers you wood com to clere all wth all speede: you may leve some of the Lords there to se what you give order for don, and you need not stay yourself any longer:—this, beseeching you to com hether on Sunday or Munday w^thout all fayle. I rest yours,

"true loving and obedent wife,

"K. Buckingham.

"Mr. Maule desires you to com to the King, though you stay but on night, for they were never so busie as now.

"To the Duke of Buckingham."[92]

Many were the welcomes offered to the Duke on his return. Henry, Earl of Manchester, "hoped that God had preserved him to add to his honour;" and begged him not to be discouraged, for no captain nor general could play his part better; Sir James Bagge declared that the Duke was "dearer to him than children, wife, or life;" and Mr. Mohun and Sir Bernard Granville "will put down their lives and fortunes," they wrote, "at the Duke's feet."[93]

It seems, however, from the following letter—half reproachful, yet ever affectionate—that some time passed before the Duke saw his wife, and that even then he had thoughts of returning to Rhé:—

"My dere Lord—I was in great hope by on of your leters that I should a hade the happynes to a sene you this weeke, but sences I have not had it confirmed by any more, and in this I received by my lady's mane I was in hope wood a tould me sartanly when I should a had the happnes to a sene you, but your leter not saying on worde makes me begine now to fere that you have but deceived me all this whill in giving me assurances that you deed not, and now I begine to be much greeved that you wood not a tould me the truth; but yet I cannot absolutly dispare, because I hope you will yett be as good as your word, for I confese, if you should go, I should not have a stout hart. My

Lord, these too cusens of yours desires you to accept of there servis, and lett them go wth you, for thay had rather venter ther lives wth you than stay behind, but I hope you will put them in some way for ther advancement, for thay deserve very well, and I hope will till the last. I am very well, I thanke God, and ever

"your trewe loving and obedent wife,

"K. BUCKINGHAM.[94]

"To the Duke of Buckingham."

It is a terrible state when esteem and affection are opposed; for, in a woman's heart the latter is sure to gain the ascendancy. Allowance must, however, be made for the Duke's almost overwhelming occupations at this time, and for the harassed state of his mind, which prevented him writing to his wife.

Upon arriving in Plymouth, Buckingham, however, experienced a greater act of friendship than any mere welcome in words. The warmest and most estimable of his friends was Sir George Goring, one of those true-hearted Cavaliers of whom Englishmen of every party may be truly proud. To Goring the Duke left, in some measure, the care of his mother, when he sailed for La Rochelle. Goring's blessings had followed the Duke on his voyage. "My dearest Lord," are the terms in which Goring addressed him; and he showed that he was, as he himself wrote, faithful in every point to him for whom he professed friendship.

The incident which now occurred rests on the authority of Sir Henry Wotton, the long-trusted servant of James I., and the devoted adherent of Buckingham, by whose influence he had been made Provost ofEton.

Scarcely had Buckingham set off from Plymouth, on his way to London, than a messenger, sent in haste from Goring, warned him not to take the usual road, for that his friend had authentic information that a design upon his life would be attempted on his journey. The Duke received the letter when on horseback, and, crushing it into his pocket, without the slightest sign of apprehension, rode on. He was attended by seven or eight gentlemen only; and they were merely provided with the swords they usually wore, and had no other means of defence. There was one among them, however, who was personally bound to the Duke by ties of kindness and affection; this was his nephew, the young Lord Fielding, the son of that sister who had wept when she saw that the Duke was not at chapel with the King. The most cordial union, indeed, existed between all the members of the Villiers' family; and they were bound by gratitude as well as by affection to the Duke.

31

The party rode on, when, about three miles from the town, they were stopped by an aged woman, who came out of a house on the road, and asked "whether the Duke were in the company?" Buckingham was pointed out to her; and she then, coming close up to his saddle, told him that in the very next town through which he was to pass she had heard some desperate men "vow his death;" she therefore advised him to take another road, which she offered to show him.

This circumstance, added to the warning letter sent by Goring, greatly impressed those around the Duke; and they entreated him to take the old woman's advice. But whether from his usual recklessness of consequences, or from an idea that his showing fear would provoke taunts from his enemies, does not appear; the Duke obstinately refused to comply. And yet this "strange accident," as Wotton calls it, was the more remarkable, as it was a sort of prelude to his fate, and in itself was of importance to a man whose unpopularity before he left England was now, at his return, tenfold more general than it had ever been during his career.

As they were disputing, the Duke still resolute, his young nephew, Fielding, went up to him, and entreated him to honour him by giving him his coat and the blue ribbon of the Garter, that he might wear them through the town; and he urged his request by pleading that the Duke's life, in which the welfare of the whole family was concerned, was the most "precious thing under Heaven." He declared that he could so muffle himself up in the Duke's hood, in the way his uncle was accustomed to do in cold weather, that no one could fail to be deceived—so that, attention being withdrawn, the Duke would be able to defend himself.

The Duke caught the noble-spirited youth in his arms, and kissed him. "Yet," he said, "he would not accept that offer from a nephew whose life he valued as he did his own;" then rewarding the poor woman for her good-will to him, he gave orders to his retinue how to act in case of attack, and rode calmly onwards.

Scarcely had he entered the town, when a half-drunken soldier caught hold of his bridle, as if he wanted to beg; instantly a gentleman of the Duke's train, though at some distance, rode up, and, with a violent thrust, severed the man from the Duke, who, with the others, galloped quickly through the streets. Either from his usual indifference to danger, or fearing, as Sir Henry Wotton says, to "resent discontentments too deep" to be allayed, no notice was taken of this incident of Buckingham's journey to London,[95] nor any inquiries made as to the projected assassination.

On his return to Court, the king received him graciously; no change appeared in the outward demeanour of those who met him; but his horse regiment had been composed of the sons of the noblest families in the land, and smothered regrets for the loss of "such gallant gentlemen" were as prevalent amid the higher classes, as deep resentment was in the indignant and vehement lower orders of society.

"The effects of this overthrow," Lord Clarendon observes, "did not at first appear in whispers, murmurs, and invectives, as the retreat from Cadiz had done; but produced such a general consternation over the face of the whole nation, as if all the armies of France and Spain were united together, and had covered the land."[96]

Charles was, however, resolved to see no fault in his favourite, to acknowledge no disgrace; with a confidence in the Duke that would have done honour to a private friendship, he wrote to him, saying, that with "whatever ill success he came, he should ever be welcome—one of his greatest griefs being that he was not with him in that time of trial, as they might have much eased each other's griefs." Adding, that the Duke "had gained, in his mind, as much reputation as if he had performed all his desires."[97] The terms on which they stood towards each other were those of one young man towards another—his companion in pleasures and pursuits, his fellow-traveller, his confidant—not those existing between a sovereign and a trusted subject, amenable to public opinion.

The step which Buckingham took, on his arrival in London, was to ask immediately for a public audience with the King and Lords in Council. Then he plunged at once into the subject about which the country was in a ferment. He "delivered a clear account of the passages, descending even to the good and bold actions of private soldiers." He extolled the patience of the army, and "the fair opportunity offered of turning their sufferings into glory, if their virtue had been seconded with the power and succours designed for it." He named every officer in terms of great praise; and if both officers and men were sensible of "the honours and obligations done them by the Duke, they would," Conway wrote, "live with their swords, or die with them in their hand, to pay him that duty." The King, also, put the "right interpretation on the Duke's actions." This open way of forestalling criticism, and, perhaps, impeachment, was certainly as sagacious as it was fearless.

The Duke, before leaving the coast, had provided carefully for the soldiers who were sick and wounded, and amongst whom a fearful infectious disease prevailed, so that those in whose houses men were billeted died of the same malady. A storm soon damaged fifteen or sixteen of those fated ships which had returned from Rhé: and such was the poverty of the State, that, so late as the fifth of January, 1620, we find the sailors, who had deserved so much from their country, ill from want of clothes.[98] There was no money for their pay, which was in arrears; there arose, of course, a mutinous spirit among them. The sailors were so destitute of clothing, that they would not do their duty in their ships, and many fell dead into the harbours. Still money could not be raised, although every possible expedient to obtain it was employed by the King. Among others who supplied him was Sir Francis Crane, Garter King-at- Arms, to whom Charles gave certain royal manors for security, to the extent of seven thousand five hundred pounds.

The Court was now both dull and partially deserted; the beautiful masques of Ben Jonson were no longer called into requisition: they had been discontinued since 1626, and were not resumed until two years after Buckingham had ceased to exist; and the only diversion specified for the Christmas festivity of this, his last Christmas, was "a running masque," to be performed on a Sunday, hastily got up, and of no particular note.[99]

Throughout the whole of the winter, the condition of the navy was the incessant theme of Buckingham's various official correspondents. "Many of the men," writes Sir Henry Mervyn, "for want of clothes, are so exposed to the weather, that their toes and feet miserably rot away piecemeal." Yet a fresh expedition was, so early as the twelfth of January, in contemplation; and, hearing this, the French prisoners, to whom an allowance of eightpence a-day was given, refused to go back, as they said there would soon be a fleet fitted out for La Rochelle. Meanwhile news arrived of great naval preparations in France, and the sailing from Bordeaux of ships which were to be sunk in the Channel before La Rochelle.

During all these troubles, and whilst a storm hovered over him, an heir was granted to the parents, who were anxious for the boon—and George, the second Duke of Buckingham, of the house of Villiers, was born. Owing to the death of his elder brother, Charles, when an infant, his birth was a source of great delight to the Duke and Duchess.[100] And great need was there for all that could solace the days that were now numbered. All that had been brilliant in the career of Buckingham had faded into gloom; the country was justly irritated by the measures which he had recommended— the war, the impressment of seamen, the scheme for granting to the King the tonnage and poundage for the Customs during Charles's life—were subjects which kept all classes—some from anger, some from fear—in continual agitation. The impressment of seamen had formerly been applied only to the lower classes; but they had been taught by the higher orders, who had felt the burden of oppression themselves, to understand their condition and their rights, and a determined spirit of resistance ensued; yet it must, in justice, before we draw our conclusions, be remembered, that the Government was only indirectly responsible for the present shattered condition of the navy, and for the depth of misery into which the brave sailors had sunk. Generally, the great business of setting out ships had been charged on the port towns and neighbouring shires, but it was now too heavy a burden on them to bear. The Privy Council, therefore, cast up the whole charge of the fleet, which was prepared in February, 1628, and divided it among all the counties.[101]

Neither does it appear that there was in the expenses of the navy, even during the time of war, any extravagance. The error was in the original neglect of the maritime forces, and injustice to a noble profession; the ruin incident to total indifference to its maintenance during the reign of James I. Had not Buckingham, in a few brief years, done much towards its renovation, the naval power would have been almost extinct.

Whilst at Rochelle, he had placed the affairs of the navy in the hands of commissioners. On the 28th of February (1681) the Council called for these commissioners, and gave them "the King's thanks for past services, letting them know that it was his pleasure in these stirring times to use again the ancient offices of the Admiralty."[102] The commissioners, on retiring, gave in their certificates, signed by the Duke as Lord Admiral, of the expenses of the navy, both ordinary and extraordinary, in harbours, and the ordinary at sea, containing six ships and four pinnaces, for the year 1628. It amounted to forty thousand, eight hundred, and seventy-six pounds, fourteen shillings and fourpence[103]—the rest of the fleet being supplied by merchants, and paid by local contributions. But the country was little disposed to view any point with leniency. Their grievances were, indeed, almost daily increasing; and whilst the landholders were impoverished, the loss of all commerce between England and France completely alienated the mercantile community from the Court.

A Parliament was summoned. During the preceding year the Duchess of Buckingham had apprehended great danger to the Duke in allowing the commission of inquiry into the affairs of the navy to drop; and had expressed her fears that the abuses brought to light, and unremedied, might hereafter be laid on the Duke.[104] There had been no time then, in the hurry of the ill-starred expedition to Rochelle, to complete that inquiry; but the Duchess's fears were indeed realized, when, after the Petition of Right had been passed by both Houses, the King went to the House of Lords, sent for the Commons, and then, in his chair of state, and when the Petition had been read to him, instead of giving his consent to the bill in the concise form in which the monarch, in Norman French, declares that "Le Roy le veult," delivered an evasive answer, promising much, but signifying nothing.

The indignation of the House of Commons first descended on the head of Mainwaring, afterwards Bishop of St. Asaph, who had preached, by the King's order, a sermon containing doctrines subversive of liberty. Mainwaring, although he had acted under royal authority, had been fined a thousand pounds, imprisoned, and suspended during three years.[105] After he had been sentenced, the House proceeded to pass "strong condemnation on Buckingham," whose name had hitherto not been mentioned. It must have been a singular scene, when, on the fifth of June, the House being assembled, a message was delivered to them from the King, announcing that, as he meant to prorogue Parliament in six days, he desired that no new business, which might consume time, nor lay any aspersion on His Majesty's ministers, should be commenced. A deep dejection was observed on all faces; but when Sir John Eliot, the most impassioned speaker of that period of earnest and eloquent men, rose, and was about to denounce Buckingham as the author of all the national misfortunes, he was stopped by Sir John Finch, the speaker, who, rising from his chair, his eyes full of tears, told the House that he had been commanded to interrupt every member who laid aspersions on any minister of state. A profound and melancholy silence succeeded; then, after several members had broken it, by resuming the debate, it was strange again to hear that voice which had never deceived his fellow-subjects, and to behold Sir Edward Coke rise, and remind them of former parliamentary impeachments, and tell them that it was their province to regulate prerogative and correct abuses; and he added, "If they flattered man, God would never prosper them." Then the name fell from his lips that none since the King's message had dared to utter: he denounced Buckingham; he called him the grievance of grievances; and, setting at nought the royal mandate, declared, that till the King were informed of that truth, the Commons could neither continue together, "nor depart with honour."

Thus the fears of the poor Duchess of Buckingham were finally and fully realized. One member imputed to the Duke the ruin of the shipping, in the restoration of which he had so incessantly laboured. The faults of others were thus laid on him. Another stated that there were Papists in every branch of the public service. The intolerant fierceness of Puritanical opinions, on this occasion, blazed out. Selden proposed a declaration of grievances, and suggested that, though a mantle had been

36

thrown over the charge against the Duke in the last Parliament, it ought to be resumed, and judgment demanded. Whilst the question was being put, on this motion, whether the Duke should be named as the primary cause of grievances, the Speaker begged leave to retire for a few minutes, and soon returned with a message from the King to adjourn.

The consternation at the Court must have been extreme; for Charles now retraced his former steps; again went to the House, and, giving his consent to the Petition of Right, in the usual form since the Norman Conquest, "*Soit droit fait comme il est desiré,*" was received with loud acclamations. His popularity did not, however, last very long. He took this opportunity to commit an act which was both dangerous to himself and to his friend. When, by the dissolution of a former parliament, the impeachment of the Duke had been stopped, Charles, to save appearances, ordered an information against him to be filed in the Star Chamber. He now ordered this information to be taken off the file; thus insulting the Commons, who had named Buckingham as the "grievance of grievances."[106]

It may easily be imagined how deeply chagrined Buckingham must have been during these proceedings. Among the common people his name was held in still greater detestation than even by his parliamentary opponents.

It was during this session that Sir Thomas Wentworth, recently created Viscount Strafford, distinguished himself by his eloquence, which he exerted in support of Buckingham, thus abandoning his former show of patriotism, in the fervour of which he had denounced the Council of State.

"They have taken from us," he exclaimed—"what shall I say?— indeed, what have they left us? They have taken from us all means of supplying the King, and ingratiating ourselves with them, by tearing up the roots of all property."[107]

In the midst of this declaration the Presidentship of the County of York was deemed likely to be vacated, owing to the illness of Lord Scrope, who then held it; and Wentworth had not scrupled to solicit the promise of it in the following terms of abject flattery to Buckingham. The letter is addressed to Lord Conway:—

"MY MUCH HONORED LORD,—The duties of the place I now hold not admitting my absence out of these parts, I shall be bold to trouble your lordship with a few lines, whereas otherwise I would have attended you in person. There is a strong and general beleaf with us here that my Lord Scrope purposeth to leave the Presidentshippe of York; whereupon many of my friends have earnestly moved me to use some means to procure it, and I have at last yielded to take it a little into consideration, more to comply with them than out of any violent inordinate desire thereunto in myself. Yett, as on the one side I have never thought of it unless it might be effected, wth the good liking of my Lord Scrope, soe will I never move further in it till I know also how this may please my Lord of Buckingham, seeing, indeed, such a seale of his gracious good opinion would comfort me much, make the place more acceptable; and that I am fully resolved not to ascende one steppe in this kind except I may take along with me by the way a special obligation to my Lord Duke, from whose bountye and goodness I doe not only acknowledge much allready, but, justified in the truth of my own hartte, doe still repose and rest under the shadow and protection of his favour. I beseach y'r Lorp., therefore, be pleased to take some good opportunity fully to acquaint his Grace hearunto, and then to vouchsafe, with y'r accustomed freedom and nobleness, to give me your counsel and direction, wh. I am prepared strictly to observe, as one albeit chearfully embracing better means to doe his Majesty humble and faithful service in the parttes whear I live, yet can wth as well contented a mind, rest wher I am, if by reason of my manie imperfections I shall not be judged capable of neuer appointment or trust. There is nothing more to add for the present save that I must rest much bounden unto y'r Lorp. for the light I shall borrow from y'r judgement and affection hearin and soe borrow it too, as may better enable me more effectually to express myself hereafter.—Y'r Lorp. most humble and affec^{ate} kinsman to be commanded,

T. WENTWORTH.

To the Right Honble. my much honored Lord the Lorde Conway, Principall Secretary to his Majestie."[108]

This favour being granted, and Sir Thomas having been created a Viscount, he appeared in the upper house as an advocate for the ministers whom he had, only a few months previously, denounced; but the adherence of Strafford was of little benefit to Buckingham, as his new ally was the most unpopular of men. One unhappy result, however, this unprincipled alliance produced. The new partisan ingratiated himself with

Charles during his late and brief support of Buckingham; and the seeds were laid of that influence which so tended to undermine the future stability of the Crown, and pioneered the way to Charles's fall.

The most unjust aspersions were now circulated throughout all society. It was Buckingham's custom to cast away, as unworthy of consideration, all reports that were brought to him. On one occasion, hearing that two Colonels, when before St. Martin's Fort, had said to a third that they observed the Duke often go in his barge to the fleet, and that they believed he would steal away to England some day; and that if he did, they swore they would hand out the white flag, and deliver up the town and island to Tonar, the Governor; the Duke called a council of war, the accused being absent, and charged these gentlemen with their words. They flatly denied them on their swords. The Duke, without further inquiry, believed them, and dismissed the court. Nor did he ever pay any attention to things said about him, either in the Commons or in the camp.

In the same way he appears to have treated James Howell, who, presuming on having been in his service, and on the affabilities of the Duke, and a facility of character which had its advantages as well as disadvantages, wrote an impertinent letter, saying, that in his "shallow apprehension" it might be well for the Duke to part with some of his places, and so to avoid opprobrium. "Your Grace," he remarked, "might stand more firm without an anchor." Then he next threw out some suggestions as to the better regulation of the Duke's family and private affairs; and ended by saying that he knew the Duke did not, nor need not, affect popularity. "The people's love," he added, "is the strongest citadel of a sovereign prince, but wrath often proved fatal to a subject, for he who pulleth off his hat to the people giveth his head to the prince." And he ends by referring to "a late unfortunate Earl," who, a little before Queen Elizabeth's death, had drawn the axe across his own neck; he had become so unpopular, that he was considered dangerous to the State. This very unpleasant reference was taken, at all events, amicably by Buckingham. The fate of Essex was often supposed to shadow forth his own; and the rapid rise, the more rapid fall, the generous, careless nature, the very early doom of both, to have suggested that parallel between the Earl of Essex and Buckingham, in which Lord Clarendon has placed the characters of both before the reader in delicate touches.

In one respect they were very different. Essex, when attacked, even before going to Ireland, wrote an apology, which he dispersed with his own hands. Buckingham left his fame to his contemporaries, and to posterity, just as they choose to view it. On an offer once being made to him to write a justification of his actions, he refused it, says Lord Clarendon, "with a pretty kind of thankful scorn, saying that he would trust to his own good intentions, which God knew, and trust to Him for the pardon of his errors;" that he saw no "fruit of apologies but the multiplying of discourse, which, surely," even Lord Clarendon observes, "was a well-settled matter."[109]

But there were dangers lurking in his path which no defence could avert. Personal danger did not appal him. Slander did not affect him. Yet a forgotten, morbid, disappointed man was the instrument of destiny; and even in this crisis Buckingham seems never to have shrunk from the assassins, even in imagination: he knew that he had already escaped great perils—and that consciousness gave him security.

CHAPTER III.

FELTON—HIS CHARACTER—UNCERTAINTY OF HIS MOTIVES —CIRCUMSTANCES UNDER WHICH HE WAS BROUGHT INTO CONTACT WITH BUCKINGHAM—MOTIVES OF HIS CRIME DISCUSSED—THE REMONSTRANCE—THE FATE OF LA ROCHELLE—BUCKINGHAM'S UNPOPULARITY— RETURNS TO RHE—MISGIVINGS OF HIS FRIENDS— INTERVIEW WITH LAUD—WITH CHARLES I.—HIS FAREWELL—HE ENTERS PORTSMOUTH—FELTON—THE ASSASSINATION—ORIGINAL LETTERS FROM SIR D. CARLETON AND SIR CHARLES MORGAN—THE KING'S GRIEF.

CHAPTER III.

Whilst all these events were pending, dark designs were being formed and cherished in the distempered mind of one far from the Court, and probably wholly forgotten by him to whose destiny he gave the final stroke.

Hitherto Buckingham had escaped all bodily harm. He had rallied speedily from illness, and was in the full vigour of his life; he had returned unhurt from the perilous service at Rhé; he had repeatedly crossed the Channel, and tracked even the great ocean when the science of navigation, as well as of ship-building, was imperfect, and when a thousand dangers encompassed his course: he had escaped the pestilence by which the army lost many of its best men. And yet his days were numbered.

In the remote county of Suffolk the unhappy John Felton was born. He was the youngest son of an ancient family, and in somewhat narrow circumstances, and had been a lieutenant in a regiment of foot, under the command of Sir John Ramsey, in the expedition against Rhé. He was a man of great reserve, which, though he had long led a soldier's life, in the course of which he appears to have risen from the ranks, was still silent and gloomy. In person he was diminutive, with a meagre form, and a face rendered almost ghastly from the expression of that deep, habitual, and apparently causeless melancholy to which we give the term morbid; and thus singularly did these outlines of his character correspond with the circumstances of his daily life. So strange was it to discover in the young soldier the characteristics attributable to a cloister rather than to a camp, that one turns to the mournful plea of insanity for explanation. But no defence of that nature, or on that ground, was ever attempted for Felton; unhappily, so much has lunacy increased in modern times, that it forms now one point in almost every case of unaccountable crime. In the days of our ancestors it was different. Such an excuse was rare, and only applied to imbecility, or to mania, when too apparent to be disputed.

To this day, indeed, there has been found no adequate motive for the deed, which Felton long contemplated in the depths of a soul that never gave utterance to its joys or sorrows, and exchanged no sympathies with others. Whatever "may have been the immediate or greatest motive of that felonious conception," Sir Henry Wotton declares, "is even yet in the clouds."[110] The origin of that dark design has, nevertheless, been referred to a disappointment in Felton's military career. This he subsequently denied, by saying that the Duke had always shown him respect. Whilst at Rhé, Felton's captain having died in England, he naturally applied to Buckingham for promotion. The Duke, however, consulted the colonel of the regiment, and, by his suggestion, gave the company to an officer named Powell, who happened to be lieutenant of the colonel's company, and a man of great bravery; and Felton himself acknowledged the justice and expediency of this preference of Powell to himself. So that, to follow the same authority, the idea of any rancour being harboured, owing to this arrangement, can have no foundation.[111] But the notion has been taken up by historians adverse to Buckingham—and such are in the majority—rather to heighten the impression that he suffered for an act of injustice, for which his death was, more or less, a retribution, than from any certain conviction on the point.

There was also another cause assigned for the crime which Felton meditated. In his native county there was a certain knight whom the Duke had latterly favoured; and between this individual and Felton there "had been ancient quarrels not yet healed," which might be festering within his breast, and worked up by his own grievance into frenzy. But this explanation is also rejected by Sir Henry Wotton, whose evidence is the best that can be given, as proceeding from a man of principle, and a contemporary and friend of Buckingham's.

Three hours before his execution, however, Felton, either as a palliation to others, or to excuse the deed to himself, alleged that the book written by Dr. Egglisham, King James's Scottish physician, in which the

Duke was portrayed as one of the foulest monsters upon earth, unfit to live in a Christian court, or even within the pale of humanity, had a great effect upon his mind, in inciting him to what he deemed an act of heroic virtue. The fact, indeed, it is plain, was, that his religious convictions had an all-powerful influence upon his judgment, which was warped by the gloomy bigotry which casts a shadow over the noblest and most encouraging hopes of the Christian. The tenor of this unhappy man's life had been marked by seriousness and religious observances; but it was the religion which condemned all who differed—the religion, not of love, but self-righteousness and hatred.

During the leisure of peace—if peace that can be called in which all the elements of civil war were being engendered—the Petition of Right— that great measure, which even Clarendon allows, "was of no prejudice to the Crown"—received the King's assent. Not contented with what they found might prove a bare declaration of the law, the Commons drew up a Remonstrance, addressed to the King, in order that the too great power of Buckingham might be diminished. The promotion of Papists, the protection of Arminians, under the patronage of Neal and Laud, were the chief subjects, and were calculated to arouse and inflame the passions of a fanatic, like Felton, and to have suggested the reasoning that was soon warped, by prejudice and hatred, into the form and conception of guilt. There were other subjects of complaint in that celebrated Remonstrance, which touched him also—the standing commission of general continued to Buckingham in time of peace, the dismissal of faithful officers from various places of trust, the failures at Cadiz and at Rhé—these were but a small part of that important document, but they were the portion most likely to excite such a mind as that of Felton. He stated, indeed, that the idea of assassination, which he had repelled by stern efforts of conscience —for he was a man misled and mistaken, but not devoid of certain principles, and he dared to make use of that solemn and misguiding word, conscience—was revived, with irresistible force, by the Remonstrance. Never, hitherto, had the members most distinguished for oratory in parliament reasoned with so much force, and so much research, and so great a depth of legal argument, as on the Petition of Right, and its successor, the Remonstrance. It was the era of good taste and profound argument in that great assembly.[112] All tended to strengthen Felton in the conviction that the Duke was a traitor and oppressor, whom any patriot would do well to assassinate.

Then he read works which maintained the lawfulness of ridding a nation of an oppressor; and the voice of conscience was heard no more— a false heroism was thenceforth the spectre that lured him onwards.

Never was there a more striking instance of the influence of one mind over another than that which the books of the day had over the mind of Felton; never was there a more prominent exemplification of the responsibilities of a writer, even if his words chance to have only an ephemeral reputation, than this man's crime.

The resolution was then formed—Buckingham's life was to be sacrificed for the public good. Sir Henry Wotton seems to think that every plea adopted by Felton in explanation of this design was to be distrusted. "Whatever were the true motives, which, I think, none can determine but the Prince of Darkness itself, he did thus prosecute the effort."

He bought for tenpence, in a cutler's shop on Tower Hill, a knife—that instrument, the blow of which paralyzed England—and sewed the sheath into the lining of his pocket, so that he could at any time draw out the knife with one hand—his other being maimed and powerless.

Being thus provided, he watched in gloom and privacy (for he was very poor) the opportunity over which he brooded.

Meantime, Buckingham was mingling, in the full confidence of his fearless nature, in the affairs of that world which he was so soon to quit for ever. His unpopularity was at its acmé, and if he feared not for himself, there were friends who trembled for his safety. Sir Clement Throgmorton, a man of great consideration and judgment, one day asked a private conference, and advised the Duke to wear a coat of mail underneath his his outer garment. The Duke received the suggestion very kindly, but gave this reply, "Against popular fury a coat of mail would be but a weak defence, and with regard to an attack from any single man, he conceived there was no danger." "So dark," says Wotton, "is destiny."

This consciousness of being the object of universal hatred probably increased the keen desire which now possessed the Duke's mind of retrieving the discredit into which his failure had plunged him. During the whole of the spring, preparations for a fresh descent on La Rochelle had been in contemplation. As good a squadron as that which Admiral Pennington had previously commanded was ready at Plymouth by the end of February, ten ships having been pressed into the service. Several new vessels were built, notwithstanding that the workmen of the navy at Chatham complained that they had not received any pay for seven months. Buckingham was, at one time, on the point of visiting Plymouth, but went to Newmarket instead.[113] During the session of Parliament his brother-in-law, the Earl of Denbigh, was dispatched with a fleet to the relief of La Rochelle, which was blockaded by the French, but he returned without even attempting to effect anything; and the unfortunate town was left to its fate. Richelieu, besieging it by circumvallations, constructed a mole across the mouth of the harbour, leaving room only for the ebb and flow of the sea; and destruction seemed inevitable. It was, therefore, a very probable means of recovering his credit at home, for the Duke again to attempt the relief of those who, as Protestants, represented a cause dear to English hearts. Independently of this, it is not unlikely that old rivalship with the sagacious Cardinal may have influenced Buckingham to undertake a second expedition to La Rochelle.[114] It is, perhaps, not to be wondered at that Buckingham's name should be covered with so much opprobrium after his death, when the fate of the heroes who defended La Rochelle is remembered. In the October of the year in which the Duke perished, La Rochelle, long refusing to yield, was forced to submit. The inhabitants surrendered at discretion—even with an English fleet, commanded by Lord Sidney, in sight. Of fifteen thousand men who had been enclosed in the town, only four thousand survived famine and fatigue, to lay down their arms before the generals sent by Richelieu.

To make a last effort for these valiant sufferers was, therefore, the wisest determination that Buckingham could form. The fleet which Lord Denbigh had commanded was in good condition, and all at home had learned experience through failure. He had taken that severe lesson to his own heart. Had Buckingham been spared to relieve La Rochelle, and to recover for England the honour of her sullied reputation, his errors would doubtless have been forgiven.

Before leaving London, the Duke went to take leave of Laud, then Bishop of London. Laud had now, both in civil and ecclesiastical matters, a great influence over the King: of this Buckingham was fully sensible.

Sir Henry Wotton, who had made some inquiries whether the Duke had had any presentiment of his death, relates a touching scene between the Duke and Laud.

"My Lord," Buckingham said, "you have, I know, very free access to the King, our sovereign; let me pray you to remind his Majesty to be good to my poor wife and children."

At these words, or perhaps rather on looking at the expression of countenance with which they were uttered, the Bishop, with some uneasiness, asked the Duke whether he had any forebodings in his mind which he did not like to betray?

"No," replied the Duke; "but I think some adventure may kill me as much as any other man,"

The day before he was assassinated, the Duke being ill, Charles the First visited him whilst he was in bed. After a long and serious conversation in private, they separated, Buckingham embracing the King "in a very unusual and passionate manner;" and he also showed great emotion on taking leave of Lord Holland, "as if his soul had divined he should see them no more."

The twentieth of August was his birthday. He had completed his thirty-sixth year—that period which has been marked by a great writer as the departure of youth[115]—it might have been, perhaps, in Buckingham's case, the beginning of wisdom extracted from experience.

It was the age of omens and other superstitious weaknesses; and supernatural warnings were not wanting to heighten the effect of the tragedy that was soon to be acted. Neither did they who foreboded evil to the Duke wait until after the event to bring forth their ghostly revelations. One day, some little time before the Duke's death, he was playing at bowls with the King in Spring Gardens. Buckingham, as he usually did, even in Charles's presence, kept his hat on, a piece of presumption which irritated a Scotsman named Wilson, who, in his wrath, tossed off the Duke's hat, and declared he would punish impertinence wherever he met it in the same way. On looking round for this man, he had vanished, and was nowhere to be found. The courtiers marvelled at the incident, and regarded it as ominous of the Duke's fate; but he laughed at them for their folly, and showed no fear.[116]

His indifference was regarded as infatuation; in fact, it proves that the Duke was, in some respects, superior to those whom he most respected. There was no lone spinster in the country more given to believe in dreams and omens than Laud; and his diary contains perpetual references to his dreams. Every slight incident had its peculiar meaning, foreshadowing some great event. Nor does Lord Clarendon rise above the tone of the times, in his relation of that famous ghost story which forms one of the most prominent incidents of Buckingham's latest days.

Old Sir George Villiers had now been dead eighteen years, and perhaps few of his family, and certainly not his wife, who had been twice married, ever wished to see him again. There was a certain Mr. Nicholas Towse, however, living in Bishopsgate Without, London, to whom the aged knight appeared in the spirit, during the year 1627, making choice of that individual as the depositary of secrets beyond the grave, because he had known him whilst he was a boy at school in Leicestershire, near Brookesby. As a mark of friendship, therefore, the apparition of Sir George favoured Mr. Towse with his revelations, and stood one night at the foot of his bed, dressed in the costume of the time of Elizabeth. There was a candle in the room, and Mr. Towse was perfectly wakeful. On beholding Sir George, he uttered, according to his own account, the natural inquiry, "What he was, and whether he was a man?" To which the apparition answered, "No." Then Towse, in considerable emotion, asked, "Was he a devil?" To which the apparition still answered, "No." Then Mr. Towse, with increasing agitation, said, "In the name of God, tell me what you are?"

"I am," replied the spectre, in doublet and hose, "the spectre of Sir George Villiers, the father of the Duke of Buckingham;" adding, that because he believed Mr. Towse loved him, and was sensible of the former kindness that he had shown him, he had selected him as the bearer of a message to the Duke of Buckingham, warning him in such a manner as to prevent much mischief and present ruin to the Duke.

Whilst the apparition was speaking, Towse became more and more convinced of his identity, and more fully conscious that the long defunct master of a noble house stood before him; nevertheless, he refused to do Sir George's bidding, saying that it would bring ridicule on him to carry to the Duke such a message. But the ghost earnestly entreated him to comply, assuring him, after the manner of ghosts, that there were certain passages in the Duke's life known only to himself and his son, and that the revelation of these would plainly show the Duke it was no "distempered fancy, but a reality, that he wished to disclose."

That night was one of irresolution, if not of incredulity; but, on the next, the unhappy Towse, thus picked out for so ghostly a service, promised to go to the Duke. He went, indeed, and found out Sir Thomas Freeman and Sir Ralph Bladden, the Duke's chamberlains, by whom he was presented to the Duke. Then followed some private and agitated interviews between Buckingham and Towse, and the cautions of the ghost were fully and forcibly communicated: they related chiefly to Buckingham's patronage of Laud, and suggested some popular acts which the Duke was to perform in Parliament—and, in short, contained advice that any reasonable man might have offered. But nothing that was said by Mr. Towse made the slightest impression on the Duke, except, when certain passages of his life were referred to, with which the ghost had primed Mr. Towse, he owned he had believed "that no living creature knew of them but himself, and that it must be either God or the devil that had revealed them." The Duke then offered to get Mr. Towse knighted, and to have him made a burgess in the forthcoming Parliament. But Mr. Towse, finding that the obstinate favourite was deaf to his advice, left him, prognosticating that the Duke's death would happen at a certain time —which prognostic was fulfilled.

Mr. Towse then returned to Bishopsgate Without; and, there is much reason to believe, laboured under mental malady; for the visits of the apparition were now so frequent that he grew familiar with him, "as if it had been a friend or acquaintance that had come to visit him." And from this very unpleasant guest Towse learned to see in perspective many events that had not then dawned on England; more especially the troubles of Prynne, who was Towse's father-in-law—which was contrary to all rule, as a ghost should keep to one subject. On the day of Buckingham's death, also, Mr. Towse and his wife being at Windsor Castle, where Towse had an office, they were sitting in company, when he started up, exclaiming, "The Duke of Buckingham is slain!" At the very moment that these words were uttered the blow had been given. Towse dying soon after, also foretold his own death.

This narrative, thought worthy of insertion by Clarendon, and therefore not to be completely disregarded in any biography of Buckingham, is taken, however, from a letter penned at Boulogne, by one Edmund Wyndham, in 1672, twenty years after the event.[117][118] According to Lord Clarendon, Buckingham, after hearing Towse's revelation, was observed ever afterwards to be very melancholy. That he had misgivings as to his return, we have seen; but there are few men so insensible, at such a moment, as to be quite free from presentiment of evil—more especially one on whom the eyes of the country were directed in resentment, and regarding whom the Commons was then preparing a Remonstrance.[119]

Felton, meantime, was intent on pursuing his scheme. The frank and kindly manner of the Duke towards his officers and soldiers at Rhé, his personal courage, and his participation in the hardships all had undergone in that expedition, had failed to propitiate the assassin, who was, in fact, stimulated by the fiercest of all incentives—political hatred, justified by the plea of religion. He set off, therefore, to Portsmouth, and, partly on horseback, and partly on foot, accomplished that journey; and perhaps the desperate state of his fortunes added to his gloomy views and reckless designs, into which one thought of self-preservation never entered. At a few miles from Portsmouth he was seen sharpening the fatal knife on a stone; he arrived at that city with the determination that, should his scheme of assassination fail for want of opportunity, he would enlist as a volunteer, in order to accomplish it eventually.

There was, of course, considerable bustle in the town; and on entering it, when the ghastly murderer stood unobserved amongst the crowd, there was too numerous a train about the Duke for Felton to reach him. Fearful of observation, he kept himself indoors one morning after his arrival; but, on the ensuing day, repaired to the house where Buckingham was staying. The Duke was at that time at breakfast, and little attention was paid by a number of suitors and applicants who were waiting for him in the antechamber, to the diminutive being who was watching, with his dark purpose, among the unconscious crowd. As there were several military men, amongst whom was the Duc de Soubise, with Buckingham, as well as Sir Thomas Fryer, much animation pervaded the conversation, in consequence of a report having reached Portsmouth that La Rochelle had been relieved. Soubise and his followers believed that this report was set on foot by some agents of the French, in order to induce the English to relax in their preparations, until the mole, which it was Richelieu's plan to form at the mouth of the harbour, should be completed. He and the other foreigners spoke with vehemence, and in tones which the English, who were listening, deemed to be those of anger. The Duke, it appeared, was inclined to believe the report, and the eagerness of Soubise was not, therefore, to be matter of surprise, since his interests, and those of his adherents, were irrevocably engaged in the approaching expedition. At length, however, the conference ended; Soubise took his leave, and Buckingham rose to quit the chamber where he had breakfasted.

It was, probably, with a pre-occupied mind that he thus prepared to go out; and it is very possible that he scarcely observed a small figure, which he may not even have recognized, which was lifting up, as he passed on, the hangings between the room and the antechamber. This was Felton. Buckingham, on his way, stopped an instant to speak to Sir Thomas Fryer, one of his Colonels, who was a short man—so that, in order to hear his reply, the Duke bent down his head somewhat. Fryer then drew back, and, at that moment, Felton, striking across the Colonel's arm, stabbed Buckingham a little above the heart. The knife was left in the body; the Duke, with a sudden effort, drew it out, and exclaiming, "The villain has killed me," pursued the assassin out of the parlour into the hall or antechamber, where he sank down, and, falling under a table, drew a deep breath, and expired.

Then the utmost confusion ensued. The English, misled by what had passed at breakfast, accused Soubise and his followers of the murder; and they would have been instantly sacrificed to the fury of the populace, had not some persons of cooler feelings interposed in their behalf. No one had seen the murderer; he had come in unnoticed, and had withdrawn in like manner. At this moment, a hat, into which a paper was sewn, was found near the door; it was eagerly examined, and some writing on the paper read with avidity, and these words were deciphered:—

"That man is cowardly, base, and deserves neither the name of a gentleman nor soldier, who will not sacrifice his life for the honour of God, and safety of his prince and country. Let no man commend me for doing it, but rather discommend themselves; for if God had not taken away our hearts for our sins, he could not have gone so long unpunished.

"JNO. FELTON."[120]

Whilst the bystanders were reading these words, the body of the Duke had been conveyed to the inner apartment, from which he had issued, having been first laid on the table of the antechamber, or hall; and in this inner chamber it was left, without a single person, even a domestic, to watch over his remains, or to give him that tribute of sorrowing respect which is due to the poorest. And this singular neglect has been regarded as a proof of indifference in those who, but a few minutes previously, were crowding round the powerful Minister and General. But it was, in fact, one of those accidents which often bear a very different construction, when they are considered relatively to the circumstances of the hour, to that placed on them. Sir Henry Wotton, to whom the fact was mentioned by one of the Duke's friends, speaks of it as "beyond all wonder;" but accounts for it by the horror which the murder had excited, added to the astonishment at the sudden disappearance of the murderer, who had glided from the terrible scene like an actor who has done his part, and makes his exit. For a time, however, whilst high words were heard between the Frenchmen and their accusers, whilst murmurs from the street below, of the eager and infuriated crowd, were changed into yells of vengeance, that cold corpse lay unheeded; "thus, upon the withdrawing of the sun, does the shadow depart from the painted dial."[121] All were, indeed, in the house, occupied in asking again and again the question, Where could the owner of the hat be?—for he, doubtless, was the assassin. Whilst they were thus talking, a man without a hat was seen walking with perfect composure up and down before the door. "Here," cried one of the crowd, "is the man who killed the Duke," upon which Felton calmly said, "I am he, let no person suffer that is innocent." Then the populace rushed upon him with drawn swords, to which Felton offered no defence, preferring rather to die at once, than to abide the issue of justice. He was, however, rescued by others less violent

—a circumstance which was thought very fortunate for the popular party, on whom a stigma might have rested had the murderer been killed; and Felton being secured, was conveyed to a small sentry-box; he was

50

instantly loaded with heavy irons, which prevented his either standing upright or lying down in that narrow prison, where he remained sometime, whilst the mob were raging without in the streets.[122]

The Duchess of Buckingham was in an upper room of that house in which the husband whom she had "loved," to use her own words, "as never woman loved man," was murdered. She had not, when it happened, risen from her bed.[123]

The following very graphic account, written by a very devoted friend of Buckingham, Sir Dudley Carleton, presents, in several details, a somewhat different delineation of this scene of murder, to that which has been related, collected from various sources, although, in various instances, it is confirmatory of the statements usually received.[124]

"S^R—If ye ill newes we have heard (doe not as their use is) out flye these lres,[125] they will bring you ye worst of ye strangest I think you ever received: sure I am, whatever passed my pen. Our noble Duke in ye midst of his army he had ready at Portsmouth as well shipping as land forces, in ye height of his favour with our Gracious Master, who was herd by at this place and in the greatest joy and alacrity I ever saw him in my life at ye newes he had received about of ye clock in ye morning on Saturday last of ye relief of Rochell, in that fort, that ye place might well attend his coming, wherewith he was hastening to ye King, who that morning had sent for him by me upon other occasions;—at his going out of a lower parlour where he usually sat, and had then broken his fast in presence of many standers by (Frenchmen with Monsieur de Soubise, officers of his army and those of his own Trayns) was stabbed unto ye heart a little above ye breast with a knife by one Felton, an Englishman, being a Reformed Lieutenant, who hastening out of ye doore and ye duke having pulled out ye knife which was left in ye wound and following him out of ye parlour into ye hall, with his hand putt to his sword, there fell down dead with much effusion of bloud at his mouth and nostrils. The Lady Anglesea,[126] then looking down into ye hall out of an open Gallery, which crossed ye end of it, and being spectator of this tragical fight, went immediately with a cry into ye Duchesses Chamber, who was in bed, and then fell down on ye floor, so surprized ye poor Duchesse with this sad … matin….[127] The murderer in ye midst of ye noise and tumult, every man drawing his sword and no man knowing whom to strike, nor from whom to defend himself, slipt out into ye kitchen and there stood with some others unespyed, when a voyce being currant in the court to wch ye window and doore of ye kitchen answered (a Frenchman, a Frenchman), and his guilty conscience making him believe it was "Felton, Felton" (who being otherwise unknown and undiscovered might well have escaped) he came out of ye kitchen with his sword drawn, and presenting himselfe, said, I am the man: some offering to assayle him and one running at him with a spit, he flung down his sword and rendered himselfe to ye company, who being ready to handle him as he deserved by tearing him in pieces I took him from them, and having committed him to ye custody of some officers, when I had taken ye best order I could for other affairs in so great confusion, jointly with Secretary Cooke I examined ye man and found he had no particular offence against ye Duke, more than all others for want of some small entertayments were owing him: but he grounded his practise upon ye Parliament's Remonstrance as to make himselfe a Martyr for his Country, which he confessed to have resolved to execute ye Monday before, he being then at London, and came from thence expressly by the Wednesday morning, arriving at Portsmouth ye very morning, not above half an hour before he committed it. We could not then discover any complices, neither did we take more than his free and willing confession: but now His Majestie hath ordayned by Commission ye Lord Treassurer, Lord Steward, Earl of Dorset, Secretary Cooke and myselfe to proceed with him as ye nature of ye fact requires, and wee shall begin this afternoon: meane while I would not but give you this relation to ye end you may know ye truth of this bloudy act, which will flye about the world diversly reported to you, and you should not find it strange such a blowe to be struck in ye midst of ye Duke's friends and followers: you must know ye murderer took his time and place at ye presse near ye issue of ye room, and many of us were stept out to our horses, as I my selfe was to go to Court with the Duke. The murderer gloryed in his acte ye first day; but when I told him he was ye first assassin of an Englishman, a gentleman, a soldier, and a protestant, he shrunk at it, and is now grown penitent. It seems this man and Ravillac were of no other Religion (though he professeth other) than *assassanisme*; they have the same maxims as you will see by two writings were found sowed in his hat, wch goe herewith.

"From Lord Viscount Dorchester to" [not addressed.][128]

In another letter, addressed to the King of Bohemia by Sir Charles Morgan, it was also shown in what sanguine spirits the Duke was, and how he was forming good resolutions, when he received the fatal blow which cut him off from all hope of retrieving the errors he so candidly confessed, or of completing the work of reformation, in various departments, which he hoped to accomplish. Although we may feel assured that the blow was suffered to fall for some purpose of mercy, yet never did any sudden death seem more untimely.

The King was only about six miles from Portsmouth, whence he intended doubtless to witness the departure of a friend whom he never ceased to lament. He was at prayers when Sir John Hippesley came suddenly into the Presence Chamber, where service was that day performed, and whispered the news into his Majesty's ear. Charles did not permit a single feature of his face to express either astonishment or distress; and, when a deep pause ensued, the appalled chaplain thinking to spare his Majesty the distress of remaining during the service, he calmly ordered him to proceed with the prayers—and, until those were concluded, preserved the same undisturbed demeanour. Some there were who argued, from this perfect mastery over his feelings, that the King did not regret the death of one who had rendered him so unpopular, and from whom he could not unloose the bonds which early habit and youthful friendship had drawn so closely as to convert them into shackles. But the deep sorrow which Charles felt was shown in his affectionate care of those whom his favourite loved; nor was it, as some supposed, without a stern effort that he controlled his emotions whilst he remained amid those assembled in prayer. No sooner was the service over, than he suddenly departed to his chamber, and, throwing himself on his bed, gave full vent to a passion of grief, and, weeping long and bitterly, paid to the poor Duke the tribute of his anguish,—lamenting not only the loss of an excellent friend and servant, but "the terrible manner of the Duke's death." And he continued for many days in the deepest melancholy.[129]

Of course, in those days, this fearful event was said to have been foretold, not only by a ghost, but in dreams, and by presentiments. Sir James Bagg, one of the Duke's most trusted servants, has left the following proof of his belief in dreams:—

"RIGHT HONORABLE—Hand in hand came to my unfortunate hand yo Expps.[130] and my noble friend Mr. Secretarie Cooke's, and yo[r] Honors leynes could not be but welcome although they brought vnto mee the sadd and heavy newes of that damnable act of that accursed ffelton, wc[h] hath so seated itself in my heart as it will hould memorie there, of the untymilie losse of my deere and gracious Lord to my unpacified sorrow untill my Death; for as I partook wt[h] him of his comforts living, I will have a share of his sorrowes after him. Oh my Lord! his end was upon Satterdau morning. The daie of his dissolving tould mee by a dreame, discribed in all. It wanted but the damned name of Felton. But that fiende unworthy of it was entituled by the name of Souldier. This Dreame tould my Wife and dearest friends, did not a little trouble mee, but now the trueth thereof torments me.

"Yo leynes my only comforte brought wt[h] them his Mat[131] commands. In all I doe obey them," &c., &c.

The letter is addressed thus from Sir James Bagg—"For his Lordship," and dated, "Augt. 28th, 1628."[132]

Amongst the Duke's relations the Countess of Denbigh was most beloved by him, and his affection was warmly returned. On the very day of his death he wrote to her. Whilst she was penning her answer, her paper was moistened with her tears, in a passion of grief so poignant and so despairing, that she could only account for it by believing those transports of sorrow to have been prophetic. She wrote to him these words:—

"I will pray for your happy return, which I look to with a great cloud over my head, too heavy for my poor heart to bear without torment. But I hope the great God of Heaven will bless you."[133]

On the day after the Duke's death, the Bishop of Ely, who was the devoted friend of Lady Denbigh, being considered the fittest person to break the intelligence to her, went to visit her, but hearing that she was asleep, waited until she awoke, which she did in all the perturbation produced by a terrible dream. Her brother, she said, had seemed to pass with her through a field, when, hearing a sudden shout from the people, she had asked what it meant, and was told that it was for joy that the Duke of Buckingham was ill. She was relating this dream to one of her gentlewomen when the Bishop entered her chamber. The scene that followed may be easily conceived. Whatever were the ill-starred Duke's failings, he died beloved by those most dear to him.

His sister's apprehensions were, indeed, perfectly justifiable, and they might well intrude into those hours of silence in which thoughts of the absent or unhappy most frequently trouble our minds. Had the Duke again been saved from the chances of war, what might have been his fate at home in case of his return unsuccessful? Already had he hardly escaped from the indignation of the people: even then, in the remote county of Carmarthen, they were raising reports that the King had been poisoned by the Duke—reports that had been believed by the simple inhabitants of Wales. The fury of party had much to answer for in the excitement of bad passions, the end and mischief of which can never be foreseen.

The greatest obscurity hung over the motives which prompted the act, unless it be explained by the practical aberration of a mind which, still bearing the outward semblance of reason, has evil thoughts, fostered by strong passions. The connections of Felton were not only poor—his mother appears to have been illiterate. To them, probably, his designs were never imparted, although they lived in the metropolis; yet it is evident, from several circumstances, that they knew of his animosity to the Duke, and were, to a certain extent—without any complicity— prepared to hear of some fearful act on the part of their unhappy relative.

Whilst the Duke's family were overwhelmed with anguish, another humble mourner almost sank under the blow. This was Elianore Felton, the mother of the assassin. She was a native of Durham, of which city her father had once been mayor, but she was then residing in London. On the 24th of August, in the church in St. Dunstan's, in the Strand, an aged woman and her daughter attended afternoon service. These poor women were Elianore Felton and Elizabeth Hone, the mother and sister of Felton.

During the singing of the psalms, whilst the congregation were standing up, some disturbance took place in the church. Elianore Felton, turning to a gentleman near her, inquired what was the cause? She was told that the Duke of Buckingham was killed; upon which, although the name of the assassin was not then mentioned to her, the unhappy woman fainted.

It is probable that, knowing her son's sentiments towards the Duke, and being aware of Felton's fanatical opinions and moody temper, a panic, causing that sudden fainting, seized her. Her daughter, also, as the poor mother confessed in her subsequent examination, swooned also. These facts are very remarkable, and seem to show that she and her mother were aware of Felton's intentions. No further information was gathered from these gentlewomen by those around them, until, in about half-an-hour, upon the church becoming fuller, there ran another whisper through it, purporting that a certain Lieutenant Felton, or Fenton, had killed the Duke. Then, as Elizabeth Hone confessed, she did much weep and lament, supposing that it was her brother that had done the deed. She had, however, the presence of mind to conduct her mother home, before she told her that it was her son who had committed murder, and plunged the nation into consternation, and his family into ruin.

No proof whatsoever of any conspiracy was to be elucidated from the unfortunate relations of the culprit. Debt and disappointment had, according to their evidence, driven Felton to desperation. How many of the evil accidents of life issue, as far as one can see, humanly speaking, from pecuniary mismanagement. Felton, on the Wednesday before the Duke was killed, had gone to his mother's lodging, and told her of his intention to get the money due to him for pay from the Duke; adding, that "he was too deeply in debt to stay longer in town." Eighty pounds, it appeared, was then owing to him. This, and the loss of his Captaincy, were all that he had alleged to his own family against the Duke; he owned to no other grievance. The mother and sister, and brothers, were, however, committed to prison, although Edmund Felton, the brother of the delinquent, affirmed that he had not seen him for ten weeks previously to the murder; that John Felton had been estranged from him, and did not let him know where he lodged. There was no attempt in the examination, which took place before Thomas Richardson and Henry Finch, to screen the culprit by a plea of insanity; all his brother said was, that his disposition was "melancholie, sad, and heavy, and of few words."[134] Alone had he conceived, planned, and put into execution the deed of guilt; yet such was the hard disposition of the times, that it was proposed to extract a confession from John Felton by torture; but Charles interposed, and forbade the application of that horrible test,[135] and it was never again attempted in this country.

The nation was paralyzed by the death of the Minister, Admiral, and General. "During Buckingham's presence at Court," as Mr. Bruce, in the preface to the "Calendar of State Papers," remarks, "he reigned there as the King's absolute and single Minister. Every act of the Government passed by or through his will. The King was little seen or heard of on State affairs. He seldom ever attended a sitting of the Privy Council, except to carry out some object of his favourite." The void, the loss, may easily be conceived, after the death of the Duke. Charles, however, not only entered warmly into public affairs, but into the care and concerns of those children whom his friend had solemnly bequeathed to his charge.

His first office, however, was to honour the remains of one so suddenly cut off, whilst in the prime of life. The process of embalming was then deemed indispensable; the Duke's body, therefore, was submitted to that, happily, now disused operation; his bowels were interred at Portsmouth, where Lady Denbigh erected over them a memorial. Thus the place of his death was marked.

The corpse was then conveyed to York House, where all that could be viewed of that once noble form was exhibited underneath a hearse. Eventually it was entombed under a splendid monument in Westminster Abbey, on the north side of Henry VII.'s Chapel; and his Duchess, notwithstanding her second marriage, and his two sons, were buried in the vault beneath the tomb with their father.

The Duchess of Buckingham was near her confinement when this tragedy occurred. When Charles first visited the young widow, he promised her that he would be a "husband to her, and a father to her children." One son alone was living at the time of the Duke's decease. This was George, the second Duke of Buckingham of the house of Villiers. The character of this young nobleman, to whom Horace Walpole imputed "the figure and genius of Alcibiades," has been "drawn by four masterly hands. Burnet has hewn it out with his rough chisel. Count Hamilton touched it with slight delicacy, that finishes while it seems to sketch. Dryden catched the living likeness. Pope completed the historical resemblance." Lastly, Sir Walter Scott, in our time, has depicted this singular being with admirable skill, if not with perfect fidelity. He was scarcely a year and seven months old at his father's death.

One daughter, Lady Mary Villiers, survived the Duke. In the third year of the reign of Charles I., Buckingham having then no male heir, caused a patent to be made, limiting to her the title of Duchess of Buckingham, in default of male issue, his infant eldest son, Charles, having died in 1626, and George not being then born.

Lady Mary's life, so happy, seemingly, in her infancy, when, as "little Moll," she was King James's plaything, was not, in one respect, felicitous. Her first marriage, to Charles Lord Herbert, son and heir of Philip, Earl of Pembroke, was hastened, and performed privately in the chapel at Whitehall, because the young bride had formed an attachment to Philip Herbert, a younger son, who "did more apply himself to her," as she stated, than the elder suitor.

But her mother chided her out of this fancy, and the wedding took place—the bridegroom dying of small-pox a few weeks afterwards. Lady Mary married, secondly, James, Duke of Richmond and Lennox, by whom she had a son, Esme Stuart, who died in infancy; and thirdly, Thomas Howard, brother of the Earl of Carlisle. She left no children, so that her father's desire to perpetuate in her his title was not realized. If we may believe the praise of an epitaph which was undisguisedly paid for, we must suppose Lady Mary to have been endowed with all the virtues.
[136]

Some months after the Duke's death, his widow gave birth to a son, named Francis after his grandfather, who provided for him in a fortune of 1,000l. a-year. When he grew up, however, Francis shared with his brother the misfortune that overshadowed the family, from the unexpected second marriage of their mother to Randolph Macdonald, first Earl and afterwards Marquis of Antrim. It is painful to find the widowed Duchess separated from her children, having become a Roman Catholic; and having incurred in this, and on account of the conduct of her husband in Ireland, under Sir Thomas Wentworth, the King's displeasure. Charles so greatly disapproved of her marriage, that he refused, for several years, to see her, and, when reconciled, took away her children lest they should be imbued with her religious opinions. The young Duke and his brother Francis were educated, unhappily for themselves, with the Princes, Charles II. and his brothers; and Lady Mary was received in the house of the Earl of Pembroke, her father-in-law. Such are the changes and chances of life, that in 1639 we find Katharine, (still signing herself "Katharine Buckingham") interceding with Strafford for her husband, Lord Antrim. "Any misfortune," she writes, "to my lord must be mine."[137]

For him she had sacrificed indeed the favour of the King, and the guardianship of her children.

In 1648, Lord Francis, who, with his brother, had taken the field against the Parliament, was killed, at about two miles distance from Kingston-on-Thames: standing with his back planted against an oak-tree on the road-side; and, scorning to ask quarter, he met his death gallantly, having nine wounds on his face and body. He is said to have been a most beautiful youth, and was only nineteen when he thus fell. His body was brought by water to York House, then sad and desolate, and was taken thence to be deposited in his father's vault, with a Latin inscription on the coffin, preserved by Brian Fairfax, a faithful adherent, who thought it a pity that the epitaph should be buried with him; and who has therefore given it in his life of George, the second Duke of Buckingham. The elder brother of Lord Francis, after a life of extraordinary adventure, vicissitude, study, and dissipation, died, in 1688, quietly in his bed—"the fate of few of his predecessors of the title of Buckingham." His body also lies entombed near his father. "The life of pleasure and the soul of whim," as Pope describes him, his career furnishes a wide field for reflection and investigation, to those who may dare to dive into a biography so characterized by all the worst parts of the age in which he existed, as that of this profligate man.

Mary, Countess of Buckingham, survived the Duke, her son, four years —when, with her life, her dignity expired.

John Villiers, Lord Purbeck, died in 1657, when the titles which he bore became extinct. He lived, however, to recover his powers of mind, and to act as a friend and guardian to his nephews. Lady Purbeck, his first wife, took the name of Wright, and her son, by Lord Howard, bore that surname. The once flattered heiress, whose follies and misconduct were forgiven, as we have seen, by her father, died in 1645, in the King's

Garrison, at Oxford, and she is buried in the Church of St. Mary's, in that city.[139] Notwithstanding the misery of his first union, Lord Purbeck married again; but had no issue by his second wife, who was a daughter of Sir William Thugsby, of Kippen, in Yorkshire.

Robert Wright, the illegitimate son of Lady Purbeck, took his wife's name of Danvers, in order to abandon that of Villiers, so distasteful to the Commonwealth, with which he sided.

His descendants, nevertheless, laid claim to the honours of the first Lord Purbeck—and, although their claim was refused by Parliament, assumed them, until, in 1774, the death of the last pretender to the title, George Villiers, died without issue.

Christopher Villiers, the youngest brother of the Duke, pre-deceased him, dying in 1624. His title became extinct in 1659.

Sir William Villiers, the eldest half-brother of the Duke, had never emerged from his original obscurity; but Sir Edward, his other half-brother, whom Buckingham constituted President of Munster, was highly esteemed for his justice and hospitality, and lamented by the whole province.[140] From him, through his son, who had succeeded his maternal uncle in the title of Viscount Grandison, was descended the famous (or infamous) Barbara Villiers, afterwards Duchess of Cleveland, the mistress of Charles II. Her beauty appears to have been one of the few traits of the Villiers family that she possessed.

It is remarkable that not one of the titles conferred on the family of Villiers by James I. remains to distinguish the descendants of old Sir George of Brookesby. The Earldoms of Clarendon and of Jersey are subsequent creations.[141]

The Duchess of Buckingham, as she still styled herself, appears to have lived occasionally at Newhall, for after her daughter's marriage she was very desirous of having her with her—but the King would not hear of it; and the soundness of his judgment was proved by the conduct of the Duchess. Her life was henceforth occupied in bringing over converts to the faith she professed; amongst others she succeeded in making a proselyte of the Countess of Newburgh. After the death of her father, in 1632, she inherited the title of Baroness de Ros. It is remarkable that even in her person the honours her first husband had procured for his family did not abide. She, indeed, by courtesy, bore still his title, but was actually Marchioness of Antrim and Baroness de Ros. So extraordinary an acquisition of honours, and so rapid an extinction, are not known in any other family of England, but are peculiar to the House of Villiers.

Few things disappoint the reader more than the unaccountable change in the character of Katharine, Duchess of Buckingham, after she ceased, except by courtesy, to bear that name. She seems to have hastened, not only to plunge into a second marriage, but to have at last avowed, what she had during the whole of her life denied, the tenets of the Church of Rome. Henceforth she was opposed to the monarch by whom her husband, the Duke, had been overwhelmed with benefits. This painful alteration in one so gentle, so forgiving, so affectionate in her earlier life, is one of those anomalies in life that one cannot cease to regret, without being able to explain.

CHAPTER IV.

CHARACTER OF THE DUKE OF BUCKINGHAM—HIS PATRONAGE OF ART—HIS COLLECTION—THE SPANISH COURT DESCRIBED—COLLECTION BY CHARLES I.—FATE OF THESE PICTURES.

CHAPTER IV.

Whatever may have been the failings of the Duke of Buckingham as a husband, he marked his confidence in his wife by his will. That last act of his life gave the Duchess power over all his personal property, as well as a life possession of all his mansion-houses, with a fourth of his lands in jointure. That his debts were considerable, has been amply shewn during the course of the preceding narrative. Previous to his expedition to Rhé, he had wisely put his revenues into the hands of commissioners, and placed it out of his own power to manage or mismanage his own affairs. His occupations, as a courtier, as a minister, as an ambassador, and, lastly, as a general, sufficiently excuse his want of leisure for the control of his expenses, and the system of retrenchment requisite to relieve him from harassing liabilities.

He left, however, an immense amount of capital locked up in pictures; and that famous collection which places him, as Dr. Waagen affirms, in the third rank as "a collector of paintings in this country," came into the possession of his son. It was chiefly deposited in York House—that stately structure, so complete and so princely, that in 1663, when it had become the residence of the Russian embassy, Pepys was still amazed at its splendour, although thirty-five eventful years had shaken many a grand fabric to its fall. "That," he says, "which did please me best, was the remains of the noble soul of the late Duke of Buckingham appearing in his house, in every place, in the door-cases, and the windows."

It was in the Court of Madrid that Buckingham had learned to love art, to favour artists, and to become a judge of their works. Philip IV., of Spain, inert and inefficient as a monarch, and governed by Olivares, was a man of considerable intellectual powers, and of great taste. "The denizens of his palace breathed," as a modern writer expressed it, "an atmosphere of letters."[142] At that time the Castilian stage was in its perfection; the scenery was inimitable, and the greatest expense was bestowed in representing the pieces of Lope de Vega, and of Calderon; in the same manner as the masques of Ben Jonson were aided in effect by the talents of Inigo Jones. Nor was Philip IV. a mere patron of genius; he was himself an actor and author, writing with purity and elegance: a musician, a poet, or, as he delighted to style himself, *Ingenio de esto corte.* He wrote a tragedy on the death of Essex, Elizabeth's favourite; and he often acted with other literary men of his Court, delighting to vie with them in the display of fancy and humour in the *Comedias de repente*, representations resembling those of charades in the present day, in which a certain plot was worked out, with extempore speeches.

Several of this monarch's drawings, both of figures and landscapes, long remained as proofs of that skill which had distinguished both his fathers and grandfathers. He was an incomparable judge of painting; for at Valencia he delighted the citizens: on being shewn the great silver altar of the cathedral, he remarked promptly, that "the altar was of silver, but the doors were gold"—alluding to the pictures painted by Aregio and Neapoli, which adorned the doors.

It may easily be imagined how the example of this young Prince, only in his nineteenth year when Buckingham visited Spain, must have awakened in him, as in Charles, a new sense; fresh conceptions of the beautiful, cravings hitherto unfelt, an honourable emulation. And the example of Philip had its effect on both: the reception given to Rubens, who, as an artist, was treated with far greater distinction than he would have been as a mere diplomatist, in which capacity he came; the efforts of Philip to form an academy of fine arts; the honours bestowed on Velasquez; and the enthusiasm which he shewed in the collection of fine pictures for the galleries, which he so wonderfully enriched, must have proved to Charles and Buckingham how far behind was their own country in taste and liberality. They saw that the gold of Mexico and Peru was freely given for the treasures of art, whilst royalty at home was lavish only on pageants, horse-racing, hunting, and feasting. They saw the elevating effects of art and letters, and staid not in Spain long enough to witness the results of that life-long mistake made by Philip IV., in resigning the reins of government to the hands of a minister who lost for his sovereign great possessions, far exceeding those that many conquerors have acquired.

These refined tastes, which shone forth in Philip, were participated by his young and beautiful queen, Isabella of Bourbon, his first wife, and the sister of Henrietta Maria. She was the loveliest subject of the pencil of

Velasquez. At Broom-Hall, in Fifeshire, there is a picture by him representing the exchange of this Princess, when a girl, with Anne of Austria, the sister of Philip IV.

Isabella was destined to be the bride of Philip, then Prince of the Asturias—Anne to become the wife of Louis XIII. of France.

This production of Velasquez was only one of many portraits of this lovely princess; for she was by all acknowledged to be the very star of the Court. She shared the taste of her husband, whilst his young brothers, both early instructed in drawing, warmly joined in the King's pursuits, not only in the arts, but in literature. The elder, Don Carlos, beloved, as has been stated, by the Spaniards for his dark complexion, was supposed to have excited the jealousy of Olivares by his talents—he died in 1626: the second, the Boy-Cardinal, who assumed the Roman purple and the mitre of an archbishop, was the able pupil in painting of Vincencio Carducho, and became the most intellectual of the Spanish Princes that had appeared since Charles V. He set the fashion of those half-dramatic, half-musical pieces, which were called in Spain, *Zarzuelas*.[143] The boy —whom we have seen joining heart and soul, in his purple robe, and beneath his mitre, in court revels, given in honour of Charles I., was, at that very time, a student in philosophy and mathematics; and when at the age of twenty-two he was sent to govern Flanders, and henceforth to spend the brief span of life allotted to him in camps and councils—was still, to the last, the patron of Velasquez and Rubens.[144]

Olivares the Magnificent, as he was often called, cultivated the fine arts as a means of diverting the young monarch from his own abuse of power, and the consequent discontents which marked his administration. He possessed the most magnificent library in Europe, abounding in rare manuscripts, and, domesticated in this house as chaplain, Lope de Vega passed his old age. Quevedo, Pachecho, and many others, owed much to the patronage of Olivares—a protection which they paid back in compliments, and, like Lord Halifax, he was "fed with dedications." Olivares was one of the first sitters to Velasquez; he was the patron of Murillo, and, in the downfall of this minister, these two painters did not desert their early friend, but alone clung to him in his misfortunes.

The King, his Queen, the two royal brothers, and Olivares, had all a passion for having portraits taken of themselves. Philip was born for a sitter. His face, as Dr. Waagen remarks, "is better known than his history." His pale Flemish complexion, Austrian features, and fair hair have been many times depicted by Rubens and Velasquez. He was sometimes painted on his Andalusian courser, sometimes in black velvet, as he was going to the council—even at his prayers. There was an hereditary gift of silence and composure in his race: in Philip the attribute was so signal, that he could witness a whole comedy without stirring hand or foot, and conduct an audience without a muscle moving, except those in his lips and tongue.[145] Even after slaying the bull of Xarama, famed for strength and fierceness, not for a moment did he change countenance. To this incomparable staidness and dignity was added the advantage of a tall figure, which Philip knew well how to set off by a perfect mastery in combination of colours. Black he mixed almost uniformly with white, and gold and silver. This stately monarch was never known to smile more than three times in his life—that is, publicly, for in private he was ever "full of merry discourses."

Thus, taste, letters in every branch, the noblest works of architecture and sculpture, were the themes of a court where those who had left behind them the pedantry and vulgarity of King James arrived in the vigour of youth and intellect. Velasquez was painting a portrait of the King, and one also of the Infant, Don Fernando, when Charles and Buckingham arrived at Madrid, and interrupted, by their presence and the ceremonials of their reception, the completion of these pictures. The astonished Prince and his favourite found themselves transformed into a region hitherto scarcely dreamed of, yet which they were, by natural refinement of taste, well calculated to enter. They had left King James hunting in a ruff and bombasted garments; that King hated novelties. "It was as well," Horace Walpole remarks, "that he had no disposition to the arts, but let them take their own course, for he might have introduced as bad a taste into them as he did into literature."

Walpole attributes, likewise, the absence of pictures in the houses of the English nobility at this period to the great size and height of the rooms which they erected in the sixteenth and seventeenth centuries, when vastness seems to have constituted the idea of grandeur. Pictures would have been lost in rooms of such height, which were better calculated for tapestry; and he offers, as an instance, Hardwicke—which was furnished for the reception and imprisonment of Mary Queen of Scots—and Audley-End, as proofs of the prodigious space covered by a modern gentleman's house in the days of James I., and observes how impossible it would have been to place pictures in such structures.

One may readily conceive, therefore, the enchantment that was felt in visiting the Escurial, the palace of Buen-retiro, and the noble churches and famous convents of Madrid. Charles and Buckingham beheld that capital in the height of its splendour, and witnessed its most brilliant displays; they attended the grand, picturesque services and processions; they became acquainted with the works of Titian, of Velasquez, and Carducho. That Charles cherished the remembrance of the scenes in which he had once played so romantic a part, is evident from his employing a young painter, Miquel de la Cruz, even when England was threatened with the great Rebellion, to paint for him copies of a number of pictures from those in the Alcazar of Madrid.[146] The painter was cut off by an early death, and the project was never carried out.

After visiting the halls of the Escurial and of the Pardo, Charles resolved to form a gallery of art at Whitehall; and Buckingham, at the same time, determined to decorate York House with Spanish paintings. The nucleus of the gallery of art at Whitehall was bought from the collection of the Conde de Villame. Charles, also, endeavoured to purchase a small picture, on copper, of Correggio's, from Don Andres Velasquez, for a thousand crowns, but was unsuccessful; he failed, also, in obtaining the valuable volumes of Da Vinci's drawings, which Don Juan de Espina refused to sell, saying that he intended to bequeath these treasures of art to his master, the King. The nobles in the Spanish Court were in the habit of gratifying their young sovereign with presents of pictures and statues; and a similar attention was paid both to the Duke of Buckingham and to Charles. Philip gave the Prince the famous "Antiope," by Titian; as well as "Diana Bathing," "Europa," and "Danaë," by the same master. Buckingham had several presents of value given him; but though they were packed up, these paintings were left behind, in the hurry of departure, and were never forwarded to England.

A great portion of the large sums spent by Buckingham in Spain was expended in forming that famous collection which fell, unhappily, into the hands of his son. It would appear that James I. somewhat curtailed Charles's expenditure on this head; for we find, by an entry in the State Paper Office, that Buckingham lent the Prince twelve thousand pounds during their sojourn in Spain. Nevertheless, no specimen of Spanish art was ever conveyed to England by Charles.[147] A sketch was, indeed, begun of the Prince, by Velasquez, but it is doubtful if it were ever completed. Pachecho, the father-in-law of Velasquez, states that Charles was so delighted with this portrait in its unfinished state, that he presented the great painter with a hundred thousand crowns.[148] One may readily account for its never being completed, because Velasquez, when Charles and Buckingham left Madrid, could scarcely have finished the portraits and other pictures on which he was engaged by Philip IV.

In 1847, a picture belonging to Mr. Saare, of Reading, and supposed to have been a relic of the gallery of Whitehall, was exhibited in London as this lost portrait by Velasquez. It portrays Prince Charles in a more robust form, and with a greater breadth of countenance than any other known resemblance; and was stated to have been painted in 1623, and to have been mentioned in a privately printed catalogue of the gallery of the Earl of Fife, who died in 1809, in which it was stated that it had once belonged to the Duke of Buckingham. Unfortunately, the surname of the Duke of Buckingham was not specified; and since the title has been owned, so late as 1735, by the Sheffield family, the evidence was incomplete. A very curious controversy ensued, but facts remain much in the same state as before; and the authenticity of the portrait has been strongly disputed, if not denied, by Dr. Waagen, and others. It is singular that there was no work of Velasquez among the pictures left by Buckingham.

Whilst the great enlargement of ideas and improvement in taste, resulting from the journey into Spain, is acknowledged, it must be remembered that Charles and his favourite went, prepared in knowledge, and in an honourable emulation, to profit by all they might behold and hear. In painting, Perichief tells us, Charles "had so excellent a fancy, that he would supply the defect of art in the workman, and suddenly draw those lines, give those airs and lights, which experience and practice had taught the painters." In every point he met the accomplished Philip IV. on equal grounds; in some he exceeded him. A good antiquary, a judge of medals, a capital mechanist—cognizant of the art of printing—there existed not a gentleman of the three kingdoms that could compete with him in universality of knowledge.[149] He was as ready for war as for peace; could put a watch together, yet comprehend a fortification; understood guns, and the art of ship-building; but the dearest occupation of his leisure was the collection of sculptures and paintings.

The Crown was already in possession of some good pictures, when Charles commenced his undertaking. Prince Henry had begun the work, and the nobility, perceiving the King's love of art, imitated the Spanish nobles, and sent him presents of great value. But the great act of Charles's life as a connoisseur, was the purchase of the collection of the Duke of Mantua, which was considered to be the richest in Europe.[150]

Philip IV. constantly employed his ambassadors and viceroys to buy up fine pictures for his gallery; and Charles and Buckingham likewise, on their return, adopted a similar plan on a smaller scale, by instructing Sir Henry Wotton and Balthazar Gerbier to negociate for them in works of art. It is obvious how much the royal collection at Whitehall must have been prized; since, upon its being sold during the Protectorate, the principal purchaser was Don Alonzo de Cardenas, the agent of the Spanish King, and his purchases required eighteen mules to carry them from the coast to Madrid, whence Lord Clarendon, ambassador of the exiled Charles II. was dismissed, that he might not see the treasures of his unfortunate master thus brought into a far and foreign country.[151]

The collection of the Duke of Mantua cost Charles eighty thousand pounds—Buckingham being the agent, and probably the instigator of this purchase. The family of Gonzaga had been, in 1627, a hundred years in forming this noble gallery. Little inferior to the Medici in their liberality to artists, they were the patrons of Andrew Mantegna, of Guido Romano, of Raphael, of Correggio, and of Titian, successively. The "Education of Cupid," by Correggio, was among King Charles's purchases, as well as the "Entombment," now in the Louvre,and the "Twelve Cæsars" by Titian. Rubens purchased for him the Cartoons of Raphael, which had been sent by Leo X. to Flanders, to be worked in tapestry, and left there. Then Charles received various presents; that especially commonly styled the "Venus del Pardo," or more properly "Jupiter and Antiope;" the figures being set off by one of the grandest landscapes by Titian, known. This gem was given by Charles to the Duke of Buckingham.[152] It is now in the Louvre, as is also the "Baptist," by Leonardo da Vinci, a present originally from Louis XIII. to Charles.[153]

It was during the residence of Buckingham in Paris that he became acquainted with Rubens. Eventually he bought the whole of the collection of statues, paintings, and other valuable works of art, which that master had formed at a cost of about a thousand pounds, and which he sold to the Duke for ten thousand. But it was not often that Buckingham increased his stores so easily; so early as the year 1613, he had in his household Balthazar Gerbier d'Ouvilly, of Antwerp, a sort of amanuensis, or, as Sanderson styles him, a "common penman," whose transcribing the decalogue for the Dutch Church was one of his first steps to preferment. Gerbier became a miniature painter, and in that ostensible capacity went into Spain with the Duke; he painted, amongst other portraits of the family, a fine oval miniature of his patron on horseback, which, in Walpole's time, belonged to the Duchess of Northumberland; the figure, dressed in scarlet and gold, is finished with great care—and the horse, dark grey, with a white mane, is very animated; underneath the horse is a landscape with figures, and over the Duke's head is suspended his motto, *"Fidei curricula crux."* It was in allusion to the well-known talents of Gerbier that the Duchess of Buckingham wrote to the Duke, when in Spain, begging him, "if he had leisure to sit to Gerbier for his portrait, that she might have it well done in little."

Gerbier seems at that time to have been a special favourite with the King and Queen, who supped once at his house—the entertainment, it is said, costing the painter a thousand pounds.[154] Gerbier, like Rubens, was employed in delicate diplomatic missions; he was also an architect and an author, and the founder of an Academy for foreign languages, and "for all noble sciences and exercises," as he expressed it. As a diplomatist, Gerbier negociated in Flanders a private treaty with Spain:—as an architect, his fame rested, in the reign of Charles, chiefly on a large room built near the Water Gate, at York Stairs, in the Strand, which was commended by Charles I. almost as much as the Banqueting House. Encouraged by this encomium, Gerbier wrote a small work on magnificent buildings, proposing to level Fleet Street and Cheapside, and to erect a fine gate at Temple Bar; a plan of which was presented to Charles II., in whose reign Gerbier died. He was the rival, or believed himself to be so, of Inigo Jones. Hempstead-Marshal, the seat of Lord Craven, long since burned down, was Gerbier's last effort: he died before it was completed, and was buried in the chancel of the church at that place.

His literary works seem to have been very singular compounds of falsehood, invective, and flattery. Horace Walpole believes him to have been the author of a tract printed by authority, in 1651, three years after the execution of Charles I., entitled "The Nonsuch Charles, his character," and considers it one of the basest libels ever published. "The style, the folly, the wretched reasoning, are," he observes, "consistent with Gerbier's usual works; he must, at all events," he decides, "have furnished materials." Nevertheless, two years afterwards, Gerbier published a piece styled "Les Effets Pernicieux," written in French, and to this he affixed his name; it was printed at the "Stag," and composed apparently as a precautionary palliative to the other work, in case of the restoration of the Stuarts; and the notion seems to have succeeded, since Gerbier returned to England with Charles II., and the triumphal arches, erected on the Restoration, were designed by this singularly versatile man.[155] He had, however, the merit, as we have seen, of endeavouring to form an Academy, somewhat on the plan of the Royal Institution in Albemarle Street. Sir Francis Keynaston at that time resided in Covent Garden, and at his house the Academy was held. None but gentlemen were admitted. Arts were taught by professors, in lectures, Gerbier being one of the lecturers. The academy was afterwards removed to Whitefriars; then to Bethnal Green, whence he dedicated one of his lectures on Military Architecture to General Skippon, whom he loaded with the most fulsome, and from one who had, like himself, been overwhelmed by kindnesses from Charles I.—the most treacherous flattery.

It is unsatisfactory to refer to any statement of Gerbier's as reliable; in a work on "Royal Favourites," written in French, he stated that Dr. Egglisham had applied to him, through Sir William Chaloner, to procure his pardon, on condition of his confessing that he had been instigated by others to publish his libel on Buckingham. Gerbier stated that he had applied to the Secretary of State, but received no answer. It is unfortunate that no one could believe Gerbier, either when he calumniated or when he excused any individual.

It was by this able, scurrilous sycophant that the catalogue of Buckingham's pictures was drawn up. In it were enumerated thirteen pictures by Rubens, whom the Duke had seen when he was at Antwerp, shortly before the Expedition to Rhé. When, in 1630, the great painter came to England as a diplomatist, the Duke was dead, but the sovereign who had so greatly encouraged his tastes, did not, as Walpole remarks, "overlook in the ambassador the talents of the painter." Rubens painted, for three thousand pounds, the ceiling of the Banqueting House built by Inigo Jones—and depicting the "Apotheosis of King James;" a subject highly inconsistent for the purpose for which it is now most strangely appropriated as a chapel. Vandyck was to have adorned the sides with the history of the Garter; so that three great masters would have combined to form that noblest room in the world; but so grand a possession was not destined to be the work of former times, or the pride of our own.

After Buckingham's death, some of his pictures were bought by the King, some by the Earl of Northumberland, and some by Abbot Montague.[156] In the collection there were nineteen pictures by Titian, seventeen by Tintoret, thirteen by Paul Veronese, twenty-one by Bassano, two by Julio Romano, two by Georgione, eight by Palina, three by Guido, thirteen by Rubens, three by Leonardo da Vinci, two by Correggio, and three by Raphael, besides several by inferior masters whose productions are scarce. The great prize of the collection was the "Ecce Homo," of Titian, eight feet in length and twelve in breadth. For this magnificent work of art, in which portraits of the Pope, the Emperors Charles V. and Solyman the Magnificent are introduced, the Earl of Arundel had offered Buckingham seven thousand pounds in land or money. The proposal was refused, and the "Ecce Homo" shared the fate of many of the other pictures in the year 1648.

George, the second Duke of Buckingham, among whose few good

qualities was a loyal adherence to that family to whom his father owed all, after being allowed by the Parliament a period of fifty days to choose between desertion of the Stuarts and outlawry, chose the latter. His estates were seized, but his father's pictures, many of which still hung on the now gloomy walls of York House, were sent to him in his exile at Antwerp, by an old servant, John Traylinan, who had been left to guard the property. These were now sold for bread. Duart, of Antwerp, purchased some of them, but the greater number became the possession of the Archduke Leopold, and were removed to the Castle of Prague. Amongst them was the "Ecce Homo;" which has been described as embodying the greatest merits of its incomparable painter.[157]

Buckingham's collection contained two hundred and thirty pictures. One may conceive how grandly they must have adorned York House, where in every chamber were emblazoned the arms of the two families, lions and peacocks, the houses of Villiers and Manners, who were for a few brief years united by one common bond under that roof.[158] Neither pains nor money were ever spared by Charles, or by Buckingham, to enrich their collections. Charles, with his own hands, wrote a letter inviting Albano to England. Buckingham endeavoured to attract Carlo Maratti, who had painted for him portraits of a Prince and Princess of Brunswick, to the English Court; but Maratti excused himself on the plea that he was not yet perfect in his art.[159] Little could the King have foretold that his treasures at Whitehall would have been sold, as Horace Walpole expresses it, by "inch of candle;" or the Duke that his son and heir should have parted with his father's collection to save himself from starvation in a foreign country. Such events seem to confirm Sydney Smith's counsel to a friend, not to look forward more than to a futurity of two hours' duration.

Charles I., less happy than Buckingham, had the chagrin to hear that his favourite's beloved collection was partially sold, three years before his own death. It seems, as Walpole expresses it, "to have become part of the religion of the time to war on the arts, because they had been countenanced at Court." In 1645 the Parliament ordered the two collections to be sold; but, lest the public exigencies should not be thought to afford sufficient cause for this step, they passed the following acts to colour their proceedings:—

"Ordered, (July 23, 1635,) that all such pictures and statues there (at York House) as are without any superstition, shall be forthwith sold."[160]

"Ordered, that all such pictures as shall have the representation of the second person in the Trinity upon them shall be forthwith burnt."

"Ordered, that all such pictures there, as have the representation of the Virgin Mary upon them, shall be forthwith burnt."[161]

This, Walpole remarks, was a worthy contrast to Archbishop Laud, who made a Star Chamber business of a man's breaking some painted glass in the cathedral at Salisbury. Times were changed; Laud, however, looked on the offence as an indication of a spirit of destruction and irreverence;—unhappily, he was right.

Such was the fate of Buckingham's pictures: a brief notice of the proceedings which dispersed the far more valuable collection of the King must not be omitted. Immediately after Charles's death, votes were passed for the sale of his pictures, statues, jewels, and "hangings." It was then ordered that inventories should be made, and commissioners be appointed to appraise, secure, and inventory the said goods. Cromwell, to his honour, attempted to stop the dispersion of these valuables; but he had matters of even greater importance to engage his attention, and the sale, about the year 1650, appears, as far as the paintings were concerned, to have been completed. From that time no further mention of them is to be found in the Journals of the House of Commons.[162]

All the furniture from the ill-fated King's different palaces was brought up, and exposed for sale; and, as far as relates to the jewels, plate, and furniture, the affair was not concluded until 1653. It must, indeed, have been a melancholy sight. Cromwell, through his agent, was one of the principal purchasers. The price of each article was fixed, but, if any one offered a higher sum, preference was given. Cromwell, who resided alternately at Whitehall and Hampton Court, bought the Cartoons for 300*l*. The order against "superstitious" pieces was not, it seems, strictly observed; for a painting of Vandyck's, "Mary, our Lord, and Angels," sold for 40*l*.[163] The celebrated portrait of George, the second Duke of Buckingham, and his mother, by Vandyck, one of the finest productions of that master, was valued at 30*l*., and sold for 50*l*. Many of the finest pictures were bought by Mons. Jabach, a native of Cologne, settled in Paris, who sold his collection afterwards to Louis XIV. "The Entombment," by Titian, which he secured, and "Christ and the Disciples at Emmaus," are in the Louvre. Amongst the pictures in the Mantua collection, was the large "Holy Trinity;" it was bought by De Cardenas, the Spanish Ambassador; and on its arrival Philip IV. exclaimed, "That is my pearl"—and the picture has, ever since, been known by that name.

There were, also, valuable allegorical sketches by Correggio, which are among the valuable collection of drawings and designs in the Louvre.

The Imperial Gallery of the Palace Belvedere, in Vienna, contains several fine pictures from the Whitehall collection. They were bought at the sale by the Archduke Leopold William, Governor of the Netherlands, and afterwards Emperor of Austria. Reynst, an eminent Dutch connoisseur, Christina, Queen of Sweden, and Cardinal Mazarin, were amongst the purchasers—but bought still more largely of the jewels, medals, tapestry, carpets, embroidery—many of which went to adorn Mazarin's palace in Paris. Bathazar Gerbier, and other painters, also purchased pictures—and thus, by their aid, and that of some few Englishmen, the wreck of this noble collection may still be traced in this country, but the greater portion was lost to it for ever. Some miniatures were restored;—the States-General, during the reign of Charles II., bought back the pictures formerly sold to Reynst, and presented them to Charles II.

By the exertions of that monarch, seventy of the best paintings that his father had possessed again adorned his various Palaces. St. James's, Hampton Court, and Windsor were enriched with the works of those masters in whose productions Charles I. had so greatly delighted. But in Whitehall, the gallery of which was hung with the works of Leonardo da Vinci, Raphael, Titian, Correggio, Vandyck, Holbein, Rubens, and many others, had been deposited the finest specimens of their works. England seems fated never to contain a collection suitable to her wealth, her intelligence, and her wishes—for in 1697 that ancient palace, so often partially burnt, was destroyed by fire; and within its old walls and many chambers perished the various collections of Charles II., both of pictures, medals, and sculpture.[164]

Charles I., like all good judges of art, was extremely careful of his pictures. Hitherto the Court revels had been held in that famous gallery which Charles II. afterwards debased into a resort for gamblers and infamous women of rank; and the Banqueting-house was next appropriated to them. But during the Christmas of 1637, when two masques were to be performed, the King being one of the chief dancers, a building, the mere boarding of which cost two thousand five hundred pounds, was erected in the main court at Whitehall, because the King would not have "his pictures in the Banqueting-house burnt with lights."[165]

The noble portrait by Vandyck, of Charles on horseback, was reclaimed from Seemput, a painter, who had bought it at the sale; and some few paintings which Catherine of Braganza had coolly shipped off to Lisbon, were stopped by the Lord Chamberlain in their embarkation.

When the convulsions under which the country groaned had ceased, and on the arrival of the Restoration, the nobility, though not encouraged by the reigning monarch, introduced the custom of adorning their country seats with paintings. "But the pure and elevated taste," as Dr. Waagen expresses it, "of Charles I. had degenerated; the names of famous masters were indeed to be found, but not their works."[166]

Architecture and sculpture were also arts which owe infinitely to the judicious patronage of Charles, assisted by Buckingham. Among the Mantua collection was a whole army "of old foreign emperors, captains, and senators," whom Charles I., as Walpole tells us, "caused to land on his coasts, to come and do him homage, and attend him in his palace of St. James's and Somerset House."[167] But the King also discerned and rewarded native genius; and when he planned the noblest palace in the world at Whitehall, sent for no foreign architect, but summoned Inigo Jones to his service.

"England," says Walpole, "adopted Holbein and Vandyck; she borrowed Rubens; she produced Inigo Jones." Originally a joiner, Jones was brought out of obscurity, according to many accounts, by the patron who first extended a hand to assist George Villiers in his struggles in life. William Earl of Pembroke was the friend alike of the young courtier and of the son of the clothworker—the immortal Inigo. Either by the Earl of Arundel or by Pembroke—it is not certain which—Inigo was sent to Italy to learn landscape-painting; but at Rome he soon discovered the inclination and bent of his genius. It is of no use to stop the pure and flowing stream, and thus to make it turbid. Inigo "laid down his pencil, and conceived Whitehall." Nature had not, he felt, destined him to decorate cabinets; his vocation was to build palaces. He was, however, still in danger of living in remote splendour. Christian III. enticed him to Copenhagen, whence James I. sent for him, and whence he was brought to be the Queen's architect in Scotland. Patronized by Prince Henry, he was in despair at the death of that royal youth, and went again to Italy. It was in the interval between his two journeys to Rome that he perpetrated some buildings in bad taste; to which the appellation of "King James's Gothic" was affixed.

His first task, as Surveyor of the Works, to which office James appointed him, was to build, for twenty pounds, a scaffolding, when the Earl and Countess of Somerset were arraigned; his next, to discover, by King James's pedantic mandate, who were the founders of Stonehenge. In 1619, he was entrusted with the direction of the Banqueting-house at Whitehall, which was finished in two years, and ordered to draw up a plan for the whole structure.

Horace Walpole, who was a true royalist whenever the arts were concerned, if not slyly in every other respect, thus speaks of that great but vain effort to build in London a palace worthy of the country. "The whole fabric," he says, referring to Jones's designs for Whitehall, "was so glorious an idea, that one forgets in a moment, in the regret for its not being executed, the confirmation of our liberties obtained by a melancholy scene that passed before the windows of that very Banqueting-house."[168] The misfortunes of this eminent man now began. Inigo Jones was a Roman Catholic, and, as such, was peculiarly obnoxious to the Parliament party. His very name, too, was mingled with associations of those arts and that magnificence, which, from being the cause of envy, were now the objects of detestation to certain of the people. "Painting had now," says Walpole, "become idolatry; monuments were deemed carnal pride, and a venerable cathedral seemed equally contradictory to Magna Charta and the Bible." Even the statue of Charles at Charing Cross was regarded as of ill-omen, and taken away lest it should bring back unpleasant recollections.

"The Parliament did vote it down,

And thought it very fitting,

Lest it should fall and kill them all,

In the house where they were sitting."

It had become a matter of wonder that society could ever have tolerated those masques patronized by James, by Charles, and by Buckingham, in which the masks, costumes, and scenes were designed by Jones, and the poetry written by Jonson. These representations had been indeed interrupted by the quarrel between Inigo Jones and Ben Jonson; and in the civil war they ceased entirely. With the royal family and their followers literature and the arts were banished; they were restored with the monarchy, but good taste was not revived. "The history of destruction" superseded that reign of elegance and learning which had a brief duration under Charles, and which, whilst Buckingham was at the head of affairs, was the main-spring of every impulse. "Ruin was the harvest of the Puritans, and they gleaned after the reformers." Of course vengeance fell on the unfortunate royal architect and stage manager, Inigo Jones. His face had been seen at every gorgeous revel; his hand was traceable in many a country seat, even in the picturesque college of St. John's at Oxford; he had designed the chapel of Henrietta Maria at St. James's; he had erected the arcade and church of Covent Garden: every familiar scene was haunted with his presence.

The party that condemned him felt neither gratitude nor pity; two years before the King's death, he was fined 500*l.* for malignancy. Afraid of a sequestration of all his revenues, he is stated to have buried his money, as did Stone, the painter, in Scotland Yard; and to have removed it, when fearful of discovery, to Lambeth Marsh. He lived to see Cromwell occupy Whitehall, which he had hoped to renovate; and to hear that Charles had suffered beneath the very windows of that fine and perfect fragment of a palace which was still, in spite of all the terrors of that execution, called the Banqueting-house; he lived to be called "Iniquity Jones," by the successor of that Earl of Pembroke who had once been his generous patron; he lived to learn that the wit, the poetry, the scenery that had combined to render the masques at Burleigh a feast not only for the senses, but for the intellect, were construed into heathenism. All gallantry and romance were gone—and gone for ever; wit, indeed, flourished after the Restoration, but it was wit without decency or feeling. The old man must have felt that he had lived too long. Somerset House had been with great difficulty saved from the destruction of the Parliamentary decree; it gave poor Inigo, who still appears to have nominally held his former office, a refuge wherein he could lay down his head and die. He was buried in the church of St. Bennet, at Paul's Wharf; a monument erected there to his memory was destroyed in the Fire of London, and the great architect of the Banqueting-house remains without any memorial, save the works of his genius.

Vandyck was not settled in England, under the patronage of Charles I., until after the death of Buckingham. Mytens, whose position as the King's principal painter was, as he believed, encroached on by the celebrity of Vandyck, was patronized by Buckingham, for whom he painted a portrait of Sir Jeffrey Hudson.

This little wonder of the seventeenth century was nine years old only at the Duke's death. He had been domesticated at Burleigh on account of his diminutive stature, which did not, at that time, exceed seven or eight inches. Jeffrey was the plaything of the Court: at the marriage-feast of Charles I., the Duchess of Buckingham had him inserted in a cold pie, and served up at table to the Queen, by way of presenting him to the royal bride, who took him in her lap, and kept him. Until the age of thirty, this little personage never grew. He then suddenly shot up three feet nine inches, which he carried off with infinite dignity, and remained at that height. He was still the butt of all the idlers at Whitehall, and the theme of a poem, by Davenant, called "Jeffresdos," the subject being a battle between the dwarf and a turkey-cock.

Henceforth he became important—went over to France on a mission of great confidence, to fetch an experienced *sage-femme* for the Queen— was taken by the Pirates off Dunkirk on his return—was rescued, only to encounter the incessant raillery of the courtiers, which, to a man of his present size and importance, became exasperating. Faithful and trusty, he went with Henrietta Maria into France, and there, being goaded on by renewed insults from a Mr. Crofts, sent a challenge. Crofts came to fight him provided only with a squirt; the duel was to be on horseback, and with pistols, that Jeffrey, or, as he had now become, Sir Jeffrey, might be more on a level with his antagonist. By the first shot, Crofts was struck dead. The next event in this adventurous life was the capture of Jeffrey by a Turkish rover, during one of his voyages; he was sold as a slave, and taken into Barbary; he was, however, ransomed, or set free, so as to resume his attendance on the Queen. After the Restoration, he was suspected of being concerned in the Popish plot, and confined in the Gate House at Westminster. Here, a life that had been rendered worthy of record even by his very littleness was closed, in 1682; his old enemy, a gigantic porter at Whitehall in Charles's time, with whom the little creature was in incessant strife, having long since been displaced—and another giant, Oliver Cromwell's porter, established in his stead.

On Mytens the office of his Majesty's "picture-drawer in ordinary, with a fee of 20*l.* per annum, was conferred in 1625, procured by the agency of Endymion Porter, who was the servant and relative of Buckingham, from the Duke."[169]

Incited by the example of the Earl of Arundel, who employed a Mr. Petty to collect antiquities in Greece, Buckingham despatched for the same purpose Sir Thomas Roe, telling him, in explaining his wishes, that "he was not so fond of antiquity as to court it in a deformed or unshapen stone."[170] Lord Arundel had begun to "transplant old Greece into England." His agent, Petty, was indefatigable, "eating with Greeks on their work days, and lying with fishermen with planks," so that he might obtain his ends. This valiant antiquary lost all his curiosities on returning from Samos, and was imprisoned as a spy, but, regaining his liberty, set forth again to his researches with the energy of a Layard.[171]

The principal medallist in the time of Charles I. was Andrew Vanderdort, a Dutchman, also patronized by Prince Henry. Upon the accession of Charles, Vanderdort was made keeper of the King's cabinet of medals, with a salary of 40*l.* This cabinet or museum was contained in a room in Whitehall, running across from the Thames towards the Banqueting-house, and fronting the gardens westward. By Vanderdort the coins of the realm were designed; and to the commission to perform that work was added an injunction that he should superintend the engravers. To Vanderdort was once confided the preparing of the catalogue of the Royal collection, written in bad English, and preserved in the Ashmolean Museum, at Oxford. It is related of him, that, being entrusted with a miniature by Gibson, the "Parable of the Lost Sheep," he laid it up so carefully, that, when asked for it by the King, he could not find it, and hung himself from grief.[172]

It was owing to the suggestions of Buckingham that the great portrait-painter, Gerard Honthorst, was invited by Charles I. to England. Honthorst of Oxford. was a native of Utrecht, but had completed his education at Rome. He had many pupils in painting of high rank, and amongst them were Elizabeth of Bohemia and her daughters, the Princess Sophia, mother of George I., and the Princess Louisa, afterwards Abbess of Maubissen, being the most apt scholars of that family. It was owing to the early culture of the arts which both the sons of James I. had enjoyed, that it became an easy task for Buckingham to incite Charles to the patronage of great masters in afterlife. Solomon de Caus, a Gascon, was the instructor of Prince Henry, and probably of Charles, who inherited the pictures and statues which his brother had collected. Honthorst probably improved by his lessons the taste that had been already so well cultivated. At Hampton Court, a large picture on the staircase sometimes rivets attention, without conferring pleasure—for the taste for allegorical paintings has long since been extinct. It delineates Charles and his Queen as Apollo and Diana in the clouds; the Duke of Buckingham, as Mercury, is introducing them to the Arts and Sciences, whilst genii are driving away Envy and Malice. This, and other paintings, were completed by Honthorst in six months; the King giving him three thousand florins, a service of silver plate for twelve persons, and a horse. He also painted portraits of the Duke and Duchess of Buckingham, sitting with their two children; and it was likewise the Duke's fancy to have a large picture by him, representing a tooth-drawer, with many figures introduced around the operation.

Horatio Gentileschi, a native of Pisá, was one of those who contributed alike to the collection of Charles and to the glories of York House, which, long before Buckingham's death, had, we are told, become the admiration of the world.

Gentileschi was treated with a degree of liberality that was quite congenial to the feelings of Buckingham: he was invited to England, and rooms were provided for his use, and a considerable salary advanced to him. Some of the painted ceilings in Greenwich Palace were his work; and he ornamented York House in a similar manner. When it was dismantled, one of the ceilings was transplanted to Buckingham House, in St. James's Park, the seat of Sheffield, Duke of Buckingham. He also painted the Villiers family, and, by the Duke's order, a Magdalen, lying in a grotto, contemplating a skull—a strange subject for the worldly and high-spirited Buckingham to select. But the delight of Charles and of his favourite was Nicholas Lanière, meritorious as a painter, engraver, and musician. It was Lanière who composed the music for some of Ben Jonson's masques, in recitative. Lanière, after the death of Charles, set to music a funeral hymn written by Thomas Pierce. As a composer, he was salaried by Charles with two hundred a-year. He had, however, also painted pictures for King James; and it is stated that Buckingham, not being able to induce that monarch to reward him adequately, gave Lanière three hundred pounds at one time, and five hundred at another, from his own means.[173] Lanière had been instrumental in the negociation for the Mantua collection. After the death of Charles he was one of those painters who viewed with deep concern the dispersion of the Whitehall collection; and bought several pictures at the sale of what he had contributed to enrich.

Whilst ceilings were painted, pictures distributed on richly-carved panels, and in spacious galleries, there was even an attempt in those days to decorate with frescoes the exterior of houses, as in Bavaria, where even the dwellings of superior farmers are sometimes adorned in that manner. Francis Cleyn, a Dane, was called to England in the reign of James I., in order to improve also the manufacture of tapestry at Mortlake, to which James had contributed two thousand pounds. Hitherto, Sir Francis Crane, the proprietor, had worked only on old patterns; Cleyn brought new and original designs to the aid of the tapestry-workers. Five of the cartoons were sent by Charles to be copied. Cleyn also painted the outside of Wimbledon House in fresco; he designed one of the chimney-pieces in Holland House, and gave the drawings for two chairs, carved and gilt, with shells for backs, still there. In every possible department art was called into play. Drawings for the great seals were made by Cleyn. He published books for "carvers and goldsmiths." Nothing was to be tasteless, clumsy, or inappropriate; and, with this spirit abroad, it is not surprising that the little that the Rebellion spared should be models for our own conservative generation.

Whilst Villiers employed portrait-painters on himself and on his family, he did not forget the old man at Brookesby, long since gone to the grave. Cornelius Jansen, by his order, painted a portrait of his father;

probably from some family picture. It was in the possession of Horace Walpole, "less handsome," he says, "but extremely like his son."

The patronage extended by Charles I. to architects[174] was often directed by Buckingham; for the King and the favourite had but one soul between them. To exalt and improve the art of painting, they summoned foreign architects as well as painters to England, remunerated them liberally, and treated them with the courtesy due to one of the noblest of professions. Charles delighted to dabble with his brush on the canvas, his hand directed by the master, with whom he sat for hours. Buckingham's few leisure days were devoted to his buildings and paintings. Amongst the English builders who worked at the Banqueting-house, under Inigo Jones, was Nicholas Stone, who was in 1619 appointed master-mason to the King, at the usual salary, of twelve pence a-day; but the extra work he executed for Charles was amply paid; and his salary during the two years he worked at Whitehall amounted to four shillings and tenpence the day.
[175] Nicholas Stone designed four of the dials at St. James's and Whitehall.[176] He rebuilt the fountains at Theobald's and Nonsuch; his drawings are, it is to be feared, lost. He was the statuary employed by the Countess of Dorset to set up at Westminster the monument of Spenser the poet, for which he was paid forty pounds. His great talent lay in tombs; amongst others, he erected one for the Countess of Buckingham, the Duke's mother, three years after her son's death, in 1631, in Westminster Abbey, for which he received 560*l.* Doubtless, therefore, he was continually employed by Buckingham, and Stone's various performances must have been just what the Duke required. He was the modest architect, who did not disdain to form and chisel the piers for gates—Inigo Jones designing them,—at Holland House. He built the great gate of St. Mary's Church at Oxford, and the stone gates for the Physic Garden in that city, —also designed by Inigo. The figure of the Nile at Somerset House was by Stone; his skill, like that of Inigo, is familiar to us, though we may almost have forgotten the hand that had so much "cunning." At York House, at Wanstead, New Hall and Burleigh, his fine face, with his love-locks, his plain collar, and tight doublet, were, we may be sure, often to be seen before ruin and desertion darkened those once splendid homes of Villiers.

Few men, it must be acknowledged, in so brief a space, have done more for the arts in this country than George Villiers. By Charles, his friend and sovereign, who survived him twenty years, much more was effected. Without their unceasing efforts, without even the almost pardonable extravagance that was directed to purposes so refined, England would almost have been devoid of paintings by the greatest masters, and, what would be almost worse, destitute of the love and reverence for high art which has come down to us from the time of Charles I., and which is now cherished, though unconsciously, in the breast of the poor artisan, as in that of the richest peer or commoner. The crowds who not only throng, but enjoy, the galleries of Hampton Court— and, still more, the humble visitors from the Faubourg St. Antoine and the Marais to the Louvre, on Sundays, in Paris—prove that a love of what is true and holy, and even sublime, in pictures, exists intuitively in the uncultivated mind, as well as in the highest intelligence of the soul. Those who called from its latent recesses this love of art in the seventeenth century are greatly entitled to the gratitude of that age to which the luxuries of music and painting are become necessities.

CHAPTER V.

CHAPTER V.

After considering the benefits conferred by Charles I. and his favourite on art, and detailing their patronage of eminent masters, one turns, naturally, to the literature of the day, and more especially—as subsidiary to music and painting—to the drama.

The accession of James I. opened fairer prospects to dramatists than they had enjoyed in the days of Elizabeth, who paid as grudgingly for her amusements as for the services of her statesmen. To her "Master of the bears and dogs" she assigned a salary of a farthing a day only.[177] Yet the office was sometimes held by a Knight; and, during the "princely pleasures of Kenilworth," of which bear-baiting formed a prominent feature, by no less opulent a person than Edward Alleyn, the actor, and founder of Dulwich College. Little but honour, therefore, had accrued, in the time of Elizabeth, to poets and play-writers; and the struggling authors were obliged to have recourse to a more liberal patronage than that of the Court—until James I., somewhat "of a poet, but more of a scholar," promoted, with an extravagant zeal, the diversions which his taste disposed him to enjoy. Plays, which his predecessor had deemed likely to draw her younger subjects from the manlier recreations of bear- baiting and hunting, were patronized in high quarters, and were henceforth the fashionable diversions notwithstanding the invectives of the Puritans, both of the Court, and in the provincial castles of the nobility at a distance from London.

Independently of the delights of the masque, which comprised both music, dancing, and poetry, there were pleasures to be found in the drama which accorded with the tendencies and failings of that period.

It was an age of personality, a disposition to which existed as strongly in the unrefined court of James, and even among his northern retainers, as in the brilliant galleries of Versailles, encouraged by Louis XIV., and led by the dangerous and witty St. Simon. "The great eye of the world," says an able writer, "was not then, any more than now, so intent on things and principles as not to have a corner for the infirmities of individuals."[178] Wilson, Weldon, Winwood, Osborne, Peyton, Sanderson, circulated what were in many instances fabrications about the higher classes; whilst the crimes and absurdities of the lower orders were celebrated by the ballad-mongers, or dramatized for the stage. Many of those ballads transmitted to us, which were exempted from the fate of "damn'd ditties," were founded on authentic domestic tragedies, the actors in which have long since passed into oblivion. The ballad, which afforded the multitude a pleasing insight into the fact that their superiors were no better than themselves, was the most popular literature of the day. Sung to doleful tunes, with a nasal twang, they called forth the satire of the dramatist, who aimed at a higher species of personality, and who deprecated these, often scurrilous, productions; which were, at length, checked in the time of Swift by the imposition of a penny stamp on every loose sheet. The ballad was a source of dread to the tavern bully, whose iniquities it exposed.

"If I have not ballads made of you all, and sung to filthy tunes, may this cup of sack be my poison," says Falstaff.

"Now shall have we damnable ballads out against us,

Most wicked madrigals."

Humorous Lieutenant.

Whilst the attention of society was not altogether fixed on exalted members only, it was found difficult to restrain satire, and even calumny, from introducing living characters on the stage, and from depicting them with hateful qualities, and in invidious situations.

In vain did the Master of the Revels, who was under the peculiar influence of the Court, endeavour to control the disposition to personality which characterized even many of the plays acted before James I. and his son. In these compositions the public acquired that insight into conduct and peculiarities which is now derived from periodical papers, or from diaries, letters, and autobiographies, in which our age is especially fertile.

Amongst the dramatists of James and Charles's reigns, we may take, as the most remarkable, Philip Massinger, Ben Jonson, Beaumont and Fletcher, and John Ford, the greater part of whose works were produced during the life of King James and of Charles I. and II.

The biography of each of these celebrated men elucidates much of the manners and temper of the times, and their history comprises that of this species of literature during the commencement and middle of the seventeenth century.

Philip Massinger was the son of Arthur Massinger, a retainer in the household of the Earl of Pembroke. A retainer was often a gentleman of good birth but small means, and this was probably the condition of Arthur Massinger, who, from his carrying letters from his master, the Earl, to Queen Elizabeth, could not have been a man of low origin, else he would not have been admitted to the honour of conveying any dispatch to one who placed so much importance on lineage in those who entered her presence. That custom was still in force, which surrounded a nobleman, not with menials, but with a middle-class of bondmen, who thought service no degradation. It was esteemed a turn of fortune when a youth of gentle birth could be introduced into some noble house, to learn therein politeness, chivalrous attention to ladies, and to imbibe, from example and precept, that loyalty which was then considered a sort of virtue. The education and training of a page is now confined to royal courts; but there were, in England, in those days of the Tudors and Stuarts, many minor courts, which exacted, in miniature, the duties and service that existed in the palaces of the monarch. And of those stately and wealthy patrons, none were more respected than the Herberts, Earls of Pembroke, to whom Arthur Massinger wrote himself "Bondman."

That wholesome discipline which it is difficult in our own time for a parent to preserve over his family was maintained to the advantage of a page who rose from a lowly to a confidential situation. Massinger's lines in the "New Way to Pay Old Debts" refer to the subjection under which the youth groaned, but to which the matured actors on this world's stage looked back with gratitude:—

"Art thou scarce manumised from the porter's lodge,

And now sworn servant to the pantofle,

And darest thou dream of marriage?"

New Way to Pay Old Debts.

Yet in this servitude the father of Philip Massinger lived and died. These grand establishments, in which the noble head saw around him none but persons of gentle blood and breeding, would long since have ceased to be congenial, even if they still existed, to the English notions of independence, by which servitude is confounded with slavery. But they had this advantage—the son of a retainer was supposed to have a claim on the illustrious noble, who estimated his father's fidelity and offices;

and that this was the case with Philip Massinger, might seem probable from the advantages of education which he was enabled to derive; and the value of which he had learned to appreciate, in the proximity to the really noble and intellectual family of Herbert. It appears from Philip Massinger's dedication of the "Bondman," that he never had any personal communication with Philip, Earl of Pembroke and Montgomery; but that is no proof that he may not have been indebted for the advantage of a university education to the far more intellectual and estimable Henry, Earl of Pembroke, his father's patron, as appears from the following passage in the dedication of the "Bondman" to the Earl of Montgomery:—

"However, I could never arrive at the happiness to be made known to your lordship; yet a desire born with me, to make a tender of all duties and service to the noble family of the Herberts, descended to me as an inheritance from my dead father, Arthur Massinger. Many years he happily spent in the service of your honourable house, and died a servant in it, leaving his to be ever most glad and ready to be at the command of all such as derive themselves from his most honoured master, your lordship's most honoured father."[179]

It would be agreeable to reflect that Massinger had passed his childhood and youth, partly at all events, in the classical region of Wilton Castle, which Sir Philip Sidney had almost sanctified to the Muses by his presence, and whence he had issued forth on that expedition in which he died a hero's death. But those were not the days in which the childhood and youth of celebrated men were recorded, and of Massinger's not a trace remained. We only guess at the early influences which formed his imaginative, yet vigorous mind. We only conjecture that his taste was directed to poetry by the taste of those whom he must have learned first to respect. We are not sure, yet we are glad to believe, that whilst his mind took on afterwards the impressions of the age in which he lived, it was in earliest youth incited by the author of the "Arcadia," and by the acquirements of her to whom that poem was dedicated, to culture and exercise, until circumstances brought its powers into full activity.

The dedication of the "Bondman" was written in 1624; and whilst it shews that the poet had never seen Philip, Earl of Montgomery, it does not follow, as has been stated, that he was *not* reared at Wilton during the life-time of Henry, Earl of Pembroke, the "noble father" of Philip, who, as a younger son, was created Earl of Montgomery, and long known by that title only. Henry, who was succeeded by his eldest son, the second Earl of Pembroke, died in 1600; and since Massinger was born in 1584, it is extremely probable that he passed his childhood at Wilton, although, in compliance with the custom of the age, he was probably sent out to nurse. Even the name of his mother is unknown. Few authors of so much merit as Massinger have been, as Hartley Coleridge observes, "so little noticed by contemporaries;" and none so soon forgotten by succeeding times.

There can, however, be but little doubt that Philip Massinger imbibed at Wilton that value for letters which is so soon caught by children from the society of the intellectual; and that a gentler influence than that of Earl Henry stimulated the natural inclinations of his mind. A learned education for women of rank was in vogue for nearly a century after the Reformation: with Protestantism came in the notion that the female understanding was worthy of high cultivation; and our earliest and most superior women, in those times, were prepared for their important part in life by a sound and almost masculine training. Witness the learning of Lady Jane Grey, of Queen Elizabeth, of Joanna, Lady Abergavenny, whom Walpole believes to have been the "foundress of that noble school of female learning, of which (with herself) there were," he says, "no less than four authoresses in the three descents."[180] Among the learned and the virtuous none was more esteemed in her time than Mary, the sister of Sir Philip Sidney, and the third wife of Henry, Earl of Pembroke, the son of Arthur Massinger's patron. She was one of those ornaments of her age who added lustre to her station without forfeiting one feminine attribute. What was then called a "polite education" comprised not only the acquisition of light literature, but that also of classical learning. From her mother, Lady Mary Dudley, this admirable woman inherited a noble and congenial spirit; from her father, Sir Henry Sidney, surpassing abilities, moral excellencies, enlarged views, generous motives. That father, superior to the venal courtiers of his time, spent his whole fortune in his endeavours to benefit Ireland and Wales, of the affairs of which he held the administration. In her brother, Sir Philip Sidney, the Countess of Pembroke found a companion in all her pursuits, as well as in affection. Hence, as Spenser wrote, their minds grew in unison:—

"The gentlest shepherdess that liv'd that day,

And most resembling, both in shape and spirit,

Her brother dear."

In conjunction with him, this gifted woman is said to have translated the Psalms;[181] of which effort Daniel says:—

"Those hymns which thou dost consecrate to Heaven,

Which Israel's singer to his God did frame,

Unto thy voyage eternity hath given,

And makes thee dear to Him from whence they came."

Several of these are extant; one of them was published in the *Guardian*;[182] and it corresponds with a Psalm printed in the "*Nugæ Antiquæ*" as the Countess of Pembroke's.[183] It has been regretted that these productions are not authorized to be sung in churches; for the present version, Mr. Hartley Coleridge remarks, "is a disgrace and a mischief to the establishment." These translations are preserved in the library at Wilton.

The Countess was residing there when the "Discourse of Life and Death," by Mornay, which she translated from the French, was printed. This was in 1590, when Philip Massinger was six years of age. She survived until 1621; and, since she extended her patronage both to arts and letters, it is probable that she not only befriended Ben Jonson, but that she encouraged and assisted the struggling dramatist, whose father had been so favoured or retained in her husband's house. Ben Jonson's well-known lines on her tomb have challenged various criticisms. Whilst by some they are deemed a tribute "which have never been exceeded in the records of monumental praise,"[184] by another critic they are considered "too hyperbolical, too clever, and too conceited to be inscribed on a Christian's tomb."[185]

"Underneath this marble hearse

Lies the subject of all verse—

Sidney's sister, Pembroke's mother;

Death, ere thou canst find another,

Learned, and fair, and good as she,

Time shall throw a dart at thee."

At all events, Massinger imbibed from his father's connection with the Herbert family, one taste—that for theatricals. Amongst the retinue of the great peer, was a company of itinerant performers, "the Earl of Pembroke's players;" and though the childhood of Massinger is indeed a blank, it maybe inferred that the attractions of the theatre, or rather of the hall, in which that portion of the Earl's household must have been frequently occupied, were such as to fascinate a boy of an imaginative turn of mind. He is stated to have been shy, melancholy, retiring, and studious; that he received a classical education, as a boy, is also stated; but when that education was received, who directed that thoughtful and dreamy mind to poetry, or how he, who was evidently designed for a scholastic career, should have devoted himself to the profession of a playwriter, does not appear to have been ascertained, even by the indefatigable Gilford.

But it was an age of great mental energy, and there was sufficient in the rich harvest won by Shakspeare, or in the rare delights afforded by his works, to account for the direction of young Massinger's genius.

It has been conjectured, also, that he acted occasionally in those plays the parts of which were then usually sustained by boys: of this there remains not a single proof, and nothing is *certain*, in so far as the events of his youth are concerned, except that he was entered at St. Alban's Hall, Oxford, in 1601-2.

It must not be supposed that this fact at all implied what in the present day it might appear to indicate. It did not follow that Massinger was to enter one of the learned professions, because he became a commoner in that small, ancient society of St. Alban's Hall; nor was it a proof that the young man had parents who were in affluent circumstances, as a University career now seems to imply. Oxford was then a place for cheap education, and many of the "poor scholars" at the various colleges underwent, as Strype shews us, great hardships. On the other hand, it was not uncommon for the profession of letters to be in those days a man's only calling; and an academical training was his best commencement in that arduous course, since a certain display of erudition was undoubtedly one of the characteristics of the period.

The exhibition to college was, according to Anthony Wood, given to Massinger by the Earl of Pembroke; but others allege that Massinger derived the means of subsistence at Oxford from his father.

In those schools, where a man for the first, and perhaps for the only, time in his existence, frames his own success, independently of the patronage of others—in those schools, famed for strict impartiality, and where the battle is really to the strong—Massinger, nevertheless, did not appear. He left Oxford without taking his degree; for he had made the mistake, fatal to a poor man, who has to rest upon the endowments of that grand old university for his support, of not adopting the studies which the university prescribes to the exclusion of others. It was, indeed, a sin in the eyes of that zealous antiquary, whose tomb, in a corner of the anti-chapel of Merton College, is so often overlooked, save by those who honour his labours, and who view his merits, thus enshrined, with regretful reverence—that he gave his mind, as Anthony Wood tells us, "more to poetry or romance, for about four years or more, than to logic and philosophy, which he ought to have done, as he was patronized *to that end.*"

He adds, without further comment than this, "that, being sufficiently famed for several specimens of wit, he betook himself to writing plays." Massinger left Oxford in 1606—he was then twenty-two years of age.

For some time his history is again a blank, and his exertions and struggles, whatever they may have been, fell upon a serious, religious, thoughtful temperament, devoid of the elasticity with which Shakespeare fought and conquered the trials of fate. Play-writing was, at that time, almost the only means by which ready money could be obtained, and had the patronage of the Court in full activity, when Massinger cast himself into his future and only career. James I., soon after his accession, licensed the company of players who had hitherto been styled the "Lord Chamberlain's," but who were henceforth to be called "the King's servants"—amongst whom were Shakspeare, Burbage, Heminge, and others. Queen Anne adopted the "Earl of Worcester's company," and Prince Henry that of the Earl of Nottingham, the hero of the "Armada." The Court, and even provincial nobles and gentry, although Protestantized, kept, with as scrupulous attention as ever, the great feasts of the Church; and on these, as in former times a mystery or morality was given, so now a play was often performed. "The stage," says Hartley Coleridge, "was evoking and realizing the finest imaginations of the strongest intellects."

Whether Massinger ever acted or not, is as doubtful as every other incident of his early life. It was not until 1614 that a glimmering of his actual condition in life is seen through the darkness, and the disclosure is melancholy and discouraging. There is something touching, as well as dreary, in the gloom that one can only diversify with scenes of penury and imprisonment for debt. At last the light breaks out; and, in the words of the following appeal, the history of some years of disappointment is disclosed:—[186]

"To our most loving friend, Mr. Philip Hinchlow, Esquire, these,—

"Mr. Hinchlow—You understand our unfortunate extremitye, and I doe not thinke you so void of cristianitee but that you would throw so much money into the Thames as wee request now of you, rather than endanger so many innocent lives. You know there is X*l.* more at least to be receaved of you for the play. We desire you to lend us V*l.* of that; which shall be allowed to you, without which we cannot be bayled nor I play any more till this be dispatch'd. It will lose you XX*l.* ere the end of the next weeke, besides the hindrance of the next new play. Pray, sir, consider our cases with humanity, and now give us cause to acknowledge you our true friend in time of neede. Wee have entreated Mr. Davison to deliver this note, as well as witness your love as our promises and always acknowledgement to be ever your most thankful and loving friends,[187]

"PHILIP MASSINGER.

"R. DAVISON.

"NAT. FIELD."

This letter is the only one with the signature of Philip Massinger extant. It was addressed to a pawnbroker—such was Philip Hinchlow, who, besides exercising that ancient profession, was also engaged in theatrical speculations, his advances being chiefly made upon the wearing apparel and properties, of which he acquired a large portion in this way. "A comfortable sort of person," remarks Hartley Coleridge, "for three poets to be obliged to." Especially when they, as it were, pledged to him the labour of their brains; and that when they were either already in prison, or afraid of that crisis in their miserable destiny. Nathaniel Field, the writer of this letter, was Massinger's partner in the production of the "Fatal Dowry;" he had a share in the Globe and Blackfriar's Theatres, in conjunction with Burbage, the original *Richard III.*, *Hamlet*, and *Othello*; and with Lowin, the original *Falstaff*. Field was also an actor, and he performed in Ben Jonson's masque, "Cynthia's Revels," in 1600, when he appeared as one of the children of the Queen's chapel. Robert Daborne was a man of good descent, a scholar and a clergyman, although the author of several plays; nor was he the only clerical dramatist in an age which was, indeed, "not an innocent one"—for Cartwright, also a play- writer, was a divine, and, as Fuller states, "a florid and seraphical preacher."[188]

It has been remarked that the "Fatal Dowry" was like the production of a man in debt. Massinger might refer to his own case when he wrote:—

"I will not take

One single piece of this great heap. Why should I

Borrow that I have no means to pay; nay, am

A very bankrupt, even in flattering hope,

Of ever raising any."

In addition to his poverty, to hard work, and the degradation of debt, Massinger was fully conscious that he had not, in giving up the certainty of a profession, attained a position in society. The dramatist's occupation was scarcely, in those times, considered a creditable employment.[189] By the Puritans it was deemed sinful—by learned men, idle and trifling; and although lawyers and academicians, courtiers and ladies, and even the Queen and Princes of the blood, took the conspicuous parts, there was still a certain disrepute attached to the very instruments by means of which the stage was brought into what is justly called its "palmiest state."

There were perhaps various reasons for the slow success of Massinger as a dramatist, and for that adverse fate the bitterness of which breaks forth in all his works. The age was Puritan; and he was supposed to have exchanged the Protestant principles with which he had entered Oxford for Romanist opinions—or rather, what we should now term Tractarian. That he may have been, as Mr. Gifford infers, from his leaving Oxford without a degree, a Roman Catholic, is borne out by no fact, although seemingly attested by the subjects of his plays—the "Virgin Martyr," the "Renegade," and the "Maid of Honour," and from some passages in his other dramas. The bare suspicion was enough to make an author unfashionable at the time when the religion of the poet's ancestors was the object of hatred and terror, and the laws against recusants were in all their hateful force. The plots of Massinger's plays were, however, almost invariably taken from French or Italian novels, or from old legends, which embodied Romanism, and must, if Protestantized, have assumed the form of satire. Another drawback to Massinger's popularity was the strong Whiggism which manifested itself in his plays, and which was so greatly at variance with the tone of the Court and of the higher classes during the early part of the reign of James I. He had not the reverence for constituted authority which marked the sentiments of Shakspeare, whilst his devotion to birth (not to *rank* alone) savoured of the son of the retainer in a great house, where the servant generally is a far greater worshipper of the old descent than the real possessor of the ancient pedigree.[190] Thus, whilst this ill-fated man, full of genius, full of virtue, and of a deep sense of religion, was always tempting the slings and arrows of fortune, he was distrusted by the Puritans as a favourer of the Romish faith; he was avoided by the loyal as an enemy to passive obedience; and he must have been regarded with disgust by the rich city merchants and traders, for his contempt for newly-acquired wealth, and his merciless exposition of their assumption, in his dramas.

Massinger, therefore, lived and died in poverty. The language of complaint became habitual to him; he spoke of his despised state with agony—yet his patrons were many and honourable; but he addressed each successively in dedications which were masterpieces of pure English, as his last hope—his dependence on whom "ate into his very soul." To Sir Robert Wiseman, of Thorrell's Hall, in Essex, he "freely, and with a zealous thankfulness, acknowledges that for many years he had but *faintly subsisted*, had he not often tasted of his great bounty."[191] In his dedication of "The Picture" to the noble Society of the Inner Temple, he thanks them, "his honoured and selected friends," for their "frequent bounties." He lived upon presents; and of the comforts of a certain income he had not, probably, even one year's experience. It is impossible to think of such a career without pain—starving one day, repulsed with condescension from the halls of the rich, another. He has depicted feelingly, indeed, the gentleman reduced to penury, in the "New Way to Pay Old Debts," and the insults heaped on him by over-fed sycophants.

"*Overreach* (to *Wellborn*)—

Avaunt, thou beggar!

If ever thou presume to own me more,

I'll have thee caged and whipp'd.

"*Amble* (to *Wellborn*)—

Cannot you stay, to be serv'd among your fellows

From the basket, but you must press into the hall?"

The "basket" contained broken meat, which was placed in the porter's lodge of great houses, to be distributed to the poor.

So, in the "Fatal Dowry," *Pontalier* says to *Liladum*:—

"Go to the basket, and repent."

It is with true feeling that Massinger put into the mouth of *Wellborn* these pleading lines:—

"Scorn me not, good lady!

But, as in form you are angelical,

Imitate the heavenly natures, and vouchsafe

At the least awhile to hear me. You will grant

The blood that runs in this arm is as noble

As that which fills your veins; those costly jewels

And those rich clothes you wear, your men's observance

And women's flattery, are in you no virtues;

Nor these rags, with my poverty, in me vices."

His life, however, was not without its solace. Happily for the literary men of the age, Ralegh had comprehended what is most essential both to mind and body, and in founding the meetings at the Mermaid had provided for the dramatist, poet, and philosopher, suitable relaxation. The place of meeting was at the Mermaid, in Bread Street, Cheapside. Here Shakspeare, Ben Jonson, Beaumont, Fletcher, and many others, enjoyed the rare companionship of Ralegh, during the brief intervals in which he was not either engaged at the Court, or in distant expeditions. Here wit was the current coin of the company; toil was cast aside; "away with melancholy," was the burden of the guests, who had probably many a care hidden in the core of their hearts. To Shakspeare's joyous nature, and to the sanguine and then unbroken spirit of Ralegh, the sorrows of the past, the terrors of the future, might easily be forgotten, or suspended over a cup of rich Canary; or, as night drew on, after a beaker of sack- posset. But one may picture to oneself the diffident, yet proud Philip Massinger, in his black doublet and plain white linen collar, with shabby tassels hanging from it, feasting, perhaps, at another man's expense— trying to shine in these "wit-combats"—trying to forget "the basket," and to seem prosperous; but, with the remembrance of the five pounds borrowed upon the security of his capital of brains, with a heavy sigh, as the delightful bard of Avon talked of retiring, on his fortune of two hundred a-year, to the quaint old town, his birth-place.

It must, however, have been a delicious opportunity of looking into minds as various as they were original. Beaumont has described the surface:—

"What things have we seen

Done at the Mermaid!—heard words that have been

So nimble and so full of subtle flame,

As if that every one from whence they came

Had meant to put his whole wit in a jest,

And had resolved to live a fool the rest

Of his dull life ...

... and when that was gone,

We left an air behind us, which alone

Was able to make the two next companies

(Right witty, though but downright fools) more wise."

A modern writer has compared these meetings to the "*Noctes Ambrosianæ.*" Happier far the wits of modern days, than the gifted men who, in the time of the Stuarts, were fain to cringe to patrons for their subsistence. None but unsuccessful authors will rail at modern publishers, when they remember the infinite miseries, with few signal exceptions, of those who were unhappy enough to depend on individuals and not on the public, whose will and taste the publisher alone studies.

Intemperance was, in those days, not only the sin of the middle-classes, but that of the Court; and both James and his Queen are said to have indulged in it. Massinger seems to have held what were rare opinions in his time, and to have been an advocate for total abstinence:—

"O take care of wine!

Cold water is far better for your healths,

Of which I am very tender."—*The Picture.*

He wrote rapidly, and his pen was never idle; yet he lived in miserable poverty. There is no record either that he was married—no indication that, like every other poet, he had an unfortunate or unrequited attachment. His pilgrimage had one solace, that of a fervent religion; which had, probably, much of the superstitions which were mingled, in those early days of Protestantism, with the reformed faith. The Church of England was then "an untrimmed vessel, lurching now towards Rome, and now towards Geneva;" it is therefore no wonder if many of the young, the impassioned, the imaginative, inclined to that form of faith and of worship which wore at least the semblance of venerable seniority.
[192]

There is not a line in Massinger's works that can either convict him of Romanism, or stamp him as a Protestant. Like many of his contemporaries, his romantic fancy was captivated by the picturesque ceremonial, the saintly observances, the *dramatic* services of the Romish Church; and to this was probably added a disgust to that puritanic fervour by which not only the drama—to which there were, in fact, many just exceptions to be made—but all that was enchanting in life, poetry, secular music, revelry (not necessarily corrupting), was condemned as sinful, and all intellectual luxury prohibited and anathematized.

The Herbert family continued to be friends to Massinger—at all events, to lend him the support of their name. He dedicated "The New Way to Pay Old Debts," the most celebrated of his plays, to Robert, Earl of Carnarvon. "I was born," he says, "a most devoted servant to the thrice noble family of your incomparable lady, and am most ambitious, though at a proper distance, to be known to your lordship." Robert, Earl of Carnarvon, who had married the Lady Katherine Herbert, although a friend and favourer of the Muses, and also Grand Falconer of England, is long since forgotten—whilst the poet, who addressed him "at a proper distance," is remembered with pride and interest.

There was so close an intimacy at one time between the Earl of Pembroke's family and that of the Duke of Buckingham, that it seems strange that no trace of Massinger's having been patronized by him are to be discovered. In fact, the annals of Massinger's life present little except the dates of his works. The eldest son of the unworthy Philip, Earl of Pembroke and Montgomery, the poet's chief patron, was married in 1634 to Lady Mary Villiers, then a mere girl. It is true that this alliance was formed six years after Buckingham's death; but it was probably concerted before that event, after the fashion of the day, in which the infant in the cradle was often affianced by ambitious parents, and the nuptials solemnized at ten or twelve years of age. Charles, Lord Herbert set out on his travels directly after he had married his young wife, and died of small-pox at Florence in 1636. Massinger wrote a poem on his loss, among others, to his little bride:—

"True sorrow fell

With showers of tears—still bathe the widowed bed

Of his dear spouse."

The elegy, as it has been observed, had better not have been written; and his "dear spouse" very likely at that time preferred balls and revelries to her husband.

It was, however, not impossible that Villiers, to please the Herbert family, may have been the means of introducing Massinger to Charles I., who justly estimated his great merits, and proved a more generous as well as a worthier patron than the Earl of Pembroke and Montgomery.

The political tenets of Massinger brought him on one occasion into considerable danger. They were, nevertheless, such as we should now term moderate; but they were irrelevantly introduced into his dramas, at a time when liberalism was almost regarded as next to treason. In 1631, Sir Henry Herbert, the Master of the Revels, refused to receive a play of Massinger's because it contained what that functionary called "dangerous matters," as to the deposing of Sebastian, King of Portugal, and "thereby reflected upon Spain." Even the name of that piece is unknown, although the Master of the Revels took care that the fee of twenty shillings for reading it over was paid to him. In 1638, when the question of the Ship-money was dividing the nation from the Court, Massinger, unable to control his indignation at the oppressive measures of Charles I., produced another play, called "The King and the Subject," founded on the history of Don Pedro the Cruel. It contained, amongst other free and bold passages, these lines:—

"Monies? We'll raise supplies which way we please,

And force you to subscribe to blanks, in which

We'll mulct you as we shall think fit. The Cæsars

In Rome were wise, acknowledging no laws

But what their swords did ratify—the wives

And daughters of the senators bowing to

Their will as deities—"

It was evident to all who had occasion to peruse the play in manuscript, that Don Pedro was intended for the King. It was submitted, however, to Charles, who was at Newmarket; he read it, and then, in his own hand, marked the objectionable passage, and wrote underneath these words, "This is too insolent; note that the poet make it the speech of a King, Don Pedro, to his subjects." This is one instance of the kind nature of the often mistaken King, who avoided condemning the play to oblivion.[193] That he encouraged Massinger—that he perceived, beneath the bitterness of a struggling man, a noble independence of character, is evident from Massinger's plays being, in the commencement of that reign, the fashionable representations at Court. A bespeak at Court was the most signal proof of success, and was all that could be desired by an author; and Charles took an opportunity of conferring this benefit on Massinger, when the poet's feelings had been grievously wounded by the opposition made to "The Emperor of the East," on its first performance by bespeaking that play.

Massinger recorded his gratitude for the bespeak in a prologue, in which he affirms his chief aim had been to please the King, and the fair Henrietta Maria, in this production:—

"What we now present,

When first conceived in his vote and intent,

Was sacred to your pleasure; in each part

With his best of fancy, judgment, language, art,

Fashioned and formed so as might well, and may,

Deserve a welcome, and no vulgar way.

He durst not, sir, at such a solemn feast,

Lard his grave matter with one scurrilous jest,

But laboured that no passage might appear

But what the Queen, without a blush, might hear."

In 1633, just after the appearance of Prynne's "Histriomastix," Charles ordered the representation of Massinger's "Guardian" at Whitehall, on Sunday—an unwise act, in the eyes of all; a wrong one in those of most persons, who, without undue prejudice, view the Sabbath not only as a day of holy rest, but as one in which the thoughts and actions should be eminently pure, serene, and devout. We cannot but allow that the Puritans had much reason on their side in condemning this profanation, which was, one can scarcely doubt, instigated by Queen Henrietta, or intended to please her. The plays of Massinger were peculiarly unsuited to the Sabbath, from their grossness.

It is not easy to say what amount of indelicacy the ladies of that period could listen to "without a blush." Their confusion was, indeed, hidden beneath a black velvet mask. Even eighty or ninety years afterwards, the incomparable Queen Mary, the consort of William III., and her maids of honour, listened, under that protection, to the comedies of an age, perhaps, if possible, still more licentious in its plays than that in which Massinger wrote. Nor was it until the mask was abolished by law that the presence of women was recognized as controlling impropriety. In the reign of Anne, influenced by the correctness of the Court, as well as by the presence of ladies, unexceptionable plays, of loftier tone, by Steele and Addison, were placed on the stage. It is to be hoped that Queen Henrietta scarcely comprehended what she heard in a language of which she knew but little before her arrival in England; or perhaps, with the French notions, that a married woman, however young, may go everywhere and hear everything, even if only just emancipated from a convent or the nursery, she may not have thought herself and her attendants degraded by what they heard.

The Queen's partiality for Massinger was soon known by another demonstration on her part. On the site of the old Monastery of Blackfriars, which had been signalized by the sitting of the Black Parliament, in the reign of Henry VIII., by the trial of Katharine of Arragon in its hall, and by the condemnation of Wolsey, James Burbage, and his company, known as the Earl of Leicester's players, had erected a theatre. It was within the precincts, but not the jurisdiction, of the City; and the Lord Mayor, after ejecting Burbage from the City, tried in vain to drive them out of Blackfriars. The Puritan inhabitants of the precincts were also inimical to the playhouse, and petitioned the Lords and Council against its continuance there.[194] Nevertheless, Queen Henrietta bespoke "Cleander," a lost play of Massinger's, and went to see it acted at Blackfriars. She was justly censured for this imprudence—not, indeed, for her inconsistent patronage of dramas unfit for women to hear or read —a sin which that age perceived not—but for a public attendance at a theatre, on the stage of which the young gallants of the time chose to sit, perched on stools, with tobacco pipes in their mouths—or congregated in twopenny refreshment-rooms, where ale and tobacco were sold.

It does not appear that the patronage of the Court gave permanent independence to Massinger. After the production of his last drama, "The Fair Anchoress of Pausilippo," his career was over. He latterly lived at the Bankside, a residence probably chosen by him from its vicinity to various theatres—to Blackfriars, from its proximity to Blackfriars Road; to the Globe Theatre, in which Shakespeare had a share; to Paris Garden, to the Rose, to the Hope, and the Swan. The Chirk, near the Church of St. Saviour's, even in the time of Charles I., was the seat of all manner of low dissipation—bear-baiting, among the rest—and consequently of misery and vice. The district was not sanctified even by the holy edifice of St. Saviour's; that noble church, the finest specimen of the early English style in London, the crypt of which is one of the un-seen sights of the metropolis, having, happily, escaped the restoring hand of some reprehensible churchwardens, who have done their best to spoil the nave, and to reduce it to the level of their own ideas. To his obscure home, near St. Saviour's, Philip Massinger retired on the evening of the 16th of March, 1639-40, to rest, in his usual health. He was found dead in the morning in his bed. No friendly hand closed his eyes—no kind voice whispered into his ear words of hope and peace in Heaven, of which he had known so little on earth: no record of the mortal disease which thus struck him down—what would be called, in our time, prematurely—has been found. His death was, like his life, a blank. The parish register tells us all that can be told: "March 16, 1639-40.—Buried Philip Massinger, *a stranger*." He was followed to the grave by actors, and buried in the churchyard of St. Saviour's, then called St. Mary Overie, from an old suppressed priory. No stone marked his grave. His funeral was too poor for his remains to be interred within the church, where Lancelot Andrews and Henry Sacheverell preached, and where their bones repose; and where the poet Gower founded a chantry, and erected a tomb. Massinger was interred among the poor and the humble; perhaps his old companions of the playhouse, in after-days, slept, also, near his nameless grave.

His burial cost 2*l.*—a sum large enough, in those days, to ensure it, in Mr. Gifford's eyes, a considerable amount of state and ceremony; and the word "stranger," which grates so painfully on the feelings of those who reverence genius, is said by that authority to be usually affixed to the name of any one not belonging to the parish of St. Saviour. Yet, that his contemporaries put no epitaph on his tomb, that there was nothing but the sod over the cold clay, that no tradition even exists to show where he once lay, seems to prove that the Puritans were in the ascendancy on that sad day when the "stranger" was conveyed to his last home; and that they were meet ancestors of those who have since "restored" the old church, and have cleverly concealed the beauties of its interior.

Massinger had great qualities. He was religious, and of rare honesty and independence; yet his religion did not purify his thoughts, nor tend, consequently, to chasten his productions—and his circumstances wore away his real independence, as his dedications testify. His conceptions of what was noble, of what was virtuous, are beautifully expressed in those plays, which are yet so full of coarseness as to be unpresentable; and whilst he never loses any opportunity of exalting virtue, he seizes every occasion of depraving the taste, if not the mind. In this respect he is far more culpable than Shakspeare; the age had deteriorated: James I. was coarse, and liked coarseness in others; his Court and his amusements all partook of that characteristic, which increased after the old chivalric style had declined. The elegance and purity in the works of Sir Philip Sidney and Spenser were succeeded by coarseness in those of Massinger, Ford, and Ben Jonson. When Massinger ceased to write freely—and, in so doing, to indulge every fancy, fair or foul—he wrote feebly. Of this "The Roman Actor," to play which he "held to be the most perfect birth of his Minerva," affords an example. It is free from indelicacy, but presents few of Massinger's striking excellencies. The plot is bad; the scene in which the character of *Paris* might have been so powerfully developed, when tempted by *Domitian*, is poor. The tortures of the senators on the stage, and the appearance of their ghosts afterwards, savours of the love which Massinger had for the horrible—with the delineation of which he seems to have consoled himself for his forbearance in other points. Nevertheless, whilst the secondary characters in "The Roman Actor" are poor and indistinct—whilst those of the primary actors are striking and truthful— the timid tyranny of *Domitian*, and the ambition of *Donitia*, are admirably worked out.

The inordinate taste for revolting incidents on the stage was a great feature of the times; the contemporaries of Somerset and his wife were habituated to the excitement of fearful mysteries, of crimes, and sins half-disclosed, yet awful in the dimness of partial discovery. The frequent occurrence of murders, sometimes designedly, "but more often in hasty broils," in that day, presented subjects which, to us, seem extravagant, but which were highly acceptable to the bravadoes, who, smoking on the stage, brandished their rapiers, and were ready to avenge a quarrel at the sword's point. In nothing is the difference of manners so marked between those days and these as in the matter of *honour*. In those times, honour was perpetually in every man's mouth—personal courage was prominently brought forward; and hence, every play had its braggart or its coward; and, as we see in the works of Beaumont and Fletcher,[195] honour had its code, its professional counsel, and its practical paid supporters. But, with this code, this practice, moral courage had little to do; the code of honour drew the main limit of caste, and the burgher and the tradesman were beneath it. So important was it, however, to observe the new code *aux ongles*, that a manual or grammar of its rules was applied to satisfy the captious on nice points. Thus, when *Adorio*, in Massinger's "Maid of Honour," laments that his honour and reputation should suffer from having taken a blow in public from *Caldoro*, accompanied with the infamous "mark of coward," he is referred by *Camillo*, to whom he pours forth his vexation, to Caranza's "Grammar" for directions, in much the same manner as a lawyer would quote Lord St. Leonards on a point of law—or travellers call on Murray as their authority.

When *Adorio* talks of what he "would do" in the matter, *Camillo* answers:—

"Never think on't,

Till fitter time and place invite you to it.

I have read Caranza, and find not in his Grammar

Of quarrels that the injured man be bound

To seek for reparation at an hour;

But may, and without loss, till he hath settl'd

More serious occasions that import him.

For a day or two defer it.

Adorio.—You'll subscribe

Your hand to this?

Camillo.—And justify't with my life.

Presume upon't.

Adorio.—On then; you shall o'errule me."

Women were not let off so easily; happily for them, more was expected from them than from men. Without referring to Caranza, their honour consisted not only in chastity, but in constancy to vows, and resistance to the temptations of wealth; and these attributes were sufficiently rare to make the "Maid of Honour" an exceptional character.[196] Massinger, however, assures us that English women, even in those days, asserted a superiority in intellect and character: it is true, they had no opportunity of travelling, and stayed at home; but they learned from their lovers and brothers the customs of those foreign countries which it was then dangerous to traverse.

Most men of rank or fortune, nevertheless, made the "grand tour" before marrying; or left their young betrothed mistresses in their native counties. In the "Guardian," *Calipso* says:—

"Why, sir, do gallants travel?

Answer that question; but at their return

With wonder to the hearers to discourse of

The garb and difference in foreign females—

As the lusty girl of France, the sober German,

The plump Dutch frow, the stately dame of Spain."

It has been asked whether Massinger and Shakspeare ever met?—whether, as Hartley Coleridge inquires, they ever "took a cup of sack together at the Mitre or the Mermaid;" and whether Massinger was ever umpire or bottle-holder in the "wit-combats" described by Fuller? But upon this, as well as on many other points, there is no light. We know not whom Massinger loved, nor whom he hated; we would fain believe, with Coleridge, that his life was not passed without some true affection—a link between passion and virtue; we would willingly believe that, like Tasso, he loved one above him in rank—or one below him—rather than that he had never loved at all. But his works repel the surmise. True love is vehement—but it is delicate; and it would have elevated his thoughts, and purified his expressions. Massinger may have done justice to the intellect and companionship of his countrywomen, but he had no reverence for the most beautiful part of their nature; and in this, as in other respects, is far below Shakspeare.

The obscurity which overshadowed all Massinger's career has rendered any communication, as we have seen, between him and Buckingham, doubtful; but it was far otherwise in respect to Ben Jonson —whose works are so replete with allusions to the Villiers family, and to their attributes, amusements, and bounties, that no biography of George Villiers can be complete without a more copious reference to the works of this dramatist than can be conveyed in the passing notices which have been given of his masques, in the course of the preceding narrative.[197] Ben Jonson was ten years older than Massinger; and was born in 1574. Whether from his surname, or his Christian name, or from his after-life, it is not easy to say, but one generally looks upon Ben Jonson as a man of low birth. But such was not the fact. His grandfather, a man of some family and fortune, was a gentleman in the service of Henry VIII.; his father was in holy orders, "a grave minister of the Gospel."[198]

The family had originally settled at Annandale, in Scotland; but Ben Jonson was born in Westminster. He had the misfortune to come into the world a month after his father's death. It was, perhaps, a less adverse circumstance that his mother, two years afterwards, married again. Her views were not exalted, and she took for her second husband—tired, it might seem, of the genteel poverty of the cloth—a master-bricklayer. Not even has Fuller, not even has Gifford, been able to ascertain in what part of the suburb of Westminster "Ben" was born. Fuller, however, consoles us; he could not trace the poet in his *cradle*, but he could "fetch him," as he observes, in his "short coats." About two years old, Ben was *discovered*—that is to say, the haunts of his infancy were—"a little child in Hartshorn Lane, near Charing Cross."

This neighbourhood was as poor as that of Westminster Abbey; and the parish of St. Martin's-in-the-Fields, which then extended to Whitehall on the south, to Marylebone on the north, to the Savoy on the east, and to Chelsea and Kensington on the west, when first rated to the poor in Queen Elizabeth's reign, contained only two hundred persons sufficiently wealthy to pay those rates.[199] It afterwards became the greatest cure in England, until several of its parishes were separated from the patron saint, St. Martin's.

Here, however, Ben Jonson was brought up—getting such education as he might from a school in the church of St Martin's. It is stated, however, by Gifford, to have been a "private school." He might possibly have been one of the private pupils on a foundation school. Some unknown benefactor, however, removed the future poet from St Martin's, and placed him at St. Peter's College, Westminster, which was founded by Queen Elizabeth, in 1660—"a public school for grammar, rhetorick,
—*poetry* (which the maiden Queen was too wise to despise) and for the Latin and Greek languages."

This removal was the visible cause of all Ben Jonson's eminence. Camden, the historian, was then one of the masters of that school, from whose ranks issued Cowley, George Herbert, Dryden, Churchill, Cowper, Southey, and many others less celebrated. Ben Jonson always retained an affectionate remembrance of Camden's instructions:—

"Camden, most reverend head, to whom I owe

All that in wits I am, and all I know."

He dedicated his best play, "Every Man in his Humour," to Master Camden, "Clarencieux," ending his dedication thus:—

"Now, I pray you to accept this; such wherein neither the confession of my manners shall make you blush—nor of my studies repent you to have been the instructor; and for the profession of any thankfulness, I am sure it will, with good men, find either praise or excuse, from your true lover, Ben Jonson."[200]

From Westminster, Jonson went to Cambridge, probably to St. John's; but even of this important fact no certainty exists, for the university register is imperfect, and from 1600 to 1602 there is an hiatus. It is merely conjectured, from there being several books containing the name of Ben Jonson in the library of St. John's, that he entered that College. Here, however, he only stayed, according to Fuller, some weeks; funds were wanting for his support—a circumstance which seems to shew that he was not sent up to Trinity College on the foundation, as otherwise he would have had an exhibition at Westminster. His parents were unable to supply means; and the young student, thirsting for distinction, was obliged to return and follow his step-father's calling. Never was there a situation so pitiable, and the condition of this aspiring scholar was compassionated by other scholars of happier fortunes than himself. Camden generously relieved him; Thomas Sutton, who, having bought the Charter House from Lord Suffolk, nobly devoted it to an hospital and school, "the master-piece of Protestant charity," as Lord Bacon styled it,

—also, according to some accounts, consoled, and compassionated, and assisted Jonson. It has even been said that "Ben" was engaged to attend the eldest son of Sir Walter Ralegh, as a tutor; but of this no certainty exists. All that is absolutely known is, that he was sick of the trowel and the hod, whilst his mind was running on Horace and Virgil; and that to escape what he deemed degradation, he enlisted, went off to the Low Countries, and served a campaign in that scene of war, which was a sort of school to the young English soldier.

His heart went, to a certain extent, along with this new profession. "Let not those blush that have, but those that have not, a lawful calling," says Fuller,—and Jonson seems to have thought so likewise. He returned, however, at nineteen, poor as ever, with the same scholastic tastes; and the master-bricklayer being dead, he repaired to his mother's house.

He next tried the stage. It has been, in all times, the refuge of the unthrifty. But Jonson's appearance was unfavourable to that attempt. His very ugliness, one would have thought, might have been an advantage. Mr. Gifford repels with fury the imputation on Jonson, that his hero was frightful; yet the description he gives himself of Ben Jonson is by no means attractive. His complexion, which had been clear and smooth in boyhood, was disfigured by a scorbutic humour, and ultimately by scars, from what the Germans are pleased to call the "Englische Krankheit." His features are said not to have been irregular or unpleasing, but appear in his portraits to be large and coarse. One eye looked askance; his forehead was, however, noble; his person was broad and corpulent—after forty it became unwieldy; and his gait, he himself owned, "ungracious." In early youth his worst points were not, probably, prominent; he had a delightful voice and emphasis. "I never," said the Duchess of Newcastle, "heard any man read well but my husband; and I have heard him say, 'he never heard any man read well but Ben Jonson, and yet he hath heard many in his time.'"[201]

Nevertheless, "Ben" was not a good actor. Critics differ as to the nature and duration of his theatrical employ. And Gifford, who takes every question relative to his hero as a personal matter, is indignant at the statement that he was a strolling player, or ambled by the side of a waggon, and took *mad Jeronymo's* part; but, as most companies were then itinerant, and, as even now, first-rate actors and actresses make provincial tours, there seems little call for the venom and wrath poured out by the indefatigable biographer, who points, with satisfaction, to the bulky figure of Jonson, and asks how he could possibly act "little *Jeronymo*," that "inch of Spain"?[202]

Whatever was his position—whether, as Anthony Wood says, "he did recede to a nursery or obscure playhouse, called the *Green Curtain*," in Shoreditch; or whether, as Gifford declares, that statement is a mere fable, and that his aims were higher—seemed now of little moment, perhaps, to Jonson himself; for his efforts were interrupted by a duel. His antagonist is supposed to have been a brother-player, who brought to the field a sword ten inches longer than poor Ben's. They fought, and Ben killed the gentleman with the long sword, but was himself severely wounded in the arm; he was sent to prison, and brought, as he described it, "near to the gallows."

Poor Ben was now, probably, fain to cry out with *Antonio* in the "Maid of Honour":—

"But redeem me

From this captivity, and I'll vow

Never to draw a sword, or cut my meat hereafter

With a knife that has an edge or point; I'll starve first."[203]

This imprisonment had a signal effect on Jonson's destiny; he fell into melancholy, and was visited in his despondency by a Romanist priest, who applied himself to his consolation first, and to his conversion afterwards. Jonson had been religiously brought up, and it was not from indifference that he renounced the faith of his parents and entered the Romish Church. Such conversions were frequent in the early days of the Reformation. Jonson was no controversialist; wiser men than he fell into the same error, and, like such, atoned for it. The great light of our Church, Jeremy Taylor, became for some time a Romanist, but returned to the Anglican faith; Chillingworth and others wandered also, and also returned. The readiest converts are often those of deep and earnest feelings, which act on excitable minds, only superficially informed on the great doctrines of Scripture.[204] Jonson's imprisonment was aggravated in its misery by a system of espionage which the necessities of the times induced. The plots against Elizabeth's life usually originated in the seminaries of the priests. Jonson was warned by his gaoler that he was watched.

He was eventually released, but by what agency does not appear.

He quitted prison, and married a young woman of his new persuasion; and there appears to have been no great reason to repent his choice. His wife was shrewish, but respectable; and the poet's prosperity commenced with his marriage.

From this time until the period when the Court festivities brought him into frequent collision with Villiers, Jonson's productions were successive occasions of triumph. Nevertheless, money did not flow into his coffers; and he was continually obliged to pledge, as Massinger did, the labour of his brain—two sums of four pounds, and twenty shillings, being advanced to him by Henslowe, the father-in-law of Alleyn, the player, upon the plots of two plays being presented and approved. Still poor Jonson had his enemies and traducers. The scene of "Every Man in his Humour" was originally laid in Thrace; the names were Italian, but wishing still further to ensure its success, Jonson changed them, and brought the scenes to London. Nevertheless, he was still attacked about his Italian story. There seems, then, to have been as great an objection to works of imagination based on foreign plots as in the present day. In "Volpone," Jonson carefully avoided introducing any material not purely English.

He was still a struggling author, with few friends except players and playwrights, and with many enemies, owing to his vehemence of temper and imprudence of speech. But of his animosity to Shakspeare, and of the poet's alienation from him, there seems no proof; and indeed Shakspeare is reported to have stood godfather to one of his children—although the improbable anecdote connected with that act is discredited by Gifford.

Jonson's acquaintance with Shakspeare is stated by Rowe to have begun with "a remarkable piece of humanity and good-nature on the part of the immortal bard." Jonson, who was then, as Rowe observes, "entirely unknown to the world," had offered "Every Man in his Humour" for representation; it was carelessly looked over, and returned in a supercilious manner by the person who had read it, with the uncourteous answer "that it would be of no use to the company." Happily, however, Shakspeare chanced to cast his eyes on the manuscript, and found in the play something that powerfully engaged his attention. Generous, as well as gifted, he recommended both Jonson and his drama to the attention of the actors, and to that of the public also.[205]

The old play, with the Italian names, the scene laid at Florence, had been first brought out at the Rose Theatre; and it was, apparently, the amended drama, which, from the numerous alterations, had become again Jonson's property, according to the custom of the time, that attracted the notice of Shakspeare.[206] Be that as it may, "Every Man in his Humour" was acted at Blackfriars in 1598, and Shakspeare's name appears at the head of it as one of the performers. This was about sixteen years before the Bard of Avon sought for repose on the banks of his beloved river, and in his native town.

Henceforth the literary world was divided by the factions which penetrate even into the studies of the lettered; and a sort of rivalship was set up, in which, it appears, the partisans of the two great dramatists were far more rife than the parties concerned.

The contending critics endeavoured to exalt the one at the expense of the other. Pope observes, "It is ever the nature of parties to be in extremes; and nothing is so probable as that, because Ben Jonson had much the more learning, it was said on the one hand that Shakspeare had none at all; and because Shakspeare had much the most wit and fancy, it was retorted on the other that Jonson wanted both; because Shakspeare borrowed nothing, it was said that Ben Jonson borrowed everything; because Jonson did not write extempore, he was reproached with being a year about every piece; and because Shakspeare wrote with ease and facility, they cry'd he never once made a blot."[207]

Yet, without attempting to enter into a controversy long since passed away, and doubtful in origin and extent, it is satisfactory to find Jonson's vindication from unworthy motives in his famous lines, "To the Memory of my Beloved, the Author, Mr. William Shakespere, and what he hath left us:" in which he truly calls him the "Soul of the Age."

Jonson's "Every Man in his Humour" was honoured, after it had been played several times, by the presence of Queen Elizabeth, who was one of Jonson's earliest patrons. Nevertheless, in "Cynthia's Revels," which was brought out during the following year, the poet satirized the formal and affected manners of the Court.

Whitehall was never gay after the execution of Mary Queen of Scots; the joyousness of Elizabeth's nature, which she had inherited from her father, was gone.

When mirth went out, pedantry came in. Euphüism was for a time in vogue; the Queen, pensive one hour, fretful the next, looked passively on the change; but to her courtiers—among whom Jonson now began to mix

—the satire in "Cynthia's Revels" was, probably, highly acceptable. Among the most reprehensible usages of the day was that of bringing up children to perform on the public stage, as well as in the Court. In 1609 authority was given to "William Shakespeare, Robert Daborne, Nathaniel Field, and Robert Kirkham," to provide and instruct a certain number of children to perform in tragedies, comedies, or masques, within the Blackfriars, or in "the realm of England." Shakspeare, who soon withdrew from the superintendence of this juvenile company, has referred to them in "Hamlet," thus marking his disapprobation of the system.[208]

"But there is, sir, an aviary of children, little eyases that cry out on the top of question, and are most tyrannically clapp'd for it. These are now the fashion, and so besottle the common stages (so they call them) that many wearing rapiers are afraid of goose-quills, and scarce dare come thither."

These children were, in some respects, well cared for. They were selected from the young choristers in the Royal Chapel, and, by an order, so early as the reign of Edward IV., they were to be sent to Oxford or Cambridge, on the King's foundation, at the age of eighteen, should their voices be changed, or the number of choristers be over-full. "Many good people," observes Hartley Coleridge,[209] "who are scandalized at the Latin plays of Westminster, will be surprised that in the pious days of England, in the glorious morning of the Reformation, in 'great Eliza's golden time,' under Kings and Queens that were the nursing fathers and nursing mothers, the public acting of plays should be, not the permitted recreation, but the compulsory employment of children devoted to sing the praises of God—of plays too, the best of which children may now only read in a 'family' edition of some, whose very titles a modern father would scruple to pronounce before a woman or a child."

These children were first impressed from the cathedrals by Richard III.; and even Queen Elizabeth issued a warrant, under the sign-manual, "authorizing Thomas Gyles," the master of the children of Paul's, "to bring up any boys in cathedrals or collegiate churches, in order to be instructed for the entertainment of the Court." The children of the Queen's Chapel must, therefore, henceforth form a principal feature in the representations of Ben Jonson's masques, as we picture them to our minds, either in Whitehall—consumed by fire long since—or at Althorpe, or at Burleigh-on-the-Hill, or in the stately Castle of Belvoir. Under those vaulted roofs their young voices warbled the exquisite poetry of Jonson to the music of Lawes, or—be it not recorded without shame, nevertheless—were obliged to utter words of raillery, bitterness, and indelicacy, which were usually, as Heywood in his apology for actors confesses, allotted to the unconscious children to deliver.

Greatly as Ben Jonson hailed the accession of James I., he had soon reason to regret the wise though parsimonious Queen Elizabeth. In conjunction with Chapman and Marston, he had written a play called "Eastward Hoe." It was well received; but there was a passage in it reflecting on the Scotch. The two authors were arrested; Jonson had not any share in writing the piece, but, being accessory to its production, he honourably and "voluntarily" accompanied his two friends to prison, thus surrendering himself to justice. No very severe punishment was ever contemplated, but a report prevailed that the three delinquents were to have their ears and noses cut. Jonson is said to have been released owing to the intercession of Camden and Selden; and they are declared to have been present when, after his liberation, he gave an entertainment. On that occasion his mother "drank to him, and showed him a paper which she designed, if the sentence had taken effect, to have been mixed with his drink, and it was a strong and hasty poison." To show "that she was no churl," Jonson, in relating this story, added, "she designed to have first drank of it herself."

He escaped from some other personal attack which, in common with Chapman, he made on some individual, with only a second and also temporary imprisonment;[210] and from this time was in such constant requisition by the Court, that his imprudence went unnoticed. The "Masque of Darkness" was composed by the express command of Anne of Denmark, who appeared in it as a negress, surrounded with the dark beauties of her supposed African Court. The Queen, and the "Daughters of Night," as the noble dames who acted in that pageant were called, were placed in a concave shell, seated one above another in tiers; from the top of the shell, which represented mother-of-pearl, hung a cheveron of light, which cast a bright beam on these ladies; the shell was moving up and down upon the sea, and in the billows appeared varied forms of sea-monsters, twelve in number, each bearing a torch on his back. The Queen was attired in azure and silver, with a curious head-dress of feathers, fastened with ropes of pearl, which showed well as the loops fell on the blackened throats of the masquers, who also wore ropes of pearl on their arms and wrists. Inigo Jones is conjectured to have written the directions for the costume of this masque.[211] Jonson now received periodical sums, not only from the Court, but from public bodies and private patrons. A year seldom passed without a Royal progress; and we have seen how essential the poet had become to the often impromptu revelries in which James I. continually indulged. Yet Jonson wrote his plays and masques slowly. The "Fox" took him a year to complete. His notion was that "a good poet's made as well as born."[212] He worked out his own success, and his labours were incessant. He had a practice of committing to his commonplace book remarkable passages that struck him. Lord Falkland, one of the most accomplished of the cavaliers, expressed his astonishment at the variety and extreme copiousness of Jonson's knowledge. If a pedantic display of learning be imputed to Jonson, it must be remembered that it was, probably, in compliance with the taste of his royal patron, James, who delighted in exhibiting his classical proficiency; and who, even on his death-bed, as we have seen, answered the learned Prelate near him in Latin. It was during the first years of King James's reign that Jonson justified these classic allusions in his "Masque and Barriers," at the nuptials of the Earl of Essex to the faithless bride, also married afterwards to Somerset. "Some," he says, "may squeamishly cry out, that all endeavours of learning and sharpness in these transitory devises, where it steps beyond their little (or let me not wrong them) no brain at all, is superfluous. I am contented these fastidious stomachs should leave my full tables, and enjoy at home their clean empty trenchers, fitted for such airy tastes, where perhaps a few Italian herbs, picked up, and made into a sallad, may find sweeter acceptance than all the sound meat of the world."

These beautiful masques had the great advantage of being set to music by Henry Lawes, the composer who secured immortality to his name by the music of "Comus," composed by him. Lawes was beginning his career of fame when Buckingham first entered the Court. The son of a vicar choral in Salisbury Cathedral, he rose to be first a gentleman of the Chapel Royal, and afterwards Clerk of the Chapel, and conductor of the private music of Charles I. Henry Lawes sometimes took a part in the masques which he composed; and acted the attendant spirit in "Comus." His "ayres" and dialogues have disappointed posterity. Yet he appears to have been almost the father of English vocal music; and, as Milton declares—

"Taught our English music how to space

Word with just note and accent."

Music, like all the other delights of peace, languished during the troublous times of the Rebellion, or flourished only on the battle-field. Lawes was obliged to teach singing during that period; but he lived to compose the coronation anthem for Charles II., and to have a place of interment assigned to him in Westminster Abbey. His brother, less happy, though a skilful musician also, and often employed in conjunction with

Henry Lawes, took up arms for Charles I., in whose service he also lived, and to whom he was devoted, and fell, fighting for his sovereign, at the siege of Chester.

It was then the custom for certain great families to receive musicians, as well as men of letters, in their houses, and to employ them in their especial line—sometimes in hymeneal festivities, sometimes in composing requiems. Thus the arts and sciences, poetry, music, painting, and scenic decoration, were united, during the life-time of George Villiers, in a degree never before or since known in this country. Massinger, Ben Jonson, Lawes, Inigo Jones, were at the service of the rich and noble, and awaited their bidding. Shakspeare died just after George Villiers had received the first public proof of Royal favour—the honour of knighthood;[213] and the era of masques and revels began. Still, "a craving for mental enjoyment,"[214] as well as that derived from the senses, was diffused.

The religious changes and controversies in the preceding reigns had improved the intellect of the higher orders in England, by making some portion of learning necessary to those either engaged in polemical disputes, or who, conscientious, though unassuming, wished to form their own opinions. There was an earnestness in the awakened minds of that period. "It was a time of much vice, much folly, much trouble—but it was an age of much energy."[215] When, after the middle of Elizabeth's reign, the thirst for controversy abated, the desire for cultivation, the love of poetry, and the taste for art remained, took another direction, and tended to the improvement and enlightenment of social life. The higher classes did much to exalt these dawning predilections, until the rebellion came; after that fearful convulsion, the diversions of the great were henceforth debased in character, and their minds in taste.

Mary Countess of Pembroke was one of the earliest and most admired of Ben Jonson's friends. To her son William, the early adviser of the Duke of Buckingham, Ben Jonson dedicated his "Book of Epigrams." It is therefore almost certain that, before Jonson had appeared in public, as the composer of masques for the express entertainment of the great favourite at Burleigh, he had met Villiers at Wilton, in the society of their common friend, Lord Pembroke—"a man," Lord Clarendon writes, "very well-bred, and of excellent parts, and a graceful speaker upon any subject, having a good proportion of learning, and a ready wit to apply and enlarge upon it." When we add to this that the Earl was no cold, haughty, and pompous host, but facetious, affable, generous, magnificent, as disinterested and independent with the rich and great as he was unaffected and courteous to the humble; when we remember what Wilton even then was—the pride of the nation; when we reflect what and who were the men who were welcomed to its hospitality—men, as Clarendon observes, "of the most pregnant parts and understanding;" when we think of Ben Jonson there—probably received as a guest—whilst Massinger was still only the son of a retainer; when we picture Inigo Jones with his pencil—the sketches which he drew, praised by Vandyck; or hear the voices of the two brothers Henry and William Lawes, singing to soft airs the verses of Ben Jonson—we must believe that George Villiers had in such scenes, before he lost the friendship of Pembroke, many delights greater than the wearisome partiality of James, or even a communion with the then unformed mind of Charles.

A Platonic admiration for Christian, Countess of Devonshire, called forth in verses the romantic gallantry of the Earl of Pembroke. One cannot help rejoicing that Lawes set to music what Pembroke wrote:—

"Wrong not, dear Empress of my heart,

The merits of true passion,

With thinking that he feels no smart

Who sues for no compassion.

.   .   .   .   .   . Silence in love betrays more woe

Than words, though ne'er so witty.

The beggar that is dumb, you know,

May challenge double pity."[216]

From the society of Wilton, Villiers went forth imbued with those tastes which never yielded wholly to the grosser diversions in which his Royal patron indulged. Whilst he retained the friendship of Lord Pembroke, Villiers was, in all probability, learning to estimate the conversation and works of Ben Jonson; and henceforth, the efforts of the dramatist must, to a certain degree, be associated with the influence and protection of the favourite.

London, in spite of the repeated proclamations of King James, tending to restrain its extent, and to keep the provincial gentry in their homes, was now generally crowded at certain seasons. A number of small theatres were erected in various parts of the city, in order to supply entertainments to those who would have turned with disgust, since a finer taste had been introduced by the Reformation, from the old moralities. Shakspeare, happily, formed an engagement to produce his pieces at one theatre, but Jonson was obliged to carry his productions to various minor houses, until the success of his masques enabled him to form a higher estimate of the value of his powers. His lighter pieces are marked by grace and sweetness; but these characteristics he "laid aside," says Mr. Gifford, "whenever he approached the stage, and put on the censor with the sock."[217] The excellence of the masque in Ben Jonson's time, the great and gifted actors by whom it was performed, the fancy which was suffered to expand itself in these pieces, the scenic effect to which so vast an expense was devoted, incline us to think, with Gifford, "that all our 'most splendid shows are at best but beggarly parodies,' in comparison with those in which the Cliffords and Arundels, the Stanleys, the Russells, the Veres, and the Wroths; 'danced in the fairy rings, in the gay and gallant circles of those enchanting devices.'"[218]

After the death of Shakspeare, Jonson received, by patent, a pension of a hundred marks a-year from James. It is supposed that the honour of the laureateship chiefly or solely belonged to him. Hitherto the title seems to have been merely honorary, adopted at pleasure by any poet who was appointed to write for the Court. It had been borne by Daniel in the time of Elizabeth. It was on this occasion that Jonson applied to Selden for information concerning the origin of the title of laureate; and that Selden drew up expressly, and introduced into the second part of his "Titles of Honours," a long chapter on the custom of giving crowns of laurel to poets; at the conclusion of which he says, "Thus have I, by no unseasonable digression, performed a promise to you, my beloved Ben Jonson—your curious learning and judgment may correct where I have erred;" and adds, "where my notes and memory have left me short." A graceful and enviable compliment from such a man.

The triumphs of Jonson's genius were interrupted by his journey to Edinburgh in 1618—a journey which he performed *on foot*. Here he was the guest of Drummond, the poet of Hawthornden—under whose roof he passed the April of 1619. This journey was regarded as the greatest misfortune of Jonson's life; not only because during his stay in Scotland his wife died, but because Drummond, amongst other injuries, gave the following character of Ben Jonson to the world:—[219]

"For," he says, "Ben Jonson was a great lover and praiser of himself, a contemner and scorner of others, given rather to lose a friend than a jest, jealous of every word and action of those about him, especially after drink, which is one of the elements in which he lived; a dissembler of the parts which reigned in him, a bragger of some good that he wanted, thinketh nothing well done but what either he himself or some of his friends have said or done. He is passionately kind or angry, careless either to gain or keep; vindictive, if he be well answered as himself; interprets best sayings and deeds often to the worst. He was for any religion, as being versed in both."

The conduct of Drummond, styled by Mr. Gifford, "a cankered hypocrite,"[220] has been justified by others; his very hospitality to Jonson is termed by the infuriated biographer, "decoying him into his house." Drummond acted, in a very slight degree, in the same capacity to Jonson as that which Boswell, a century and a half afterwards, undertook in regard to the more fortunate Samuel Johnson, who found in *his* listener an admirer, and not a foe. Both these great men had the calamity of having every idle expression set down for the curiosity of an after-age; and "old Ben," as his contemporaries called him in their jovial meetings at the Mermaid, did not stand the test so well as "Old Samuel." We cannot, however, regard the visit to Scotland as the great misfortune of Ben Jonson's life, as the impassioned Gifford pronounces it.[221]

Jonson, however, returned to London, unconscious of all that after his death so agitated the literary world in the eighteenth century on his account. He met, as he wrote to Drummond, with a "most Catholic welcome from King James," who was then, like Jonson, a not disconsolate widower. The poet was writing a poem for the funeral of Queen Anne, who had just died, but was unburied. He was very keenly engaged in beginning the "Discovery," which was to contain a description of Scotland; and he signed himself Drummond's "true friend and lover." He received, in return, two letters full of kindness and compliment from Drummond, whom Gifford himself, incapable of an act of insincerity, styles thereupon, "hypocrite to the last."

Ben Jonson was now invited by Bishop Corbet to Christ Church, Oxford, where he was created Master of Arts. Thence he passed to Burleigh-on-the-Hill and to Windsor, to see the performance of his "Gypsies Metamorphosed"—and to introduce little compliments in each piece, as the *dramatis personnæ* were varied or augmented by the accession of fresh actors and actresses. About this time he wrote his poem on the "Ladies of England." It was lost—a mischance which, in the weakness of one's nature, one is apt to regret more than the destruction of a vast body of philological notes, the fruit of twenty years' labour, for which Mr. Gifford calls for especial sympathy.

Jonson was now made "Master of the Revells," and was nearly being knighted. He passed his time in going from one country seat to another; every Twelfth-day he was ordered to produce, or to repeat a masque.

Charles I. was now rising to maturity, and, like his deceased brother, Henry, he loved the poetry of Jonson, and the fancy of Inigo Jones. The match-making propensities of King James were as yet undeveloped, and had neither troubled his repose nor maddened the nation into a dread of his mistakes. Villiers was young, gay, and unmarried; and the world was at peace. Those were happy and busy days for Jonson—yet, amid all his labours, he found time to collect an excellent library. He was not only a collector, but a lender of his books—an unusual combination; a man must be generous, indeed, to unite the two characters; nay, he gave them also, liberally, to those qualified to value the rare editions which he bought. "I am fully warranted in saying," Mr. Gifford writes, "that more valuable books given to individuals by Jonson are yet to be met with than by any person of that age. Scores of them have fallen under my own observation, and I have heard of abundance of others."[222] This is rare praise. Nevertheless, since brilliant success always has its alloy, it was the lot of Jonson to suffer from the ingratitude of his coadjutor, Inigo Jones; and the excuse, perhaps, of Inigo was, that he was tried and tempted by the temper and irony of Jonson. Their quarrel was inconvenient, and must have caused some trouble in the representation of those masques and revels over which Jonson presided.

"Whoever was the aggressor," says Horace Walpole, "the turbulence and brutality of Jonson was sure to place him most in the wrong." This is a hard judgment. Let it be remembered that the circumstances of the two men were different. Jonson was poor, diseased, and in that miserable plight when a generous temper is continually checked by pecuniary difficulties. Inigo Jones had realized a handsome fortune, and was then in the full enjoyment of wealth and reputation. Unfortunately he was a poet; some of the masques printed had their joint names as the composers. Jealousies arose, which ought to have soon subsided, had either of these celebrated men known how to curb his wrath. In Jonson's case, his temper was his worst enemy; but for this defect he had an excuse which might have pleaded for him even with Inigo. In 1625, Jonson composed for King James "Pan's Anniversary," the last piece that he presented to that monarch; towards the end of that year he was attacked with palsy, and a threatening of dropsy added to his accumulated trials. Poverty and ill-health are pleas for indulgence. For the first evil, Jonson's improvidence, his hospitality, his utter want of prudence in his affairs, may justly be blamed. The last was also partially his own fault, for his habits were intemperate—and partly ascribable to an hereditarily diseased constitution. Nature, which had endowed him with that wonderful intellect, that indomitable energy, had modified her gift by the infliction of a cruel malady, which, being in the blood, was aggravated by the weakness of approaching age. The suppers at the Mermaid were now finally abandoned; and the club at the Devil Tavern, near Temple Bar, was no longer enlivened by his wit. His intellect was affected to some extent, but he recovered sufficiently to write the anti-masque of "Jophiel" for the Court; after which, none of his productions were commanded by the King during the space of three years. In his necessities, unable to leave his room, or to move without assistance, the poor invalid turned to the theatre as a source of revenue, and produced "The New Inn." It was hissed from the stage; and, notwithstanding the dramatist's plea in his epilogue that he was "sick and sad," he was persecuted with contemptuous verses, and pursued with remorseless cruelty by the many enemies that his rough manners had excited—among them, Inigo was the most inveterate.

There was, however, one kind heart that pitied him—that of Charles I. The monarch was touched by the lines which the hard critics in the theatre could hear without compassion:—

"If you expect more than you had to-night,

The Maker is sick and sad; he sent things fit

In all the numbers both of verse and wit,

If they have not miscarried: if they have,

All that his faint and faltering tongue doth crave

Is, that you not impute it to his brain—

That's yet unhurt, although set round with pain.

It cannot long hold out: all strength must yield;

Yet judgment would the last be in the field

With the true poet."

Charles sent him a hundred pounds: the poet, in the fulness of gratitude, wrote "A petition from poor Ben to the best of monarchs, masters, and men"—full of gaiety and good-humour, yet touching, even in its sparkling wit. The petition prayed that His Majesty would make his father's "hundred marks a hundred pounds," alluding to the pension granted by King James. The petition was granted, and in the patent by which the annuity was confirmed, it was said, "especially to encourage Jonson to proceed in those services of his wit and penn, which we have enjoined unto him."

A tierce of Canary accompanied this act of bounty. It was Jonson's favourite wine, and the King, from his private bounty, sent it to the sick poet. It was to be a yearly gift, not only to Jonson, but to his successors; and the wine—Spanish Canary—was to be taken from his Majesty's cellars at Whitehall, out of the stores of wine "remaining therein." Charles little anticipated that even his love of the drama should be made a cause of reproach to him at his trial. "Had the King but studied Scripture half as much as he studied Ben Jonson or Shakspeare!" was the cry of the Puritans.

Jonson might now have been tolerably happy, had not his former coadjutor, Inigo, still borne him enmity for having, during the preceding year, placed his own name before that of the royal architect. The conduct of Jones in this respect has been placed in its true light by a letter from a Mr. Perry to Sir Thomas Pickering.[223] In that letter it is stated that Inigo used his "predominant power" at Court to injure Jonson, then bed-ridden and impoverished, as the poet was. Henceforth, Aurelian Townshend, a poet scarcely known, was employed to invent the masques represented at

Court, in conjunction with Inigo Jones.

The same year that was marked by the death of Buckingham witnessed poor Jonson's "fatal stroke," as he termed it, of palsy. He never recovered this attack of 1628, and his days were overclouded by successive mortifications. Hitherto the city of London had given him a pension for his services. At the very time when it was most needed by the forlorn dramatist, it was withdrawn, but restored three years afterwards. The office for which he received this annuity was that of City Chronologer. The plea made for its cessation was that there had been "no fruits of his labours in that his place," which place was to commemorate signal events; other sources of emolument were also withheld, on the plea that the fruits of that now exhausted brain were no longer forthcoming.

But bright instances of compassion and generosity stood forth amid all this gloom. Amongst the great patrons of the drama was William Cavendish, the first Earl of Newcastle, declared by Cibber to be "one of the most finished gentlemen and distinguished patriots of his time." He had been constituted governor to Prince Charles, for whom he ever retained the most loyal affection. Of this nobleman it was said that he understood horsemanship, music, and poetry; but that he was a better horseman than a musician, a better musician than a poet. His wife, the eccentric Margaret Lucas, wrote of him that "his mind was above his fortune, his generosity above his purse, his courage above danger, his justice above bribers, his friendship above self-interest, his truth too firm for falsehood, his temperance beyond temptation."

It was by no means prejudicial to the popularity of this fine specimen of an English nobleman that "he was fitter to break Pegasus for a *manège* than to mount him on the steps of Parnassus." He wrote a work entitled, "A new Method and Extraordinary Invention to Dress Horses and Work them according to Nature, as also to Perfect Nature by the Subtlety of Art." The work, a folio, was succeeded by various comedies, several of them written when Lord Newcastle was in banishment, and acted, after his return to England, at Blackfriars. He wrote, it is said, in the manner of Ben Jonson, to whom he was a kind patron. The Earl was a singular compound of military skill and ardour with literary tastes; by him Sir William Davenant, poet-laureate after Jonson's death, was made Lieutenant-General of the Ordnance.[224]

His wife, who at the time Ben Jonson knew her was Countess of Newcastle, and afterwards Duchess, is one of the most voluminous of writers among the (now) long catalogue of literary ladies in this country. She was at once ridiculous and estimable—a combination of qualities painful to friends, but never acknowledged by her husband, who revered her talents, and tried to defend what was incomprehensible to the learned —her philosophy. In private life she was reserved, living almost entirely among her books, or in contemplation, or writing indefatigably. Even during the night, one of the Duke's secretaries is said to have slept on a truckle bed in a closet in her bedroom, in order to be ready to answer any sudden bursts of inspiration that might occur; and the summonses to John, "to get up and write down her Grace's suggestions," were frequent and wearisome. Kind, pious, charitable, generous, and really gifted, though romantic and visionary, this excellent lady's peculiarities might have furnished Molière with a model for his "Precieuses Ridicules;" but, to Ben Jonson, they were lessened by the vast amount of amiability that welcomed the poet to her stately abode, or, better still, relieved him in his poverty and want.

When the Earl and Countess of Newcastle heard of the poet's play being condemned—when they learned that various copies of complimentary verses had been addressed to him by admirers, pitying his humiliation— the Earl, worthy of the name of Cavendish (so dear to England), <u>sent to</u> request a transcript of them. The reply is very touching:
___[225]

"My Noblest Lord, and my Patron by Excellence—I have here obeyed your commands, and sent you a packet of my own praises, which I should not have done if I had any stock of modesty in store; but 'obedience is better than sacrifice,' and you command it. I am now like an old bankrupt in wit, that am driven to pay debts on my friends' credit; and, for want of satisfying letters, to subscribe bills of exchange.

"Your devoted

"Ben Jonson.

"4th February, 1632.

"To the Right Hon. the Earl of Newcastle."

Also note, same page:—

"My Noblest Lord and best Patron—I send no borrowing epistle to provoke your lordship, for I have neither fortune to repay, nor security to engage, that will be taken; but I make a most humble petition to your lordship's bounty to succour my present necessities this good time of Easter; and it shall conclude a begging request hereafter on behalf of

"Your truest bondsman and

"Most thankful servant,

"B. J."

One of these complimentary poems was written by Lucius Cary, Lord Falkland—a patriot, a soldier, and a poet, the very model of that refined spirit of chivalry which never recovered itself after the Rebellion. There must have been consolation in such a strain, from such a man; but poor "old Ben," as he was now called, was almost past consolation. He was engaged on another play, "The Majestic Lady." The world, who had then deemed the old man dead,[226] received it as the injudicious effort of a mind enfeebled. Dryden, even, who should have forborne from the poor triumph over him whom he wrongly considered a "driveller and a show," called these last plays "Ben's dotages;" but, though feebler than his former dramas, they exhibit no traces of *dotage*—that invidious and almost cruel expression.[227]

Sustained by the Earl of Newcastle, praised by the noble Falkland, pensioned by the King, one might have supposed that Jonson's last days would have been peaceful, though no longer cheerful. But he had debts; and he was forced—bed-ridden, shaken in body and mind—to write on to the very last. His latest effort was an interlude welcome of King Charles to Welbeck, on his way to Scotland; for which a tribute from Jonson's muse was commanded by the ever-friendly and munificent Newcastle.

The timely gratuity sent to the poet, when the interlude was ordered, "fell," he wrote, "like the dew of Heaven on his necessities." He wrote to his patron in terms of gratitude, warm and expressive, and creditable to himself and that benefactor.

He continued at his desk; and a fragment of the "Last Shepherd," one of his last efforts which is preserved, proves that his fancy was unclouded. Hitherto it has been painful to trace his decay—to record his distress; but now light came to his death-bed, and came from on high. Penitence, prayer, conviction of the true faith in our Holy Apostolic Church, confession of sins, hope, and rest—these were the Heavenly lights that broke over the gloom of his latter hours.

Happily—and let the fact he impressively recorded—his parents had carefully impressed on his infancy deep religious convictions.

As he lay, neglected by his former associates, and even believed by the worldly to be dead—and dead, indeed, was he to them—the impressions of his duty to his Maker grew more frequent and stronger in his affection.
[228]

To the Bishop of Winchester, who visited him during his long illness, he expressed the deepest contrition for having profaned the sacred name of his Creator in his plays. His "remorse was poignant;" and doubtless this sense of the responsibility which is devolved on great talents, which comes to many too late, was the foundation of his heartfelt penitence and sorrow. He died on the 5th of April, 1637—and on the 9th his remains were entombed in Westminster Abbey, on the north side, just opposite the escutcheon of Robertus de Ros. A common pavement stone was placed over his grave; but Sir John Young, of Great Milton, Oxfordshire, passing through the Abbey, noticed that the stone was without any inscription to mark where the great poet lay. Sir John, or, as Aubrey calls him, "Jack" Young, gave one of the workmen eighteen-pence to cut an inscription; and the words, "O rare Ben Jonson!" were carved as a temporary distinction. Meantime, the admirers of the deceased poet were collecting a subscription to defray the expense of a suitable[229] monument to "poor Ben;" but the Rebellion breaking out, the project was abandoned, and the money returned to the subscribers.

No fewer than thirty-four elegies on Ben Jonson were collected by Dr. Duppa, the Bishop of Winchester, and published under the title of "Jonson's Verbius;" and amongst the authors were Lord Falkland, Ford, Waller, George Donne, Lord Buckhurst, and other illustrious names. But perhaps there is no tribute more gratifying to the admirers of Ben Jonson than that of Taylor, the water-poet, who had met him at Leith. Jonson, be it remembered, had walked to Edinburgh, yet he could not see the humble poet without giving him what he could ill afford to bestow.

"At Leith," says Taylor, "I found my long-approved and assured good friend, Master Benjamin Jonson, at one Master John Stuart's house. I thank him for his great kindness; for at my taking leave of him, he give me a piece of gold, of two-and-twenty shillings value, to drink his health in England; and withall willed me to remember his kind commendations to all his friends. So, with a friendly farewell, I left him as well as I hope never to see him in a worse state; for he is among noblemen and gentlemen that know his true worth, and their own honours, where with much respective love he is entertained."

The sum, as Gifford remarks, was not, in those days, an inconsiderable one; and there was something graceful and touching in the kindness of one placed so high, as Jonson was in literary fame, to the humbler poet.

This sketch of Ben Jonson's life and writings may serve to illustrate the manners of those times, and the nature of that society in which George Villiers lived. In every revel Buckingham was the most distinguished courtier. In every masque, during King James's life, he played a part. He knew the poet at Wilton; there can be little doubt that the friends of Villiers were the patrons of poor Ben. The panegyrist of the Duke, Lord Clarendon, lived, as he has himself declared, "many years on terms of the most friendly intercourse with Jonson." In that conversation, praised by this historian "as very good, with men of most note," Villiers must have borne a part; whilst Camden and Selden mingled with poor Ben, with the Sackvilles, the Sidneys, the Herberts, and the numerous family of Villiers.

CHAPTER VI.

BEAUMONT AND FLETCHER—THEIR ORIGIN—THEIR JOINT PRODUCTIONS—CHARACTER OF BISHOP FLETCHER— ANECDOTES ABOUT THE USE OF TOBACCO—FORD, THE DRAMATIST—HOWELL—SIR HENRY WOTTON—THE CHARACTER OF THE DUKE OF BUCKINGHAM CONSIDERED.

CHAPTER VI.

Among the young Templars who devoted themselves to the drama during the times of George Villiers, was Francis Beaumont. Born in the same county as that in which Buckingham's family were settled, and bearing the same name as the Duke's mother, there is every probability of there being some tie of consanguinity between the poet and the peer.

Beaumont, like his colleague Fletcher, was one of ancient and honourable family; and, as such, entitled to be called to the Bar. It might be satisfactory to some of the lovers of literature to find that its pursuit, in the days of the Stuart Kings, was most frequently the choice of men of high connections, and by them considered as equal in position to the calling of the Bar, and far superior to that of the Church, or of medicine. The personal tastes of James, the passionate love of the drama evinced by Charles, by Henrietta Maria, and by Villiers, encouraged aspiring men to a display of genius which might have long been hidden in a lawyer's wig, or extinguished for ever beneath the coif. Men were less shackled then by conventionalities than in the present day.

The father of Francis Beaumont was one of the judges of the Court of Common Pleas during the reign of Elizabeth, and the family seat was Grace-Dieu, in Leicestershire. Two gifted sons emerged from this ancient Manor-house to the universities—John Beaumont,[230] who became a Gentleman Commoner at Broad-gate Hall, Oxford; and Francis, who was educated at Cambridge. Both were entered at the Inns of Court: Francis at the Inner Temple, the popular resort of Cambridge men; John, however, retired to Grace-Dieu, married into the family of Fortescue, and devoted his peaceful days to translations of the classics, and to religious poems, which even Ben Jonson eulogized. Amongst them is the "Crown of

Thorns," a poem in eight books. Whether from Buckingham's influence, or from his own merit, or from both conjoined, is not known, but he was knighted by Charles in 1626. He survived that honour only two years, dying in the same year in which Buckingham was killed.

His brother, Francis Beaumont, born in 1586, had a less peaceful career. Endowed with no ordinary abilities, he became acquainted with those whose example was not calculated to promote the due attention to legal studies. Ben Jonson and John Fletcher were then in favour with the public. Jonson in the decline of life, Fletcher almost in the dawn of his celebrity.

The Fletchers, like the Beaumonts, were a family of talent; and the famous friendship, or partnership, which produced so much, and to which we owe some of the most beautiful passages of poetry, linked to the most unreadable, was the result of that community of tastes and studies which is promoted by the education at an English university.

Fletcher, as well as Beaumont, had been at Cambridge; and his father, Dr. Richard Fletcher, Bishop of London, having been a benefactor to Benet College, that society was chosen for his matriculation. He came to London, and meeting, at some one or other of the clubs, with Francis Beaumont, they wrote plays in concert. Fletcher, who was ten years younger than his partner, had the most wit, the greatest luxuriance of fancy, the most extended conception, and lavish prodigality of improprieties. Beaumont had the soundest judgment, and employed it in cutting down young Fletcher's daring flights of fancy. Both assisted in forming the plots; since Beaumont happened to be the elder of the two, his name appears first in the literary firm, but it ought, in strict propriety, to be Fletcher and Beaumont, instead of Beaumont and Fletcher.

They worked out the plots together; and one night, as they sat in a tavern, concocting a play, Fletcher undertook "To kill the King." He was overheard by a waiter, who gave information of their traitorous designs; instantly the two young men were apprehended, and all the terrors of the law were before them—until they succeeded in justifying themselves, when the affair ended in mirth.

Beaumont, meantime, was gaining the confidence even of the formidable Ben Jonson, who submitted some of his works to his criticism before publication. The young lawyer had that skill in forming plots which seems like a natural gift, and which even good writers are unable to acquire; and he is said to have concocted some of those on which Jonson's plays are founded.

Meantime, he wrote a little drama called "A Mask of Gray's Inn Gentleman," and a poem entitled "The Inner Temple." Jonson, grateful for his aid, and admiring his talents, poured forth his delight in these lines:—

"How I do love thee, Beaumont, and thy muse,

That unto me do'st such religion use

How I do fear myself that am not worth

The least indulgent thought thy pen drops forth;

At once thou mak'st me happy, and unmak'st;

And giving largely to me more than tak'st.

What fate is mine that so itself bereaves?

What fate is thine, that so thy friend deceives?

When, even there when most thou praisest me,

For writing better I must envy thee."

But, unhappily, Beaumont's career was ended before he had attained the age of thirty. He was buried in St. Benedict's within St. Peter's, Westminster. No inscription on his tomb recalls the merits so soon closed in death; but Bishop Corbet, the author of the "Grave Poem," and Sir John Beaumont, commemorated them in epitaphs which are to be found in their works. Frances Beaumont, the poet's only daughter, survived him many years; but lost some of her father's manuscript poems as she went to Ireland by sea. Beaumont died in 1615, just at the crisis of Villiers' early career, when he became first the subject of King James's notice. Notwithstanding his premature death, his plays attained an almost unrivalled popularity. Dryden tells us that they were the most popular entertainments of the time—two of them being acted through the year for one of Shakspeare's or Jonson's; there being, he adds, a certain gaiety in the comedies of Beaumont and Fletcher, and a pathos in their serious plays, which accorded with the taste or humour of all men. Posterity, however, does not admit of the comparison; but it is impossible to say whether, if the lives of these two dramatists had been spared, their powers might not have enabled them far to exceed even the fanciful and poetical works which they found time to accomplish.

Fletcher died of the plague, in 1625, at the age of forty-five, and his remains were carried to the church of St. Mary Overie, where those of Massinger were deposited—and it has been said that they were both interred in the same tomb; but of this there is no certainty.

It is, perhaps, the greatest compliment we can pay to the present state of society to say that the plays of Beaumont and Fletcher can never be listened to by an English audience, as long as Englishwomen have one principle of delicacy, or Englishmen any respect for virtue, remaining. Those, however, who desire to judge of the poetical power of Fletcher will delight in his poem of the "Faithful Shepherdess," which Milton thought worthy of imitation in his mask of "Comus." Little is known of John Fletcher personally; but he lived in times when every nerve was touched by stirring events, and when many of the old memories which clung to men's minds were dramatic and tragical. His father, when Dean of Peterborough, had attended Mary, Queen of Scots, to her execution. The good man, looking, perhaps, for that preferment which followed, and forgetting the peril, the misery of sudden conversions, had urged the heroic Queen to change her religion, even at that solemn hour when the heart clings the most closely to the impressions of youth. He repeated his arguments; then she begged him three or four times to desist. "I was born," she said, "in this religion—I have lived in this religion—and am resolved to die in this religion."

In spite of his vehement Protestantism, the Bishop had some small and great failings; he was an inveterate taker of tobacco, which was then not only imported, but reared in Ireland and England. The Bishop probably considered tobacco to be, as Burton, in his "Anatomy of Melancholy," describes it, "a vertuous herbe, if it be well qualified, opportunely taken, and medecinally used;" but he did not follow the advice of that admirable writer in the moderation with which the snuff-box and the pipe should be indulged in. The prelate fell into an excess in the use of tobacco, to which Camden, in his History of England, imputed his death. The narcotic weed was indeed one of those luxuries of the age, which was most abused in the time of Buckingham. Burton anathematizes it—"as it is commonly used by most men, who take it as tinkers do ale; 'tis a plague, a mischiefe, a violent purger of goods, lands, healthe, hellish, devilish, damned tobacco, the ruin and overthrow of bodye and soule."[231]

But no considerations of this nature could either restrain Bishop Fletcher, or convince the gallants of the day that they were ruining either body or soul in their love of tobacco. It was very generally employed in the form of snuff by both sexes in the seventeenth century, and was allowed even in the royal presence.[232] "Before the meat came smoking to the board," says Dekker, "our gallant must draw out his tobacco-box, and the ladle for the cold snuff into the nostril, all which artillery may be of gold or silver, if he can reach his several tricks in taking it, as the whiff, the ring, &c., for these are complements that gain gentlemen no mean respect."[233] It was the custom to raise the snuff with a spoon to the nose; the snuff or pouncet-box having been long in vogue, charged, before the discovery of Ralegh, with cephalic powder, known since the time of Herodotus:—

"He was perfumed like a milliner,

And 'twixt his finger and his thumb he held

A pouncet-box, which ever and anon

He gave his nose."[234]

It was in vain that every power was combined to crush the practice of smoking, of the inveteracy of which Bishop Fletcher affords a memorable example. Monarchs united to oppose it, and it was even condemned on religious grounds; but that plea made no impression on Bishop Fletcher. Elizabeth had published an edict against it, assigning as a reason that her subjects, by employing the same luxuries as barbarians, would become barbarous. James I. published his famous counterblast to tobacco, comparing it to the "horrible Stygian smoake of the pit that is bottomless;" and imposed on it a prohibitory duty of six shillings and eight-pence per pound on its importation—an impost which Charles continued, making tobacco a royal monopoly, as it still is in France and the Netherlands—the duty having been only twopence a pound in the reign of Elizabeth. Still smoking prevailed; Ralegh had introduced it after the return of Sir Francis Drake from America, and all fashionable men practised it. Villiers, more especially, was probably among the most inveterate, after his residence in Spain; a pipe, a mug of ale, and a nutmeg were the right style at the Mitre and the Mermaid; and probably found toleration even in the hall of Burleigh, or at New-hall.

It seems hard to challenge the self-indulgence of Bishop Fletcher, or to grudge him a luxury which assisted Sir Isaac Newton in his contemplative mood, and soothed Hooker when a shrewish wife nearly drove him mad with vexation. Nevertheless, smoking, or taking snuff, is said to have ended Dr. Fletcher's days. He had also trials of another kind to his health. He was the bishop who offended Elizabeth by taking a second wife, and that wife a handsome widow, Lady Baker, of Kent. The Queen, thinking that one wife was enough for a bishop, forbade him her presence, and ordered Archbishop Whitgift to suspend him, and whether from her Majesty's displeasure, or from the effects of tobacco, he died suddenly in his chair; "being well, sick, and dead in one quarter of an hour."

The family of Fletcher were largely imbued with poetic fervour. Giles, the bishop's brother, was a man of great learning; and his two sons, John and Phineas, were conspicuous during the reign of James I. for their learning and poetry. Phineas, whose name occurs in the biography of Villiers, wrote "The Purple Island," an allegorical description of man—a much extended version of "Spenser's Allegory" in his second book. He also composed "Piscatory Eclogues and Miscellanies;" and his time was divided between the duties of his calling (for he was a clergyman) and the delight of composition. His brother Giles was, says Anthony Wood, equally "beloved of the muses and the graces." The Fletchers were, indeed, remarkable for their gifts. Benlowes, in his verses to Phineas, thus expresses his sense of their family attributes:—

"For 'twere a stain, Nature's, not thy own;

For thou art poet born; who know thee know it;

Thy brother, sire—thy very name's a poet."

The fame of Giles Fletcher rests chiefly on his poem called "Christ's Victory," which is printed with the "Purple Island" by his brother Phineas.

Another of the young lawyers whose genius irradiated the drama in the time of Villiers—was John Ford, a great genius, and a prudent man, as far as we can judge by the close of his career. Like Fletcher and Beaumont, Ford was well-born, and had a great advantage in being descended, on his mother's side, from the Chief Justice Popham. He came to London and entered at Gray's Inn, then, as Stowe tells us, "a goodly house," now the very *acmé* of dismal and decaying dinginess. It was illumined by the presence of Lord Bacon, as it had recently been by that of Lord Burleigh; and when Ford took chambers in the Inn, there were pleasant gardens for the gay young students, in which they could walk and ruminate at their leisure; whilst Gray's Inn Lane, furnished with fair buildings and many tenements, as Stowe also tells us, opened on the north with a view of the fields leading to Highgate and Hampstead; and there, too, dwelt Hampden and Pym, the vicinity of whom must have stirred up the spirits of the young disputants, whose ardour for liberty was excited during the days of the Remonstrance—the time of Buckingham's impeachment— and in those when the first tax for the navy was levied.

Ford, however, cared little, it appears, for those stormy questions, but much for the drama, and more for the law, to which he was brought up, and in the practice of which he was wise enough to continue. A young man of a dramatic turn had many temptations, in those days, to sacrifice the hopes of a slow advancement for the brilliant success of a poet's career. Ford, however, had a staid cousin at Gray's Inn, at the time when he became a member of the Middle Temple, in 1602. This relative, also a John Ford, persuaded him "to stick to the law;" and Ford, in after-life, recorded the obligation with gratitude.

Ford's first production was not dramatic. When only seventeen years of age, he wrote "Fame's Memorial," a tribute to one of the most popular, and at the same time one of the most unfortunate, noblemen of the day. The fate of the ill-starred Charles Blount, Lord Mountjoy—afterwards Earl of Devonshire—impressed the young poet so forcibly as to impel him, without any personal knowledge of this hero, to write this *In Memoriam*. "The life of Lord Mountjoy," remarks Hartley Coleridge, "is the finest subject of biography unoccupied." He was the generous rival of Essex, with whom, nevertheless, he had in early life fought a duel. Blount being "a very comely man," attracted the attention of Queen Elizabeth. He distinguished himself at a tilt, and she sent him a chess-queen of gold, enamelled, which he tied on his arm with a crimson ribbon. Essex, on seeing this, laughed scornfully, and said, "Now I perceive every fool must have a favour!" Blount challenged him, and they fought at Marylebone, where the Earl was disarmed and wounded. Nevertheless, the combatants became firm friends even in early life, and, in their later days, generous rivals.

Unhappily, an attachment was formed between the handsome Charles Blount and the Lady Penelope, the sister of Essex. She was, however, under the guardianship of what was then called the Court of Wards. She was, therefore, forced to marry Lord Rich. The result was melancholy; and she became henceforth the mistress of the brave, but unhappy, Blount, now Lord Mountjoy, and their connection was well known. On the death of Rich, the guilty pair were married by Laud, then Bishop of London. King James, on that occasion, said to Mountjoy, "You have married a fair woman with a foul heart." Perhaps he was too severe in his judgment, yet the gallant Mountjoy felt the opprobrium. His worldly prospects were marred by the union; so long as the attachment with Lady Penelope had been merely understood, the world had received her, and honoured him; but, when they were married, the guilty pair were slighted and contemned. "However bitter the cup of duty may be, duty commands us to drink it even to the dregs."[235] The sentiment is just, and Mountjoy felt it so. His error was redeemed by suffering. He died, it is said, of a broken heart, having long pined away under neglect and mortification.[236]

To the Lady Penelope, the survivor of this sad romance, Ford

addressed his "Fame's Memorial." Mountjoy's great valour in Ireland—
of which he was the true conqueror—had won him undying renown. His
domestic life touched the young poet's feelings; and upon it he wrote his
tragedy of the "Broken Heart." *Penthea's* lamentation for her "enforced
marriage" recalls, in that exquisite play, poor Lady Penelope's story:—

"*Penthea.*—How, Orgilus, by promise I was thine

The heavens do witness!

.   .   .   .   . How I do love thee

Yet, Orgilus, and yet, must best appear

In tendering thy freedom.

.   .   .   .   . Live, live happy—

Happy in thy next choice.

And oh! when thou art married, think on me

With mercy, not contempt! I hope thy wife,

Hearing my story, will not scorn my fall.

Now let us part."

For some time Ford merely assisted other dramatists in their
compositions; it was not until 1628 that he produced "The Lover's
Melancholy," which he dedicated to the "Noble Society of Gray's Inn."
This play was suggested by Burton's "Anatomy of Melancholy," from
which Ford, as well as Sterne, freely borrowed. After describing the
rapidity, the impelling necessity with which the works of Massinger and
Jonson were produced, it is agreeable to think of an author who was able
"to write up to his own ideal." Ford not only disdained all pandering to the
public taste, but even regarded the emolument arising from his plays as a
secondary consideration, after he was once fairly established in his
profession. Nor was it then thought incompatible to unite the character of
a play-writer with that of a lawyer. The Templars, and other learned
societies, were the great patrons of the drama. Often were the quaint halls
of the Temple and of Gray's Inn formed into temporary theatres for some
favourite piece; and the talk of the young Templar was always of
Blackfriars, the Curtain, or the Rose—of Will Shakespeare, and Ben
Jonson, and Ford.

Ford conceived that his powers lay in the delineation of dark and
horrible crimes; in the exhibition of a mysterious and hopeless melancholy.
The moral of his dramas, whatever aspect it may bear in our

days, was intended to be good; but the grossness of the times marred that intention, and his works show how impossible it is to be at once moral and indelicate. Even *Penthea* in the "Broken Heart," exquisitely as her character is drawn, lessens our sympathy by expressions which no woman of the present day would utter in the presence of a lover, and that lover for ever severed from her by her indissoluble bonds with another man.

But Ford wrote in the spirit and language of his time, with a high purpose, and a coarse taste. "His genius," it has been well remarked, "is as a telescope, ill-adapted for neighbouring objects, but powerful to bring within the sphere of vision what nature has wisely placed at an unsociable distance."[237]

He chose for the subject of his historical play the story of "Perkin Warbeck." With great skill he made this hero believe in his own royalty; and he has left in this play, according to the opinion of good judges, the best specimen of an historical tragedy after Shakspeare.

Ford resembled Shakspeare in some particulars of his fate. Happier in that than his associates, he was able to retire, at an early age, to his native Devonshire, where, tradition says, he lived to old age. It is stated that he married, and had children; but even of this there is no certainty. One thing alone is clearly shown, even in Ford's dim history, that he regarded literature as the relaxation, and not the labour of his life; that he steadily pursued the profession in which untiring work, honourable conduct, and fair talents generally find an ultimate reward; that he was independent of patronage; that he could treat those to whom he addressed his dedications as men whom he was complimenting, not benefactors whom he was suing; and lastly, that he was able to leave the world of law and letters before that world's enjoyments had been exhausted, or its disappointments had soured and wearied his spirit.

His last play was the "Lady's Trial;" but his fame chiefly rests on "Perkin Warbeck" and the "Broken Heart." It is a proof of the great esteem entertained for genius by the Earl of Newcastle, "poor Ben's" patron, that he was also friendly to Ford, who dedicated "Perkin Warbeck" to that nobleman.

It was not only by necessitous men of obscure extraction that poetry was cultivated in those times; on the contrary, some acquaintance with the Muses, although not thought essential in those who would fain rise to distinction as courtiers, was, at all events, deemed ornamental and advantageous. The name of Thomas Carew was distinguished in the reign of Charles I., as one of the most intellectual of his young courtiers.

He was a man of an ancient Gloucestershire family; a branch of that race settled in Devonshire, and his education was that usually assigned to youths of good birth and expectations. He was entered at Corpus Christi College, in Oxford, and his academical career was succeeded, as was customary in those times, by travelling. From the grand tour, Carew returned replete with wit, fancy, and with a high reputation for accomplishments.

He was, therefore, almost instantly noticed by Charles I., and, it is evident, enjoyed the favour of Buckingham, to whom he addressed "Lines on the Lord Admiral's recovery from sickness." Charles made him one of his gentlemen of the Bedchamber, and Sewer in ordinary— appointments which brought the poet into an immediate contact with the principal characters of the Court; and he became the intimate associate of Lord Clarendon, the eulogist of Villiers, and the friend of Ben Jonson. As a writer of love sonnets, Carew has had few equals; and he may be termed, in that respect, the Moore of his age. His charming qualities as a companion, and the elegance of his verses, are praised by Clarendon; whilst his contemporaries—even those less happy than himself—saw in him, whom they declared to be one of a "mob of gentlemen," who aspired to be eminent in polite literature, one whose career added lustre to the pursuits of literature. Strange to say, Carew was beloved and extolled by his less fortunate contemporaries; and even Ben Jonson gave him his meed of praise, which Carew returned with sympathy and admiration.

After Jonson's unlucky play, "The New Inn," had been hissed off the stage, and Jonson had vented his rage in an ode, Carew addressed the angry poet in lines full of good sense, wit, and good feeling; and yet, he hints, with a sincerity as rare as it is fearless, that his powers were somewhat weakened since poor Ben had brought out the "Alchemist."

"And yet 'tis true

Thy cousin muse from the exalted line,

Touched by the alchemist, doth since decline

From that her zenith, and foretells a red

And blushing evening when she goes to bed;

Yet such as shall outshine the glimmering light

With which all stars shall gild the following night."

Again he adds:—

"Let others glut on the extorted praise

Of vulgar breath, trust thou to after-days:

Thy laboured works shall live when Time devours

The abortive offering of their hasty hours.

Thou art not of their rank—the quarrel lies

Within thine own verge; then let this suffice

The wiser world doth greater thee confess

Than all men else, than thyself only less."

Carew, notwithstanding the highly virtuous tone of the Court in which he lived, led an irregular life; and lived to mourn, in deep repentance, for that more than wasted portion of his existence, in which he gave way to the worst parts of his otherwise fine nature. When Ben Jonson had ceased to write, Carew was selected as the poet most calculated to supply the place of that great genius in providing masques for the Court. Only one, however, produced by him, remains. It is called "Cœlum Britannicum."

Inigo Jones was again summoned to be one of the "Inventors," to place the masque on the stage, and Henry Lawes composed the airs, and superintended the musical performance; but those to whose splendour and genius the perfection of this species of entertainment was owing, were no longer there. Villiers was gone; Ben Jonson had virtually quitted "the detracting world," which he had once defied from his proud pre-eminence. The country was even then split up into factions. Happily for himself, Carew escaped their outbreak. He died in 1639, expressing heartfelt religious convictions and penitence.

Amongst the gentlemen writers, as they were styled, was Edmund Waller, who, at the time of Buckingham's death, was a young man of twenty-three years of age. The lines addressed by him to Charles I., on the extraordinary composure which the King showed on hearing of that event, are well known. Even then Waller had been a member of Parliament, and had been elected to sit in that assembly whilst he was in his seventeenth year. Waller's circumstances, his destiny, his views of life, his genius, his disposition, were as opposite to those of Massinger and Ben Jonson as can possibly be conceived. He seemed born a courtier; and every effort he made was to advance himself at first in that career, and afterwards as a politician. His first appearance as a poet, in his eighteenth year, was to congratulate King James on the escape of Prince Charles at St. Audera, when returning from Spain; and in this poem his polished verses, perfected, he alleged, by the study of Fairfax's "Tasso," were so turned as to excite the admiration of the literary world, by whom he was deemed the model of English versifiers. But, in spite of his alleged devotion to Charles, and notwithstanding his continuing to sit in Parliament, Waller sheltered himself during the storm that ensued, and went to study chemistry under the guidance of his kinsman, Bishop Morley—emerging only from his retreat at Beaconsfield to mingle in the delightful circle of wits and incipient heroes of whom the noble Falkland was the centre.

He married early; having, with a fortune of nearly four thousand a- year, espoused a city heiress, who died and left him a widower at the age of twenty-five. Then this accomplished man of the world looked out for rank, and paid his addresses, poetically at all events, to the lovely Dorothy Sidney, the eldest daughter of the Earl of Sidney. He apostrophized her as Saccharissa. She was, or he made her out to be, a proud and scornful beauty, and he turned to his "Amoret"—Lady Sophia Murray; but, though well-born, rich, favoured by Charles, and nephew of John Hampden by his mother's side, so that he seemed secure of rising under any faction, Waller's loves did not prosper in the direction to which he at first guided them; for he was wise in his generation, and could control his fancies by views of interest.

He married, therefore, a second time, "loving, doubtless, wisely and not too well;" but neither the name, condition, nor fortune of his second wife is mentioned by his biographers.

From this time Edmund Waller's career was despicable. In his heart a Royalist, he absented himself from the House of Commons whenever there was a chance of his being of service to the King, or of his committing himself. Yet he sent Charles a thousand gold pieces when the Royal standard at Nottingham was set up—and concocted, with a conspirator named Tomkyns, a plot for delivering the City and the Parliament into the hands of the Royalists. Nevertheless, he had been seconding "my Uncle Hampden" in the House, in his censure of Ship- money. When his plot—still called in history Waller's plot, for he had the chief blame—when this base conspiracy, unworthy of any cause, was discovered, Waller confessed everything, and criminated everybody. Confounded with fear, he had yet the consummate hypocrisy to talk of his "remorse of conscience," adding one to the long list of crimes which that abused word is called to sanction or excuse. It is a satisfaction to know that he was nearly being hanged—that he was expelled the House—fined ten thousand pounds—and then "contemptuously suffered to go into exile." Never was that party more fortunate than in getting rid of such a man.

He took refuge at Rouen, and lived there and in Paris until all his wife's jewels were sold—for on them he lived. He was, however, at last allowed to return home, and again he sullied Beaconsfield with his presence. He hastened to flatter Cromwell, and even to propose, in his smooth and flattering verses, the substitution of a crown of gold for bays:—

"His conquering head has no more room for bays,

Then let it be as the glad nation prays;

Let the rich ore be melted down,

And the State fix'd by making him a crown:

With ermine clad and purple, let him hold

A royal sceptre made of Spanish gold!"

Cromwell, however, was far too wise to take the bait. The sycophant thought it expedient to write an ode on his death—for he was not certain that the great man's power might not be perpetuated by his son. The instant, however, that the Restoration placed Charles II. on the throne, Waller was ready with his congratulatory ode. He dwelt on the guilt of the Rebellion; and, except that the flavour of spicy flattery was so poor as to provoke a *bon mot* from Charles II. he might have succeeded. "Poets," said the witty monarch, "succeed better in fiction than in truth." But with Waller it was all fiction.

He was soon a favourite at that easy, merry court; his poetry caused his unconquerable duplicity to be forgotten—or, if not forgotten, looked on even complacently by courtiers who held all virtue to be hypocrisy. He managed to please everybody; though a water-drinker, he was the life of Bacchanalian parties. It is owing to Clarendon that the renegade was not made Provost of Eton—a post for which he had actually the audacity to ask. He thence became the friend and ally of George Villiers, the second Duke of Buckingham, to whose age and time, rather than that of the subject of this memoir, one would gladly consign the apostate poet.

One of his worst acts was to vote for the impeachment of Lord Clarendon; and here one would gladly end the record of the misdeeds of an able and accomplished man, distinguished almost as much for his eloquence as for his poetic productions. But Waller lived on; he was favoured by James II., who seems to have been cajoled by the flatteries which his royal brother had detected. Waller again in parliament, and now eighty years old, was permitted to speak jocularly with the monarch. One day he called Queen Elizabeth, in James's presence, the "greatest woman in the world." "I wonder," answered his Majesty, "you should think so; but it must be allowed she had a wise council."

"And when, sire," cried Waller, "did you ever hear of a fool choosing a wise one?"

When it was known that the veteran courtier was going to marry his daughter to Dr. Birch, a clergyman, James sent a French gentleman to ask him how he could think of marrying his daughter to a falling church.

"The King does me great honour," was the reply, "to concern himself about my affairs; but I have lived long enough to observe that this falling church has got a trick of rising again."

He foresaw the coming crisis, but lived not to have an opportunity of writing odes to William III. and his Queen. He now composed "Divine Poems," and began to think, at the age of eighty-three, that possibly this world, and the courts of the Charles's and James's, were not everything that there was to value in life. When he found himself sinking, he said, "Take me to Coleshill" (his native place); "I should be glad to die, like the stag, where I was roused."

He was, however, too near death to be removed; and he expired at Beaconsfield, in October, 1678, and thus escaped being the witness of another revolution.

Such were some of the eminent contemporaries of George Villiers, in an age so rich in intellectual force as to constitute it, in that respect alone, one of the most remarkable periods of English history.

But there were, among the *literati* of that day, two men whose observations were peculiarly directed towards the career of Villiers— these were James Howell, the letter-writer, and Sir Henry Wotton.

Howell's well-known name is mixed up repeatedly in the various passages of the Duke of Buckingham's foreign life. Howell was the son of a clergyman, at Abernant, in Carmarthenshire; was accordingly entered at Jesus College, Oxford, the great emporium of the Jones's, Williams's, Morgans, and Howells.

He was, like many of his countrymen, "a true cosmopolite," born, says Anthony Wood, neither to "house, land, lease, or office." He had not the misfortune of having a position in life to lose, so he went to London, and became, through the interest of Sir Robert Mansel, steward to a glass-house in Bond Street, glass being a monopoly; whilst his elder brother rose to be Bishop of Bristol.

Glass being by no means in its perfection, the proprietors of the work sent James Howell abroad, in order to hire foreign workmen, and to buy the best materials for a manufacture which they wished to improve; and James Howell joyfully accepted the mission. He travelled into France, Holland, Flanders, Spain, and Italy; and, setting off in 1619, encountered George Villiers in his French tour, came across him in Spain, and heard of him all the good and bad that he has detailed in his letters to England.

He gave up his stewardship, and posted again into Spain, in 1623, and was in that country when Charles I. and Buckingham were at Madrid. Like persons in the pit of a great theatre, Howell, in his half-commercial, half-diplomatic capacity, saw a great deal which the actors in that brilliant scene overlooked.

His ostensible reason for going to Spain was to reclaim a rich English ship which had been seized by the Viceroy of Sardinia; his real occupation was that of watching the Royal "wooer," and his scarcely less conspicuous companion, Buckingham. Meantime, Howell was made a Fellow of Jesus College; and, in accepting this honour, he said he "should reserve his Fellowship, and lay it by as a warm garment against rough weather, should any fall on him." And certainly he was destined to experience the changes and chances of fortune in no ordinary degree. He returned to London, and was appointed secretary to Lord Scrope, who was made Lord-President of the North. Howell, therefore, was transplanted to York; and, whilst there, was chosen member for Richmond, an honour for which he had not canvassed. He sat, therefore, in the parliament which opened in 1627—a session so important to Buckingham, and so fraught with consequences to the country.

Still, the apparently fortunate man was without any fixed employment. He had, however, talents which were then rare in this country; he spoke seven modern languages—and, without recording his own remark, which borders on levity, on that score, it must be admitted that few Englishmen either in that age or this can do the same. His merits were, in this respect, estimated by Charles I., who sent him in the quality of secretary to Robert, Earl of Leicester, to Denmark, when it became necessary to condole with the King of that State on the death of his consort, Charles's Danish grandmother. Next, Howell was despatched to France, and subsequently to Ireland, where the Earl of Strafford appreciated his wonderful industry, and welcomed him kindly; he was intrusted by that ill-fated nobleman with business, first in Edinburgh and then in London; but his hopes of rising were crushed by the ruin of Strafford, and by the crash which ensued.

Charles, however, again despatched him to France, and made him, on his return, Clerk of the Council.

Poor Howell now believed that he had secured a permanent post, a fixed income, and a most agreeable residence, an apartment being allotted to him in Whitehall. The greater part of the old Tudor palace was then still standing; the noble gates built by Henry VIII. remained; the Banqueting-house was partially finished; all but the paintings by Vandyck, who was to have adorned the sides of that room, now used as a chapel, with paintings of all the history and procession of the Order of the Garter, were completed—that symmetrical fragment stood then as it now stands. Charles I. could as little have anticipated that George of Hanover would have made the room he destined for Ben Jonson's masques into a chapel, with the apotheosis of James I. upon the ceiling, as he could have foreseen that one day he should be led out from one of the windows of the Banqueting-house to Whitehall-gate, where "cords to tie him down to the block had been prepared, had he made any resistance to that cruel and bloody stroke."[238]

Equally unconscious of his royal patron's doom as of his own fate, Howell established himself in that palace, the only danger of which seemed to be the frequent inundations of the Thames, by which Whitehall was often half submerged. But shortly afterwards the King left that palace to which he never returned but as a captive; and Howell also departed. But, coming back to London on private business, he was, in 1643, thrown into prison, his papers were seized, and he was committed in close custody to the Fleet.

This ancient prison had been, until that time, a place of durance for persons sentenced by the Council Table, then called the Court of the Star Chamber—so that Howell had the additional vexation of being apprehended by one of the warrants which he would himself have issued had the troubles of the Rebellion never commenced;—had things remained as they were when Lord Surrey suffered from its pestilent atmosphere, and when the importunate Lady Dorset was silenced in what was truly called by Surrey, "that noisome place."

The Star Chamber was, however, it appears, abolished before the time when James Howell, descending Whitehall stairs, was rowed up the river Fleet, to a gate as portentous in its aspect and associations as the Traitor's-gate at the Tower; and thence conducted to what was afterwards called the Common side of the prison.[239] When the letter-writer entered its miserable courts, the Fleet had lost the dignity of a state prison for minor political offences, and was a place for debtors, and divided into two sides, the Master's side and the Common side. In the Common side, to complete the horrors, was a strong-room, or vault, which has been described "to be like those in which the dead are interred, and wherein the bodies of persons dying are usually deposited till the coroner's inquest has passed them."

Howell, as he entered the Common side, probably thought that he might live to be one of the mute inhabitants of that ghastly chamber—for he was not only suspected by the Parliament, but in debt. Wood, indeed, ascribes his captivity wholly to the curse of debt, brought on by his own extravagance; and since Howell, like many public men of the day, had no "income but such as he scrambled for," and since it was an age of careless expenditure, Wood is, perhaps, in this statement, as he generally is, correct.

The character of the man of desultory life rose under the trial. During five years the once free and happy James Howell lay in that den of misery —rendered more miserable by all that was going on in the world, of which he heard enough in his durance, perhaps too much. During that period Charles was beheaded; the gay precincts of Whitehall were stained with the blood of one whom Howell had reverenced as a royalist, but whose advisers, Buckingham, Laud, and Strafford, he had censured, as a man of the world, of sense and candour, could not fail to do. Whilst he lay in the place where Falkland had been sent for sending a challenge— where Prynne had paid the penalty for his "Histriomastix," Howell's thoughts no doubt reverted to the pleasant days of Charles's youth, in the fields near Madrid, where plumed knights ran a course—or to the arena of the bull-fight. He dreamed, perhaps, of the incomparable Infanta, or of the stately Philip, and his gallant, flattered, sanguine English guests.

But he did better. Howell is not the only writer who has tried to bind up the wounds of a broken heart by authorship; or has succeeded in dissipating the hours of a long imprisonment by communicating not only with the world of letters, which was nearly extinct in general literature during the first year of the Protectorate, but with those among the free, the sympathetic, and the celebrated who remembered the poor debtor in his cell. One of his most notable efforts was his own epitaph, beginning
—

"Here lies entomb'd a walking thing,
Whom Fortune with the Fates did fling
Between these walls."

He wrote now his "Familiar Letters, Domestic and Foreign," wisely putting no date on the epistles as to place. He composed also "Casual Discourses and Interlocutions between Patricius and Peregrin, touching the Distractions of the Times"—this work was the result of the Battle of Edge Hill—"Parables reflecting on the Times;" "England's Tears for the Present War;" "Vindications of some Passages reflecting upon himself in Mr. Prynne's book called the 'Popish Royal Favourite,'" a work which coupled his name with that of Buckingham; and his "Epistolæ- Hoelianæ." These works came out year after year. It is said by Wood that most of Howell's letters were written in the Fleet, though some of them purported to have been sent from Madrid and other places. The fact is, he wrote for subsistence; and his works were popular and productive. His statements may, indeed, have been made so long after the events they relate occurred, as to render them doubtful; yet it is acknowledged that they contain a good view of the actors in those stirring times—whilst they are almost the only letters that still preserve the memory of the writer among us.

Most of his other writings were political; one of his imaginative flights recalls, in the idea that originated it, the title of the pleasant brochure, "*Voyage autour de ma chambre*," in our own times. Howell's composition is styled, "A Nocturnal Progress; or, a perambulation of such Countries in Christendom performed in one night by strength of imagination." All the titles of his works are striking: "Winter Dream," "A Trance, or News from Hell, brought first to town by Mercurius Acheronticus;"—this was published in 1649, after the King's death. He still, Royalist as he was, bore his misfortunes cheerfully; yet his loyalty sank at last beneath the pressure of starvation, and he yielded to expediency. It was not, however, until 1653 that his constancy broke down, and that he addressed to Oliver Cromwell his "Sober's Inspections made into the carriage and consult of the late Long Parliament." One may know the views he took from the title; but when he compliments the Lord Protector, compares him to Charles Martel, and descends to flattery, Howell loses our respect. Neither does he regain it by his "Cordial for the Cavaliers," published in 1660, and answered by the "Caveat for the Cavaliers" of Sir Roger L'Estrange.

Payne Fisher, who had been poet-laureate to Cromwell, edited

"Howell's Works," in which he calls the author the "prodigy of the age for the variety of his writings." These were forty in number, and in "them all," says Fisher, "there is something still new, either in the matter, method, or fancy, and in an untrodden tract."

For the change of politics in the famous letter-writer his friends were prepared, when, after the King's death, he wrote with what some call prudence, others pusillanimity, these words:—"I will attend with patience how England will thrive, now that she is let blood in the Basilican vein, and cured, as they say, of the King's evil." Nevertheless, Howell was made Historiographer-Royal in England by Charles II., who was so lenient to his enemies, so ungrateful to his friends. The place was even created for him; but death soon caused him to vacate it. He ended his chequered life in 1660, and-was buried in the Temple Church.

Among the few who remembered George Villiers with gratitude, or who endeavoured to rescue his memory from opprobrium, Henry Wotton, his biographer, appears in a conspicuous and favourable light. Most of the eminent men of the time had been reared, and even trained, to public service, during the reign of Elizabeth, when strength of purpose, honesty, ability, and learning were the grounds of promotion in all the minor, as well as in the superior departments of the State. Henry Wotton, born in 1568, at Bocton Hall,[240] in Kent, and descended from an ancient family, was a thoroughly-educated English gentleman. After some years' instruction at Winchester School, he was entered at New College, Oxford. Close to that grand old college was Hart Hall, a sort of subsidiary establishment; and Wotton, perhaps from being a freshman, had his rooms in Hart Hall Lane. Here his chamber-fellow, as he was then called, was Richard Baker, the historian, who was entered at the same time, and born the same year, and whose predilections for letters resembled those of young Henry Wotton. The inestimable advantage of a companionship of such a nature cannot be too highly appreciated by those who watch the dawning mind of youth, and who desire them to have recourse to the only sure preventive of dissipation—employment. Baker, well known for his Chronicle, was also a writer on theological subjects, and a young man of sincere piety. His friend Wotton was then less distinguished for historical studies than for his wit and learning. For some reason, not explained, he left New College, and established himself in the then old-fashioned tenement of Queen's College, in the High Street, where he was soon complimented by being selected to write a play for the inmates of that house to perform. He produced a tragedy called "Tancredo," which was declared to manifest, in a very striking manner, his abilities for composition, his wit, and knowledge. Thus, like the gay Templar, or the student of Gray's Inn, did the young Oxonian delight in the drama— which formed, to borrow a French expression, a sort of *debût* for wits; nor did Baker, though serious and plodding, despise the drama; and even when, in after life, he had been knighted at Theobald's by King James, and Baker's reputation stood high, he vindicated the stage against Prynne, in a work entitled "Theatrum Redivivum."

Wotton, after proceeding Master of Arts in his twentieth year, left Oxford, and passed a year in France; and then going on to Geneva, formed there the friendship of Casaubon and of Beza. He remained nine years in Germany and Italy, and returned to England an accomplished and enlightened, as well as a learned man; being, says his biographer, "a dear lover of painting, sculpture, chemistry, and architecture." He was soon appreciated by Robert Devereux, Earl of Essex, then high in favour with Elizabeth; and became one of that nobleman's secretaries, and the most devoted of his friends. The parallel which he has left the world between Essex and Buckingham, and which Lord Clarendon answered, is written with an enthusiasm for the character of Wotton's first patron, which can only have sprung from intimate acquaintance, and from that true affection which generous, impulsive natures, such as that of Essex, are likely to inspire.

With Essex, Wotton remained until his patron was apprehended and attainted of treason; then he fled to France, and scarcely had he landed there when he heard that the Earl had been beheaded. He took refuge from solitude, and perhaps peril, in Florence, where the Grand Duke[241] of Tuscany received him cordially. James I. was then reigning over Scotland; a plot threatened his life, and the Grand Duke having become aware of this, by some intercepted letters, sent Wotton, in disguise, to warn James of his danger. Wotton spoke Italian perfectly; he, therefore, assumed the name and dress of an Italian, and, thus disguised, set off on his hazardous journey. Having been so deeply concerned in the affairs of Essex, he did not venture to pass into England. He travelled, therefore, into Norway, and, by that route, reached Scotland. He found the King at Stirling, and was introduced into his presence under the name of Octavio Baldi. He soon found an opportunity of disclosing himself to the King, and, after remaining three months in Scotland, he returned to Florence.

Queen Elizabeth's death brought him back to England, where his favour with the new King was ensured. When James I. saw Sir Edward Wotton, he inquired if "he knew not Henry Wotton?"

"I know him well," was the reply, "for he is my brother."

The King then asked where he was, and ordered him to be sent for.

When Wotton first saw his Majesty, James took him into his arms, and saluted him by the name of Octavio Baldi; then he knighted him, and nominated him Ambassador to Venice. But it was not easy, in those days, to avoid giving offence. The new Ambassador, passing through Augsburg, met there, amongst other learned men, his old friend, one Christopher Flecamore, who requested him to write something in his Album, a book which even then Germans usually carried about with them; Sir Henry, complying, wrote a definition of an Ambassador in the Album. The sentence was given in Latin, as being a language common to all that erudite company, but the definition was, in English, this—"An Ambassador is an honest man sent to *lie* abroad for the good of his country."

This sentence was imparted, eight years afterwards, to one of King James's literary opponents, a jealous Romanist priest, named Scioppius, who printed it in a work directed against the royal polemic, and which pretended to show upon what a degraded principle a Protestant acted. The book reached King James, who had the mortification of hearing that this definition of an ambassador, which happened to be then the correct one, whatever may now be the case, was exhibited in glass windows at Venice. For some time James was displeased, but on receiving Sir Henry's explanation, he forgave him, saying that the delinquent "had commuted sufficiently for a greater offence."

The various embassies in which Sir Henry Wotton was engaged detained him abroad until 1623, when he came home finally. A great piece of preferment was then vacant; and, by the influence of the Duke of Buckingham, it was bestowed on Wotton. This was the post of Provost of Eton; but one great obstacle presented itself—Wotton had been everything that was useful and important, but he was not in orders; nevertheless, anything could be accomplished in those days—he was made a deacon, and held the Provostship from 1623 to 1639, when he died. The appointment did no discredit to him who procured it, for Wotton was an able, honest man, singularly liberal in his religious tenets for his time. He ordered that upon his grave, in the Chapel of Eton College, there should be a sentence, in Latin, decrying the itch for disputation as the real disease of the Church. He was a great enemy to disputation. On being asked, "Do you believe that a Papist can be saved?" he answered, "*You* may be saved without knowing that; look to yourself." When he heard some one railing at the Romanists with stupid rancour, he said:—"Pray, sir, forbear, till you have studied these points better. There is an Italian proverb which says, 'he that understands amiss concludes worse;' forbear of thinking that the farther you go from the Church of

Rome the nearer you are to God."

Nevertheless, he was, like most lenient judges of the faith of others, a staunch adherent to his own. "Where was your religion to be found before Luther?" wrote a jocose Priest at Rome, seeing Sir Henry in an obscure corner of a church, listening to the beautiful service of the Vespers, and enjoying the exquisite music of a faith which appeals so much to the senses. "Where yours is not to be found—in the written Word of God," was the answer, scribbled on a piece of paper underneath the interrogation.

Another evening Sir Henry sent one of the choir boys to his priestly friend with this question:—"Do you believe those many thousands of poor Austrians damned who were excommunicated because the Pope and the Duke of Venice could not agree about their temporalities?" To which inquiry the priest wrote in French underneath—*"Excusez moi, Monsieur."*

Such was the man whom Buckingham favoured; and who afterwards repaid the obligation by a beautiful, somewhat florid, but authentic biographical account of the Duke's origin, his rise, his dangers, his services, and his death. Quaint but expressive language, genuine enthusiasm, and personal acquaintance, render this sketch one of the most delightful compositions of Sir Henry's pen. In comparing him, in prosperity and in adversity, to Essex, the master whom he loved, Wotton pays the Duke of Buckingham what he conceived to be the highest compliment. He was commencing a life of Martin Luther, and intending to interweave in it a history of the Reformation in Germany, when Charles I. prevailed on him to lay it aside, and to begin a history of England. That undertaking has something unfortunate associated with it. Rapin and Hume never lived to complete their works. Mackintosh died after leaving a noble fragment to increase our sorrow for his loss. Macaulay has expired before half his glorious task has been given to the world. Sir Henry Wotton had sketched out some short characters as materials, when his intentions and Charles's commands were frustrated by death. His "Reliquiæ Wottonianæ, or a collection of Lives, Letters, and Poems, with characters of sundry personages, and other incomparable pieces of Language and Art, by the ever-memorable Sir Henry Wotton,"[242] is a small octavo volume; yet large enough to create regret that one of such rare powers and opportunities had not written, with the candour of his nature, a history of the times in which he flourished. His "State of Christendom, or a most exact and curious discovery of many secret passages and hidden mysteries of the times," supplies in some measure that deficiency.

Successful in life, Wotton was, in his death, fortunate in being the subject of an elegy from the pen of Cowley, then a young man of twenty-one, at Trinity College, Cambridge.[243]

If we except the encouragement given by the Duke of Buckingham to the masque, and the preference evinced by him for literature as one of the essential ingredients of civilized society, the progress of letters, it must be avowed, has owed little to his direct intervention.

Clarendon, though at the time of the Duke's death patronized by Laud, was then a young lawyer, little more than twenty years of age.[244] Being brought into contact with Archbishop Laud, during the course of a cause in which he was even then retained by some London merchants, Clarendon, at that time Edward Hyde, must not only have heard much of Buckingham, but have known him personally; but the public career of the future historian did not commence till 1640. As, however, Hyde then affected the fine gentleman and the man of letters rather than the lawyer, he probably, in those characters, had opportunities of seeing Buckingham on the same footing as that on which he became acquainted with Falkland, Selden, Waller, Carew, and others; but he owed nothing, as far as we can trace, to the friendship of Villiers.

Ralegh and Bacon were above the patronage of the favourite; the one was suffered to die in prison, the other was long alienated from his early admirer and sometime pupil, the Duke. Nevertheless, there were not a few persons, as it has been seen, eminent as writers, who were indirectly assisted and protected by Buckingham, and who paid him the tribute of their gratitude or admiration. Still the aid he gave to art was far more liberal than any that he afforded to letters.

Such is the view taken of the redeeming services performed to society by a man who had much in his public career to be forgiven. With respect to the acts to which he prompted Charles, to screen himself, no defence can be offered: but for the general bearing of that King's conduct towards his Parliament, he must be deemed irresponsible, since his death neither changed his Sovereign's line of principle, nor moderated his actions. Buckingham was less a man of evil intentions than of expediency; to get out of a difficulty, he imperiled the freedom of the people, and the safety of the Crown, when he might bravely have courted inquiry, and profited by counsel. It was one of his great misfortunes that he never made a true and worthy friendship with any man so nearly his equal as to be able frankly to advise him against what Clarendon calls the "current, or rather the torrent, of his passions." He was surrounded by needy brothers, and influenced by an ambitious, unscrupulous mother. One faithful friend would not only have saved him from many perils, but might have prompted him to do "as transcendant worthy actions" as any man in his sphere. In spite of prosperity, he was of a persuadable nature; he was naturally candid, just, and generous; no record remains of the temptation of money leading him to do any unkind action. "If," says Lord Clarendon, "he had an immoderate ambition, it doth not appear that it was in his nature, or that he brought it to the Court, but rather found it there. He needed no ambition, who was so seated in the hearts of two such masters."

No man was more vilified in his private life than Buckingham. Like all persons of weak principles and impulsive nature, he was at once engaging and disappointing; warm-hearted one instant, selfish the next; the idol of his family, whom he befriended unceasingly; the object, during his life, of his young wife's most devoted affection, which he often forgot or betrayed. Nevertheless, whilst his moral character was sullied by many blemishes, it was free from the unblushing profligacy of some of his predecessors, and superior to the hypocritical sensuality of his contemporary, Richelieu. Happily for the age, the almost blameless early career of Charles enforced that virtue should be respected, and that vice, where it existed, should remain concealed. Buckingham probably owed to this necessity much of what, at all events, may be endowed with the praise of decorum.

The popular error of many historians, who depict him as an arrogant favourite, a remorseless extortioner, a reckless invader of liberty, the minion of his own King, and the instrument of foreign Courts, yields before the more intimate view of Buckingham's character which has been unfolded in the collections now laid open to all readers of history. That he was impetuous, but kind in nature—careless of forms, but courteous in spirit—led widely astray by mad passions, yet returning in love and penitence to his home—is now confessed. No instances have been found to substantiate against him charges of corruption, such as that which was commonly practised in those days; he was loaded with presents of land, of money—he spent freely what had been thus bestowed—and the affection borne to him by his dependents is the best earnest of his many good qualities as a master and a patron.

In his liberality to all around him, he is said by Wotton, who thoroughly understood the noble nature which he compared to that of Essex, to have been "cheerfully magnificent," whilst he conferred his favours with such a grace, that the manner was as gratifying as the gift, "and men's understandings were as much puzzled as their wits."

His disposition was full of tenderness and compassion. The man who fell by the assassin's hand had a horror of capital punishment, "Those," Lord Clarendon observes, "who think the laws dead if they are not severely executed, censured him for being too merciful; and he believed, doubtless, hanging the worst use a man could be put to." Consistent with this sweetness of character were his affability and gentleness to men younger than himself, as well as his ready forgiveness of injuries, an "easiness to reconcilement," which caused him even too soon to forget the circumstances of affronts and evil deeds, and, therefore, exposed him to a repetition.

Of all the imputations which were fixed on Buckingham, that of a desire to enrich himself, from motives of avarice, is the most completely refuted by facts. During the four years that he enjoyed the unbounded confidence of Charles I. he became every day poorer. His affairs were investigated, and the result was proved. It is, indeed, a question, and a very serious one,—how far any man is justified in spending, even on noble purposes, and certainly not in mere show, largely beyond his income, as Buckingham did; but his conduct is, at all events, more pardonable than the mere desire to collect a great fortune, from sources which he seems to have considered should be expended either in doing honour to his Sovereign abroad in his embassies—a notion paramount in those days, though out of date in ours—or by the encouragement of arts and sciences, and the duties of hospitality at home.

When we recapitulate the errors of this celebrated man—his omissions, his sins, his want of good faith, his overlooking the benefits he might have conferred on his country, until it was almost too late for repentance, his sacrifice of his Sovereign's best interests to his own will—we must, at the same time, admit great extenuation. No mercy was shown to his faults by the historians of his time, nor of the age succeeding; they wrote under a sense of the deep injuries from which the Rebellion received its first impulse. We must not look for fairness in such a ferment. Even after the tomb had long been closed over his remains, it was scarcely safe, certainly scarcely prudent, to palliate the faults, or to place the virtues of Buckingham in a fair light. We have now, however, the satisfactory assurance that Buckingham was conscious of his faults; contrite for his misdeeds; and earnest in his resolution to repair them, had his life been spared.[245]

Lord Clarendon closes his "Disparity" between the Earl of Essex and the Duke of Buckingham in these words:—

"He that shall continue this argument further may haply begin his parallel after their deaths, and not unfitly. He may say that they were both as mighty in obligations as any subjects; and both their memories and families as unrecompensed by such as they had raised. He may tell you of the clients that buried the pictures of the one, and defaced the arms of the other, lest they might be too long suspected for their dependants, and find disadvantage by being honest to their memories. He may tell you of some that drew strangers to their houses, lest they might find the track of their own footsteps, that might upbraid them with their former attendance. He may say that both their memories shall have a reverend fervour with all posterity, and all nations. He may tell you many more particulars, which I dare not do."

APPENDIX.

APPENDIX.

In the Calendar edited by Mr. Bruce (1859), there are the following details, amongst other curious particulars, of the state of affairs after the Duke of Buckingham's unfortunate expedition to Rhé:—

"Lionel Sharp to Buckingham, reports his sermon preached (at St Margaret's, Westminster), in which he had alluded to the censure thrown upon the Duke for his late failure at Rhé, and had declared that he who had ventured all that was dearest in the world for a foreign church, would, if he 'had as many lives as hairs,' venture them all for his own, with other laudatory personal allusions to the Duke. Is ready to 'do the rest' within two days, 'if he may have the place in Westminster, or on Sunday next.'"— *Vol. cii., Domestic, No. 76, April, 1628.*

This is a singular letter, not only as showing the alarm which led the Duke to have recourse to the Elizabeth plan of "tuning the pulpits," but also as an instance of the almost impious mixture of political and worldly affairs with sacred subjects.

SECOND ATTEMPT ON LA ROCHELLE.

Sir Henry Palmer to Secretary Nicholas, from on board the "Garland," before La Rochelle, under the Earl of Denbigh:—"In this letter Sir Henry states that what was here given out to be feasible they find directly impossible. On the approach of the English Fleet, the French retreated under their ordnance. The palisadoes across the river described. The Council of War determined that they should put out to sea, and spend their victual abroad. Lord Denbigh cruising between Ushant and Scilly. The writer between Portsmouth and Cape La Hogue. No man but looked back upon the poor town but with eyes of pity, though not able to help them."— *Vol. ciii., No. 50, May 8, 1628.*

Letter from the Earl of Denbigh to the same.—"Men have ever been the censure of the world who are unsuccessful from public employments. Misinformation has been the cause of this misfortune. They found Rochelle so blocked up, that in eight days' stay they never heard from them. The palisado is so strengthened with two floats of ships, both within and without, moored and fastened together from their ports to half- mast high, that, lying in shoal water, it is impossible to be forced."—*Vol.*

ciii., No. 57, dated May 9, at sea.

Various letters seem to clear Lord Denbigh of cowardice in turning back. See letters from Rowland Woodward to Francis Windebank. "The report is, that Lord Denbigh was overruled by Ned Clarke, that would not hazard the Fleet. The King was never seen to be so much moved, saying, 'if the ships had been lost, he had timber enough to build more.'"—*Vol. civ., No. 47.*

In a letter from Sir Henry Hungate to William, Earl of Denbigh, it is stated, "the King's pleasure is that not a single man should go ashore."— *Vol. civ., No. 69.*

RESPECTING THE "REMONSTRANCE."

"Message on Wednesday from the King, that he would not yield to any alteration in his answer, but would close the Session on the 11th inst. The house proceeded with the Remonstrance, until another message, which absolutely forbade them to do so. Scene which ensued:—Most part of the house *fell a-weeping*. Sir Robert Philips could not speak for weeping. Others blamed those that wept, and said they had swords to cut the throats of the King's enemies.

"That afternoon the King and the Lords were in council from two to eight on the question whether the Parliament should be dissolved. The negative was resolved on. On the following morning the Speaker explained away his message, and the house proceeded with the Remonstrance. The King agreed thereunto, and came that afternoon, gave the customary royal assent, adding other observations which are repeated. It is impossible to express with what joy this was heard, nor what joy it causes in the city, where they are making bonfires at every door, such as was never seen but upon his Majesty's return from Spain."—*Letter from Sir Francis Nethersole to the Queen of Bohemia, vol. cvi., No. 55, dated June 5. The Strand.*

"Sends a copy of the Remonstrance of the Commons. It was presented to the King on Tuesday last. The Duke was present in the Banqueting-house at the time, and on his Majesty rising from his chair, kneeled down, with a purpose, it was conceived, to have besought his Majesty to say something. But the King, saying only 'No,' took him up with his hand, which the Duke kissed, and so his Majesty retired. This was all that passed at the time, and all that is like to come of the Remonstrance. His Majesty's favour to the Duke is no way diminished, but the ill-will of the people is like to be much increased."—*The same to the same, vol. cvii., No. 78, June 19. The Strand.*

Some further particulars of this event and its effects are related in a letter from Sir Francis Nethersole to James Earl of Carlisle.

"The King took the Duke's death very heavily, keeping his chamber that day, as is well to be believed. But the base multitude in the town drink healths to Felton, and these are infinitely more cheerful than sad faces of better degrees."

Felton.

Examination of Richard Harward:—"George Willoughby taught him to write. Saw Felton at Willoughby's within a month; Felton complained of the Duke as a cause why he lost a captain's place, and the obstacle why he could not get his pay, being four score and odd pounds. Went together to the Windmill, where examinant read the Remonstrance to him, and Felton took it and carried it away."—*Vol. cxiv., No. 128.*

"Sir Robert Savage committed to the Tower for saying that if Felton had not killed the Duke he would have done it."—*Vol. cxvi., No. 95, Sept. 10, 1628.*

Report by Dr. Brian Duppa of an interview held by himself and others with John Felton in the Tower. (Dr. Duppa was afterwards tutor to Charles II.):—

"On stating to him that though he had no mercy on the Duke, the King had so much compassion on his soul as to give directions to send divines to draw him to a feeling of the horror of his sin, he fell on his knees with humble acknowledgment of so great grace to him. Throughout he confessed his offence to be a fearful and crying sin; attributed it, "upon his soul, to nothing but the Remonstrance." Being asked whether some dangerous propositions, found in his handwriting, had not stimulated him, he denied, saying they were gathered long ago out a book called the "Soldier's Epistles." He denied that any creature knew of his resolution but himself, and requested that he might do some public penance before his death, in sackcloth, with ashes on his head, and ropes about his neck."—*Vol. cxvi., No. 101, Sept. 2, 1628.*

Felton, it appears, had two letters found in his bag, perhaps duplicates. The knife was sewed into his dress. It appears that Felton was, at one time, puffed up by the popular applause. The state of rabid enmity to the Duke existing in the country, was exhibited in inhuman verses on his death, such as these:—

"Make haste, I pray thee; launch out your ships with speed;

Our noble Duke had never greater need

Of sudden succour, and these vessels must

Be his main help, for there's his only trust."

Satire upon the Duke, beginning—

"And art thou dead, who whilom thought'st thy state

To be exempted from the power of Fate?

Thou that but yesterday, illustrious, bright,

And like the sun, did'st with thy pregnant light

Illuminate other orbs?"

One of the poems of the day excited more than ordinary attention. It was addressed by the writer to "his confined friend, Mr. John Felton!" Suspicion fell on Ben Jonson; and even in the house of his friend, Sir Robert Cotton, the belief that he had written the poem found credence. Jonson was then paralytic, and his mind may have been somewhat embittered, perhaps enfeebled, but he was guiltless of this act of ingratitude to his deceased patron, and to his living sovereign, King Charles. His examination upon this charge is, as Mr. Bruce remarks in his preface, p. 8, ix., a new incident in Jonson's life. The original examination before the Attorney-General is to be found in the Calendar before referred to, vol. cxix., No. 33. See Preface by Mr. Bruce, p. 9.

"The examination of Benjamin Jonson, of Westminster, gentleman, taken this 26th day of October, 1628, by me, Sir Robert Heath, his Majesty's Attorney-General:—

"The said examinant being asked whether he had ever seen certain verses beginning thus—'Enjoy thy bondage,' and ending thus —'England's ransom here doth lie,' and entitled thus—'To his confined friend,' &c., and the papers of these verses being showed unto him, he answereth that he hath seen the like verses to these. And being asked where he saw them, he saith, at Sir Robert Cotton's house, as he often doth, the papers of these verses lying there upon the table after dinner. This examinant was asked concerning these verses as if himself had been the author thereof; thereupon this examinant read them, and condemned them, and with deep protestations affirmed that they were not made by him, nor did he know who made them, or had ever seen or heard them before. And the like protestations he now maketh upon his Christianity and hope of salvation. He saith he took no copy of them, nor ever had copy of them. He saith he hath heard of them since, but ever with detestation. He being further asked whether he doth know who made or hath heard who made them, he answereth he doth not know, but he hath heard by common fame that one Mr. Townley should make them, but he confesseth truly that he cannot name any one singular person who hath reported it. Being asked of what quality that Mr. Townley is, he saith his name is Zouch Townley; he is a scholar, and a divine by profession, and a preacher, but where he liveth or abideth he knoweth not, but he is a student of Christ Church in Oxford.

"Being further asked whether he gave a dagger to the said Mr. Townley, and upon what occasion, and when, he answereth, that on a Sunday after this examinant had heard the said Mr. Townley preach at St. Margaret's Church in Westminster, Mr. Townley, taking a liking to a dagger with a white haft which this examinant ordinarily wore at his girdle, and was given to this examinant, this examinant gave it to him two nights after, being invited by Mr. Townley to supper, but without any circumstance and without any relation to those or any other verses; for this examinant is well assured this was so done before he saw those verses, or had heard of them; and this examinant doth not remember that since he hath seen Mr. Townley.

"Ben Jonson."

Zouch Townley, to whom the verses were ascribed, was one of the Townleys of Cheshire. He escaped a prosecution, with which he was threatened in the Star-chamber, by taking refuge at the Hague. He was evidently on terms of intimacy with Jonson, to whom he addressed commendatory verses, beginning—

"Ben,

The world is much in debt, and though it may

Some petty reckonings to small poets pay,

Pardon if at thy glorious sum they stick,

Being too large for their arithmetic."

It is agreeable to find that Ben Jonson stands wholly acquitted of the charge of being the writer of the offensive and discreditable verses in question.

———

The following letter from Edmund Windham to Dr. Plot, author of the history of Staffordshire, relative to the ghost story related by Clarendon, is taken from the "Biographia Britannica":—

"S<small>IR</small>—According to your desire and my promise, I have written downe what I remember (divers things being slipt out of my memory) of the relation made me by Mr. Nicholas Towse, concerning the apparition which visited him about 1627.

"I and my wife, upon occasion being in London, lay at my brother's, Pym's, house, without Bishopsgate, which was next house unto Mr. Nicholas Towse's, who was his kinsman and familiar acquaintance—in consideration of whose society and friendship he took a house in that place; the said Towse being a very fine musician and very good company —for aught I ever saw or heard, a virtuous, religious, and well-disposed gentleman. About that time, the said Mr Towse told me that, one night being in bed and perfectly waking, and a candle burning by him (as he usually had), there came into his chamber, and stood by his bed-side, an old gentleman, in such a habit as was in use in Queen Elizabeth's time; at whose first appearance Mr. Towse was very much troubled; but after a little while, recollecting himself, he demanded of him in the name of God, *What he was?—whether he were a man?* And the Apparition replied, *Noe.* Then he asked him *if he were a devil?* And the Apparition answered, *Noe.* Then said Mr. Towse, *In the name of God, what art thou then?* And, as I remember, Mr. Towse told me that the Apparition answered him that *he was the ghost of Sir George Villiers, father to the then Duke of Buckingham, whom he might very well remember, since he went to schole at such a place in Leicestershire*—naming the place, which I have forgotten. And Mr. Towse told me that the Apparition had perfectly the resemblance of the said Sir George Villiers in all respects, and in the same habit that he had often seen him wear in his lifetime. The said Apparition also told him that he could not but remember the much kindness that he, the said Sir George Villiers, had expressed to him whilst he was a scholar in Leicestershire, as aforesaid; and that, out of that consideration, he believed that he loved him, and that therefore he made choice of him, the said Mr. Towse, to deliver a message to his son, the Duke of Buckingham, thereby to prevent such mischief as would otherwise befall the said Duke, whereby he would be inevitably ruined. And then, as I remember Mr. Towse told me, that the Apparition instructed him what message he should deliver to the Duke; unto which Mr. Towse replied that he should be very unwilling to go to the Duke of Bucks upon such an errand, whereby he should gaine nothing but reproach and contempt, and be esteemed a madman, and therefore desired to be excused from the employment. But the Apparition prest him with much earnestness to undertake it, telling him that the circumstances and secret discoveries (which he should be able to make to the Duke of such passages in the course of his life which were known to none but himselfe) would make it appeare that his message was not the fancy of a distempered braine, but a reality. And so the Apparition tooke his leave of him for that night, telling him that he would give him leave to consider until the next night, and then he would come to receive his answer, whether he would undertake his message to the Duke of Buckingham or noe. Mr. Towse passed the next day with much trouble and perplexity, debateing and reasoning with himselfe whether he should deliver this message to the Duke of Buckingham or not; but in the conclusion he resolved to doe it. And the next night, when the Apparition came, he gave his answer accordingly, and then received full instructions.

"After which Mr. Towse went and found out Sir Thomas Bludder and Sir Ralph Freeman, by whom he was brought to the Duke of Buckingham, and had several private and long audiences of him. I myselfe, by the favour of a friend, was once admitted to see him in private conference with the Duke, where (although I heard not their discourse) I observed much earnestness in their actions and gestures. After which conference Mr. Towse told me that the Duke would not follow the advice that was given him, which was (as I remember) that he intimated the casting off and rejection of some men who had great interest in him—and, as I take it, he named Bishop Laud; and that he, the Duke, was to do some popular acts in the ensueing parliament, of which the Duke would have had Mr. Towse to have been a Burgess, but he refused it, alledging that, unless the Duke had followed his directions, he must doe him hurt if he were of the parliament. Mr. Towse also then told me that the Duke confessed that he had told him those things that no creature knew but himself, and that none but God or the Divell could reveale to him. The Duke offered Mr. Towse to have the King knighte him, and to have given him preferment (as he told me), but that he refused it, saying that, unless he would follow his advice, he should receive nothing from him. Mr. Towse, when he made this relation, told me the Duke would inevitably be destroyed before such a time (which he then named), and accordingly the Duke's death happened before that time. He likewise told me that he had written downe all the discourses he had had with the Apparition; and that *at last his comeing to him was so familiar, that he was as little troubled with it as if it had been a friend or acquaintance that had come to visit him.* Mr. Towse told me further, that the Archbishop (then Bishop of London) Dr. Laud, should, by his counsels, be the author of a very great trouble to the kingdome, by which it should be reduced to that extremity of disorder and confusion that it should seem to be past all hope of recovery without a miracle; but yet, when all people were in despaire of happy days againe, the kingdome should suddenly be reduced and resettled again in a most happy condition.

"At this time my father Pym was in trouble, and committed to the Gatehouse by the Lords of the Councill, about a quarrel between him and the Lord Pawlett, upon which one night I sayd unto my cousin Towse, by way of jest, *I pray you ask your Apparition what shall become of my father Pym's business?*—which he promised to doe; and the next day told me that my father Pym's enemies were ashamed of their malicious prosecution, and that he would be at liberty within a weeke, or some few days, which happened accordingly.

"Mr. Towse's wife (since his death) told me that her husband and she, living in Windsor Castle, where he had an office, that summer the Duke of Buckingham was killed, told her the very day that the Duke was set upon by the mutinous mariners in Portsmouth, saying the … would be his death, which accordingly fell out—and that at the very instant the Duke was killed (as upon strict enquiry they found afterwards) Mr. Towse, sitting amongst some company, suddenly started up and said, *The Duke of Buckingham is slain.* Mr. Towse lived not long after; which is as much as I can remember of this Apparition, which, according to your desire, is written by,

"Sir, yours, &c.,

"EDMUND WINDHAM.

"Boulogne, Aug. 5, 1652."

The following letter has been adduced as a proof that Villiers owed his favour with Charles to an incident in the Monarch's early life—his sole dereliction from propriety, as it is said. Buckingham, it is said, was Charles's confidant, and mediator between him and King James:—

"Steenie, I have nothing now to wryte to you, but to give you thankes bothe for the good counsell ye gave me, and for the event of it. The King gave mee a good sharpe potion, but you took away the working of it by the well-relished comfites ye sent after. I have met with the partie that must not be named, once alreddie, and the cullor of wryting this letter shall make mee meete with her on Saturday, although it is written the day being Thursday. So assuring you that this business goes safelie on, I rest

"Your constant loving friend,

"CHARLES."[246]

155

"I hope ye will not shew the King this letter, but put it in the safe custodie of Mister Vulcan."

THE END.

R. BORN, PRINTER, GLOUCESTER STREET, REGENT'S PARK.

Footnotes

1. Brodie, vol. ii., p. 117.

2. Masters, 137.—Nichols' "Leicestershire," iii., p. 200.

3. Brodie, from Rushworth.

4. Hume.

5. Reliquiæ Wottonianæ, p. 212.

6. Ibid.

7. He was the son of Lawrence Hyde, of Gussage St. Michael, in the county of Dorset, and of a west country branch of the ancient family of "Hyde of that Ilk."—*See Lord Campbell.*

8. Lives of the Chief Justices, vol. iv., p. 381.

9. Heylyn, 149.

10. Lord Campbell, vol. vi., 322, *passim.*

11. Brodie, after Clarendon.

12. Brodie, vol. ii., note, from Ayscough's MSS. Brit. Mus., 4161, vol. ii.

13. Ibid.

14. Brodie, from Hacket's Life of Williams, part ii., p. 96.

15. Brodie, from Rushworth, vol. i., p. 424.

16. Letter from Admiral Pennington to Buckingham, State Paper Office, inedited.

17. Letter from Admiral Pennington to Buckingham.

18. Ibid.

19. A request which was quickly complied with, as we find in the State Paper Office: "Orders given to impress men for the fleet," addressed to Admiral Pennington.

20. Ibid.

21. Ibid.

22. Ibid.

23. Chamberlayne's State of Great Britain in the seventeenth century.

24. State Papers, edited, 1626.

25. State Papers, edited, 1626.

26. Brodie (vol. ii., p. 147) says that only ten sail of the hundred ships that formed Buckingham's fleet were the king's ships; but it seems from these letters that the number was much greater.

27. State Papers, vol. lxvi., No. 19.

28. Ibid., Domestic, vol. lxviii., No. 3; see also Preface to Calendar, by Mr. Bruce, p. 11.

29. Own.

30. Action.

31. Sir Sackville Crowe, who had been keeper of the Duke's privy purse, and was now treasurer of the Navy.

32. The spelling of this original letter is preserved here: the punctuation alone is altered.

33. State Papers, vol. lxv., No. 3.

34. Main business.

35. Vol. xvii. No. 28.

36. For the Duke's creditors.

37. State Papers, 2, vol. lxvii., date uncertain, No. 60.

38. No. 96, Ibid.

39. S. P., vol. lxvi., No. 14.

40. State Papers, vol. lxvi., No. 33.

41. Ibid., No. 35 and 67.

42. State Papers, No. 71.

43. Ibid., No. 76.

44. Vol. 68, No. 18.

45. Ibid., 105.

46. State Papers, vol. lxviii., No. 25.

47. State Papers, vol. lxxi., No. 43.

48. Ibid., No. 36.

49. State Papers, vol. lxxii., No 18.

50. Ibid.

51. State Papers, vol. lxxii., No. 28.

52. Ibid., No. 29.

53. This letter is dated July 28, which contradicts Hume's assertion that the Duke had given the Governor five days respite.—See Hume, Life of Charles I., 1627.

54. Brodie, vol. ii., p. 151.

55. State Papers, lxxii., No. 87 and 90.

56. Letter from Sir Allen Apsley to Secretary Nicholas.

57. State Papers, vol. lxxv., No. 20.

58. King James.

59. Vol. lxxv., No. 22, State Paper Office, Conway Papers.

60. Vol. lxvii., No. 60, Conway Papers.

61. State Papers, vol. lxxv., No. 53 and 57.

62. State Papers, 26.

63. Ibid., 34.

64. Ibid., lviiii., 65.

65. State Papers, vol. lxxviii., No. 71.

66. Edward Conway was the eldest son of the first Baron Conway of Rugby, in the County of Warwick, and succeeded his father, an eminent and popular Minister under James I. and Charles I.—*Burke's Extinct Peerage.*

67. Probably Lady Hatton.

68. The Governor of La Rochelle, whom the Duchess seems to have mistrusted.

69. State Papers, vol. lxxxv., No. 7.

70. Viscount Wilmot of Athlone, here referred to, was the grandfather of John Wilmot, the dissolute, yet penitent, Earl of Rochester, whose death has been described by Bishop Burnet.

71. Letter from Viscount Wilmot to Secretary Conway, State Papers, vol. lxxx. No. 55.

72. State Papers, lxxxii., vol. 18.

73. State Papers, vol. lxxxii. 39.

74. Vol. lxxxiii, No. 3.

75. Letter from Lord Wilmot to Secretary Conway, State Papers, No. 45.

76. State Papers, No. 3 and 8.

77. State Papers,—Letter of Secretary Conway to the Earl of Holland, vol. lxxxiii., No. 12.

78. Ibid., No. 17.

79. Ibid., No. 27.

80. State Papers. The letter is dated Nov. 1, 1627. Vol. lxxxiv., No. 1.

81. State Papers, Ibid., Nov. 16. Dated London, Nov. 3.

82. He was afterwards successively Baron Goring and Earl of Norwich; his son, General Goring, whose character is so ably drawn by Clarendon, predeceased his father by two years; both titles became extinct in 1672.—*Burke's Extinct Peerage.*

83. State Papers, vol. lxxxiv., No. 20.

84. Nov. 6.

85. Reliquiæ Wottonianæ, p. 227.

86. Letter of Denzil Holles to Sir Thomas Wentworth. Strafford Letters, vol. i., p. 42.

87. News Letter, State Papers, Ibid., No. 24.

88. Strafford Letters.

89. State Papers, vol. lxxxv., No. 56 and 57.

90. State Papers, vol. lxxxv., No. 67.

91. Ibid., No. 74.

92. State Papers, vol. lxxxvi., No. 80.

93. State Papers, vol. lxxxvi., No. 93.

94. State Papers, vol. lxvii., No. 96—Conway Papers.

95. Reliquiæ Wottonianæ, p. 230.

96. Clarendon, vol. i. p. 40-1.

97. State Papers, vol lxxxv., No. 10 and 11.

98. State Papers, vol. xc., No. 5.

99. State Papers, vol. xc., No. 10.

100. This event took place on or before the 2nd of February, 1628 (when Sir John Hippisley wished "the Duke joy of his young son"), and not on the 30th of January, as is usually stated.

101. See State Papers, vol. xcii., No 88. The county of Anglesea was to be charged 111*l.*; the money, as the King's letter intimated, was to be paid before the 1st of March.

102. State Papers, xciv., No. 57.

103. Ibid., 108.

104. State Papers, vol. lxii., No. 7. Dated May 7, 1627.

105. At the end of the session, Charles not only pardoned Mainwaring, but gave him a valuable living.

106. Brodie, p. 202. Hume's "Charles I."

107. Brodie, p. 170.

108. State Papers, Domestic, 1625.

109. Parallel between Essex and Buckingham—"Reliquiæ

Wottonianæ."

110. Wottonianæ Reliquiæ, p. 233.

111. Ibid.

112. Brodie.

113. Calendar, vol. xciv., No. 96.

114. Brodie—Hume.

115. Student.

116. Balfour's Annals, MSS., Advocate's Library, quoted from Brodie, vol. ii., p. 209.

117. The letter from Edmund Wyndham, of Kattisford, county Somerset, was addressed to Dr. Robert Plot, who wished to have the story correctly stated, in order to correct the false representations of William Lilly.

118. "Biographia Britannica," Art. "Villiers," *Note.*

119. See Appendix A.

120. The original letter was in possession of the late Mr. Upcott, by whom the author of this Memoir was presented with a fac-simile. It is, however, given in all the histories of this period.

121. Sir Philip Warwick's Memoirs, p. 35.

122. See Brodie—Wotton—Hume.

123. Reliq. Wotton., p. 234.

124. It shows in what manner the Duchess was informed of her husband's death.

125. Letters.

126. Lady Anglesea, the sister-in-law of Buckingham's mother, being the wife of his brother, Christopher, Earl of Anglesea.

127. There is an hiatus here in the MS.

128. Domestic State Papers, August 27, 1628. No. 21.

129. Clarendon.

130. Expresses.

131. Majesty's.

132. Domestic State Papers, Aug. 1628, No. 26.

133. Biog. Brit.

134. Domestic State Papers, August, 1628, No. 31.

135. Brodie.

136.

EPITAPH ON THE LADY MARY VILLIERS.

"The Lady Mary Villiers lies
Under this stone: with weeping eyes
The parents that first gave her breath
And their sad friends laid her in earth.
If any of them, reader, were
Known unto thee, shed a tear;
Or if thyself possess a gem,
As dear to thee as this to them,
Though a stranger to this place,
Bewail in theirs thine own hard case:
For thou perhaps at thy return
May'st find thy darling in an urn."

ANOTHER.

"The purest soul that e'er was sent
Into a clayey tenement
Informed this dust; but the weak mould
Could the great guest no longer hold:
The substance was too pure—the flame
Too glorious that thither came:
Ten thousand Cupids brought along
A grace on each wing that did throng
For place there—till they all opprest
The seat on which they sought to rest.
So the fair model broke for want

Of room to lodge th' inhabitant.
When in the brazen leaves of Fame
The life, the death of Buckingham
Shall be recorded, if truth's hand
Incise the story o'er our land,
Posterity shall see a fair
Structure by the studious care
Of two kings raised, that no less
Their wisdom than their power express;
By blinded zeal (whose doubtful light
Made murder's scarlet robe seem white—
Whose vain deluding phantoms charmed
A clouded sullen soul, and arm'd
A desperate hand, thirsty of blood)
Torn from the fair earth where it stood!
So the majestic fabric fell.
His actions let our annals tell;
We write no chronicle; this pile
Wears only sorrow's face and style;
Which e'en the envy that did wait
Upon his flourishing estate,
Turned to soft pity of his death,
Now pays his hearse; but that cheap breath
Shall not blow here, nor th' impure brine
Puddle the streams that bathe this shrine.
These are the pious obsequies
Dropped from his chaste wife's pregnant eyes,
In frequent showers, and were alone
By her congealing sighs made stone,

On which the carver did bestow

These forms and characters of woe:

So he the fashion only lent,

Whilst she wept all this monument."

137. "My Lord,—I was in hope, till very lately, that all your displeasure taken against my lord had been past; but, in letters sent me out of England, I was assuredly informed your lordship was much disgusted still with him, which news hath very much troubled me. I cannot be satisfied without sending these expressly to you. And I beseech you that, whatever you do conceive, you will deal clearly with me, and let me know it, and withal direct me how I may remove it. I must necessarily be included in your lordship's anger to him, for any misfortune to my lord must be mine, and it will prove a great misfortune to me to live under your frowns. Out of your goodness you will not, I hope, make me a sufferer, who have never deserved from you but as

"Your Lordship's

"KATHARINE BUCKINGHAM.

"Dunbere, this 2nd of September, 1639."[138]

138. Strafford Letters, vol. ii., p. 386.

139. Burke's Extinct Peerage.

140. "In the Earl of Cork's chapel at Youghal, where he was buried, there still remains the following hexastich to his memory:—

"Munster may curse the time that Villiers came

To make us worse, by leaving such a name

Of noble parts as none can imitate,

But those whose hearts are married to the State;

But if they press to imitate his fame,

Munster may bless the time that Villiers came."

Biographia Britannica, vol. vi.

141. Burke's Extinct Peerage.

142. Dr. Waagen—Life of Velasquez, p. 48.

143. From the name of his country-seat.

144. The infant Cardinal, the conqueror of Nordlingen, died in 1641.

145. Waagen, p. 62. From "Voyage en Espagne"—Cologne, 1662.

146. Waagen; Life of Velasquez, p. 82.

147. State Papers: Calendar, by Mr. Bruce.

148. Waagen.

149. Perichief.

150. Walpole, p. 183, vol. v.

151. Clarendon's History of the Rebellion.

152. Walpole's Anecdotes of Painters; Art. "Charles I."

153. In the work styled "Art and Artists," by Dr. Waagen, there is a full and most interesting account of all Charles's collection.

154. Note in Walpole, p. 189, vol. iii.

155. Walpole, p. 192.

156. Dr. Waagen says they were sequestrated; but it appears only a portion of them were sold by the Parliament—the rest fell into the hands of the second Duke of Buckingham.

157. Biographia, Art. "George Villiers," the second note.

158. See Biographia Britannica.

159. Walpole.

160. Dr. Waagen says that some of the Duke's pictures were not genuine, and many of little worth; but this is not the opinion of Horace Walpole.

161. Walpole's Anecdotes of Painting, vol. iii., p. 297—from the Journals of the House of Commons.

162. Walpole's Anecdotes of Painting, vol. iii., p. 200.

163. Ibid., p. 204.

164. Dr. Waagen.

165. Dr. Waagen.

166. Walpole, p. 188.

167. Walpole, p. 203.

168. Walpole, p. 270.

169. Walpole, p. 151, 152.

170. Walpole, p. 206. Note. From Peacham's "Complete Gentleman."

171. The fate of the Arundelian marbles is stated by Walpole to have been as follows:—They came into the elder branch of the family, the Dukes of Norfolk, and were sold by the Duchess, who was divorced in the time of George II., to the Earl of Pomfret for 300*l*. The Countess of Pomfret, great-grandmother to the present Earl, gave them to the University

172. Walpole.

173. Biograph. Brit., Art. "Villiers." Note.

174. Walpole, p. 149, *passim.*

175. Walpole, p. 166.

176. There were five dials at Whitehall; a Mr. Gunter drew the lines, and wrote a pamphlet on the use of them, in 1624. "One, too," says Horace Walpole, "may still be extant." Vertue saw them at Buckingham House, from whence they were sold.

177. Note in Hartley Coleridge's Introduction to Massinger's Plays, p. 32.

178. Hartley Coleridge, p. 9.

179. Massinger's Works, edited by Hartley Coleridge, p. 74.

180. Joanna, Lady Abergavenny, Mary Arundel, Catherine Grey, Mary Duchess of Norfolk. See "Royal and Noble Authors."

181. Horace Walpole's "Royal and Noble Authors," vol. ii., p. 308.

182. No. 7.

183. Ibid.

184. Note in Parke's edition of "Royal and Noble Authors."

185. Hartley Coleridge.

186. This letter was discovered by Malone, in Dulwich College. There is no date on it, but Mr. Payne Collier dates it in 1614, eight years before the publication of the "Virgin Martyr."

187. Introduction to Massinger's Works, p. xxxiii.

188. Introduction to Massinger's Works, p. xxxv.

189. Introduction to Massinger's Works, p. xiv; from Dr. Farmer's "Essay on the Learning of Shakspeare."

190. Introduction to Massinger's Works, p. xxxvii.

191. Massinger's Works, p. 167; in his Dedication of "The Great Duke of Florence" to Sir Robert Wiseman.

192. Hartley Coleridge's "Introduction," p. xxv.

193. The play was acted, but not printed, and has never been discovered.—See Coleridge, from Malone.

194. Cunningham's "London."

195. See "Maid's Tragedy."

196. "The Guardian." See Massinger's Works, p. 351.

197. From the State Papers, a new volume of which has lately been published, it appears that Jonson was accused of writing certain lines on Buckingham's assassination.—See Appendix.

198. Gifford's "Life of Ben Jonson," p. 2; from Anthony Wood.

199. Cunningham's London.

200. Ben Johnson's Works, p. i.

201. Gifford, from the Duchess of Newcastle's Letters.

202. From the First Part of "Jeronymo," a popular play.

203. Massinger's Works, p. 200.

204. Gifford, p. 7, note.

205. Rowe's "Life of Shakspeare," p. xxxiii.

206. Gifford, p. 2.

207. Pope's "Essay on Shakespere," prefixed to the Oxford edition, p. xix., 1745.

208. Introduction to Massinger's Works, p. xxxiv.

209. Page xxxvi.

210. Gifford, p. 23. See note by Mr. Dyce, p. 23.

211. Introduction to Massinger, p. xv.

212. "Lines on Shakespere," p. 552; Ben Jonson's Works.

213. In 1615. Shakspeare died in 1616.

214. Hartley Coleridge's "Life of Massinger."

215. Gifford's "Life of Ben Jonson," p. 59.

216. "Royal and Noble Authors," vol. ii., p. 268.

217. "Life of Ben Jonson," p. 63.

218. Ibid., p. 67.

219. Gifford's "Ben Jonson," p. 37.

220. In Laing's Preface to notes of Ben Jonson's Conversation.

221. Note by Dyce; Gifford, p. 38.

222. Life, p. 49.

223. This was communicated to Gifford by the late Mr. D'Israeli, to whom historical literature owes indeed much.

224. Grainger, Biog. Hist., vol. i., p. 194.

225. Gifford, p. 48.

226. Gifford, p. 49.

227. With a gentler feeling, Charles Lamb made numerous extracts from "The New Inn," to show that the mind that produced the "Fox" was still there.—Ibid.

228. Gifford, p. 48.

229. Gifford.

230. For some particulars of Sir John Beaumont, see Appendix.

231. Burton's "Anatomy of Melancholy," vol i., p. 235.

232. Stowe's "Annals."

233. Gull's "Horn-book," pp. 119, 120.

234. Henry IV.

235. Hartley Coleridge.

236. Ibid—Note.

237. Hartley Coleridge.

238. See Cunningham's "London," Art. "Whitehall," from Dugdale's "Troubles in England."

239. See Cunningham, vol. i., p. 311. The Author cannot avoid expressing obligations to this excellent work.

240. Otherwise Bougton Place (or Palace). See Izaak Walton's "Life of Sir H. Wotton."

241. Ferdinand I., of the House of Medici, who, in 1589, succeeded his brother Francis.

242. Collected and edited by Izaak Walton, in 1672.

243. Cowley was born in 1618.

244. He was born in 1608, and was only seventeen when he began the study of the law under his uncle, Sir Nicholas Hyde.

245. State Papers, vol. cxiv., No. 17; August 27, 1627. Calendar, edited by Mr. Bruce.

246. "Historia et vitae et regni Ricardi II.," p. 104, by Mr. T. Hearne, who tells us the letter is said to have once belonged to Archbishop Sancroft, and observes it is the only intrigue he had ever heard this Prince was concerned in.